The
SHAME ARTIST

WILLIAM KAUFFEN

BLUE MOON BOOKS
NEW YORK

Published by
Blue Moon Books
841 Broadway, Fourth Floor
New York, NY 10003

ISBN 1-56201-149-9

Manufactured in the United States of America

Contents

1

DATE RAPE

My boss Sofi Gorjus called me a Shame Artist the day she picked me up on the beach. She was impressed when I blushed right down to my tits. She said if I could look ashamed of myself for the camera, she'd use me. After that summer, I started working out of her agency GAM, Gorjus Actors and Models.

Even before the election and the video of me with candidate Tom Thomas, people on the street thought they knew me, 'caused they'd seen me every day for six months in one TV commercial or other. I was a blonde secretary who used the wrong mouthwash or deodorant. I look bright and eager to please, and my blouse is stuffed with creamy goodies. The young handsome boss might have wanted to dive into my cleavage—but when I come right up to him, he gags. Then, someone wises me up and I start using the sponsor's product.

My favorite commercial embarrassment was showing panty-lines. The wardrobe lady brought standard black panties for me to wear, just in case the ones I wore were too skimpy, which they were. She fitted a light tan skirt to my rear end. When I wiggled my butt, the men on the set gasped. The pitch was, you don't want this! I touched my fingertips to my lower lip, opened my eyes wide, and blushed. After the video of me and Tom Thomas at the motel pool, they showed snips of my commercials, a peek down my cleavage and a butt wiggle in every news broadcast for three days.

You probably remember me, Sarah Moons, as the Slut Who Sank the Republicans. Everybody agrees that, 'cept for me, Democrat Edwin Chase would've been a one-term president. But the Devil really goes to work every four years. It isn't the way they tell you. The Evil One hardly ever shows up as a mean Spanish aristocrat with a long face and a goatee, a long arrow-tipped tail, and a pitchfork. The Devil's a stud when it pleases him, and a sexy fourteen-year-old girl when it pleases her. The Devil can be your Mom's gigolo teaching you another way to stay virgin, or a traveling salesman who can make your kid sister misbehave in a train berth all night, right over your head. Sometimes, the Devil's something missing, like a good stiff prick when you need one. So says my protector Ethyl, the Queen of the Night.

Something sure was missing in the video of me *minus*

Candidate X. Eventually, the absent devil turned out to be Republican vice-presidential candidate Tom Thomas. MRG, or "merge" as everybody calls it, made the video. MRG stands for Media Realizations General. The tape starring me, alone, was on their shelf two years before the election, labeled, "Show Girl Minus Candidate X." Tom Thomas was put in later. That's the way these tapes are designed, so they can be used with anyone.

"Show girl" doesn't mean anything. I was never a show girl, like the White Coat recommending antacid pills isn't a doctor. A candidate's pet is expected to be a blonde with big boobs, long legs, good thighs and ass. In the section of my tape that got on the air, I wore a micro bikini most people didn't see on TV, 'cause the networks threw a jumpy shower-glass rectangle across my tits, and one below, too. The TV censors were so worried about anyone seeing my blonde bush curling out of my bikini, they completely fuzzed up all the front shots. You got to see my bare round backside in profile for two seconds. Nobody saw the bikini string at my waist, but it was there. In the rear shot, when we're going into the motel room, Candidate Thomas's arm covered the string around my waist, and two crazy rectangles kept bobbing up and down so you couldn't see my ass. Naturally, this jumpy teasing, like, "*Nyah-nyah*, she's naked and you can't see the good parts!" made it all sexier. I meet people who think they saw shots of me at a motel pool completely nude with Tom Thomas in a bathing suit, and me kissing him on the neck and working my way down his chest.

When the Democrats showed the video in September, two months before the election, there was a lot of interest all at once in the sex lives of the models and actresses at GAM, my agency. The Republicans claimed the tape was a fake, and that Tom Thomas was never at a motel with Sarah Moons, an actress familiar from TV commercials. They were right about that.

MRG destroyed every scrap of the original videotapes of me and Candidate Thomas they "MRG'd" into the phony broadcast version, but not before Sofi's husband Francis, a MRG big shot, made his own copy of me in the bikini hugging and kissing air. Maybe, Francis planned to sell it someday. Or maybe he figured he'd need tapes to jog his memory when Sofi stopped bringing luscious babes home to worship him.

The microphone-in-your-face pests stayed on Tom Thomas about me, but all he said, over and over, was that many women volunteered for his campaign to increase employment in America, and he was grateful for their support, but he could not recall meeting a young woman who acted in mouthwash and pantyhose commercials.

Thomas sounded like he was trying to crank up the outrage, and he looked positively green—some comic said, "Don't adjust the color on your TV," and that's the only line people remembered after all the speeches and debates.

At that point, the polls showed the Republican challengers Benedict-Thomas still ahead of the Democrats in the White House. But then someone, and I have a good idea who—Cathy—told the Democrats about the old date-rape charges that the "No Means NO!" women's committee at Belmont College brought against Tom Thomas, when I was a freshman and he was in law school. I'll bet Cathy sold Thomas's little black book to that celebrity gossip show. I was in the book with a string of letters like "bj" and "af" in circles over my name. The TV camera zoomed in on pages and pages of girls' names and little letters over them. It was totally scratched out where Cathy's name was.

Suddenly, there was a lot of interest in the sex games of rich kids at St. Deems High in Manhattan. Now, the Republicans saw they'd lost the family values issue even if they dropped Thomas, which it was too late to do, anyway. They got all worked up defending Thomas and attacking Maryanne Hawkes and "No Means NO!" and me, and never explained how they'd get people jobs, lower taxes, and cut the deficit all at the same time.

It's not my fault! I had no way of knowing that Tom Thomas, who drifted in and out of my life since I was a sophomore in high school, was going to star with me in the political killer video! They had footage of him at some private pool, and some of me in a bikini hugging and kissing the air in a MRG studio, and shots of a seedy motel with palm trees behind it, and they "MRG'd" it all in the lab!

The Democrats didn't go into the little black book with the letters showing what Thomas's high-school girls did for him. They left that to the talk shows. The Democrats claimed I was the nice girl next door until Thomas had me on the sofa in my college dorm, when I was a freshman and he was a law student. "Now, look at her!" they sneer, showing my behind wiggle.

When MRG made the solo tape of me in the bikini, everybody assumed the missing candidate would eventually be a Democrat. Then, rumors got around about Tom Thomas. It turned out Republicans don't know how to say, "Aw, shucks, boys'll be boys," like the Democrats do every four years.

Thomas gallantly tried to blame me in the TV debates by declaring, "Don't blame Ms. Moons." He pointed out I was the perfect victim, because I always acted embarrassed in my commercials. But, Vice President Jestyn retorted, that's the point, that vicious date rape left Ms. Moons looking permanently humiliated. Tom always was an idiot. He just made sure snips from my commercials got on the news six times the next day. Democrats Edwin Chase and Henry Jestyn strolled into their second term.

I was probably the first person to tell Tom Thomas he ought to go into politics. He was handsome and could sound like he knew what he was talking about when he had never thought about it before. We could both hear something in a TV movie about Arab oil and weapons, and then he'd say it like he had figured it out himself. You won't find that in the other books about us.

Now, a year after the videotape of me with jumpy

rectangles sunk the Republicans, there's five books about Tom and me, including the one I got two hundred thousand for authorizing. If you "authorize" it, it means you're no way the author. Well, I want to tell my own story about how I got to be a Shame Artist, the real Tom Thomas story, and the truth about Sofi Gorjus and Francis, and Gina, Walt, and me. I want to tell how it was growing up horny, how I went my own way, and you decide whether or not Tom ruined my morals.

Also, I want to tell what really happens every four years. Most people are too cynical. They think America's fucked 'cause of power-mad Republicans, sex-crazy Democrats, military-industrial greedy pigs, whore journalists, and stupid voters. Not true! I, Sarah Moons, am here to tell you it's all the Devil's work. The sooner you catch on to that, the better you feel about the USA.

Usually, I get into bed with a tape recorder and just talk. Rosario brings me a pot of tea every hour or so. The publisher has someone type my tapes on a computer.

You could start this book with the broken-down sofa in my college dorm they showed on TV. They walked the TV camera around shooting down at the soiled seat cushion. But nothing is duller than an old sofa, unless what the news person says helps you imagine Tom and me on it. Wouldn't you rather hear that from me?

The weekend before, at Alice's parents' chateau, was the first time in a long while that Tom and I got together, but we used to have hot times in New York while he bummed around after college. I talked him into applying to law school!

Anyway, I'm on my back on my college dorm sofa. Tom has my sweater pushed up over my tits and he's working them over. He isn't wearing anything but a knit shirt and his socks. I have one foot flung over the back of the sofa. My panties are down around my other foot, on the floor. My skirt's bunched up around my waist, I'm trying to get it off, but Tom wants to finish deflowering me.

Yes, I really was a virgin, although the Republicans scoffed at that. Then, the Democrats came back with the affidavit from Dr. Wurst that I was. The affidavit didn't say that I went to the clinic to get the Pill.

I turned on to Dr. Wurst just 'cause I was naked under the blue clinic gown, and he was so cool with three or four of us co-eds waiting in our cubicles for him to poke into us. He put on his rubber gloves, poked me good, looked thoughtful. He was concerned about my being a virgin or, as he put it, "technically a virgin," and offered to snip my cherry surgically. I said I'd rather have it popped the normal way, and a real prick was coming to Belmont that afternoon to do the honors. Dr. Wurst warned me the Pill takes a while to work.

Tom had just driven off when Maryanne Hawkes, then a junior at Belmont who happened to be on our floor recruiting freshmen for her women's lib group, saw blood trickling down the inside of my thigh. I admitted I just lost it. I had to tell somebody! Then, I remembered Maryanne was a friend of Ricky, a soph I was starting to get close to. I tried to get her not to tell Ricky. 'cause he might've been put off if someone else plucked my cherry just as we were about to get down for the first time. But I saw Maryanne was going to tell him, so when she asked, "Was that you yelling? Did he force you?" I nodded yes, thinking she'd pity me and I'd get her on my side.

Maryanne got all excited. I said too much, including about seeing Dr. Wurst, and before I knew what she was up to, she had a lawyer and they talked to the dean and a local judge, and whipped up a case against Tom for raping me. I wised up too late that you're better off without some people on your side.

I never told anyone this before, but I wasn't even on the sofa when I lost my virginity. I was kneeling on the floor in front of the sofa, kind of hunched over into the seat. It's true about me saying, "No," practically the whole time. When Tom first came in that Tuesday afternoon and we kissed, I was really glad to see him after our crazy weekend together. When he pushed my sweater up and grabbed my tits, I started saying, "No!" 'cause I wanted to walk him around the campus and show him off—he was great looking and a law student—and maybe fill him in on our weekend, intimate stuff he didn't have a clue about—and then we'd come back to my room and do it. I wasn't putting off doing it. Well, maybe a little.

But Tom goes right for it, reaches under my dress between my legs. I say, "No!" with a sinking feeling in my belly. Even when he snakes his finger into my pant-

[9]

ies, I keep saying, "No, Tom," 'cause I want my walk around the campus. I'm hot and wet down there, and he's on one knee and I'm sort of leaning over murmuring, "No." I didn't give in even when he got his thumb up in me. I tried to push Tom's hand down, and we wound up on the floor, my boobs out and my panties a damp ribbon halfway down my thighs, and then he went down on me. A lot of girls heard me scream, "No, you crazy bastard!" He licked my clit, and I came and moaned, "I love you!"

Somebody banged into the room, but I was so out of my skull I didn't know who. It was Sandra, one of my roommates. She picked up her books or whatever, gawking at us as she edged back toward the door. The idea of her watching Tom munch on me excited me. She wasn't getting anything herself and let everyone know she was horny as hell, although later in the year she did fine. I got a kick out of Sandra envying me. I was right about that, 'cause as she left, she called over her shoulder, "Me next!"

Tom told everyone I moaned, "Don't stop!" That doesn't count, according to Maryanne, 'cause men always claim that when they force a woman. Anyway, he did stop, long enough to get all his clothes off except his knit shirt and his socks. I glommed onto his cock and licked and sucked with all my heart, but this time he pulled me off by my ears. Believe me, that doesn't happen to me a lot. It reminded me he'd come for my cherry, and I panicked and scrambled away on my hands and knees. I was hobbled by my damp panties around my thighs. Tom came after me, cupping my quim under my skirt, his long sensuous fingers rolling my clit! I made it to the sofa, but it was hopeless, he was right behind me.

Everyone says I've got a world-class ass, peaches-and-creamy skin, pretty dimples above, round cheeks thrusting cheerfully back. "Gorgeous!"—they say that a lot. Everything else about me, eyes, hair, boobs, neck and shoulders, arms, thighs, even my knees, is "beautiful," but my ass is "gorgeous." One guy thought my backside smiled at him! I know what he meant! Looking over my shoulder down my cute ski slope, or when I'm back to a mirror and look between my legs, I see my ass like men do—it begs, *Pet me! Pinch me! Spank me! Fuck me!*

For a moment I held my skirt up behind me and reached under the sofa where I kept a little jar of Vaseline. I was trying to offer Tom my specialty, a way in he knew well. No, it doesn't hurt, at least not much once you've done it enough, and it's deliciously humiliating 'cause men always think they're doing something awful to you. Which makes it sexier for me. I was turned on by Tom breathing hard behind me, his big prick tickling my bare behind, when my roommates could walk in anytime. Tom threw my skirt up to my shoulders. He knelt behind me, one paw twiddling my tits like mad, one hand circling around playing with my clit 'til I came again. His prick slid up and down the crack of my ass and poked awkwardly underneath me, where I was sloppy as I can be. He basted his cock in my gravy, greasing it up so it would go anywhere. Meantime, I found the Vaseline jar. I wasn't sure what Tom had in mind, but sometimes a girl just goes along. I can never think when anyone's playing with my tits or my clit.

Also, the sight or feel of a guy's cock, when he's hard for me, is, like, hypnotic. If I'm attracted to the guy at all, by the time he gets his prick out and in my face, I'll do anything he wants. Anything _it_ wants, like I'm its slave. I adore a big hard prick and loaded balls. Meanwhile, Tom was still teasing my behind. I get obscenely excited when a man tickles my crack and gooses me sweetly. My head was down on the sofa seat, I arched my back, sticking my gorgeous ass out and up. By now, I forgot what he was here for, I forgot to shield my quim casually with my hand. I was trying to pass the Vaseline back to him, just like the old days. All at once, Ow! Tom slammed into my cunt! I was stunned! I didn't feel anything for a moment, except filled up in a new way. All I could think was, _I'm not virgin anymore! I'm like everyone!_

His cock felt hot and incredibly good. The hurt was minor. I put a kiss on my fingertips and reached 'way 'round back and patted his butt with it. He fucked me hard. I liked his groin slamming against my hiney. I always liked that! I pressed back against him gently when he shoved in deep and squeezed when he, like, screwed it around in me. "I feel you squeezing," he said.

The door banged open, again, and my other roommate Diane and her friend Judi came in. "I need my sneakers," Diane said. "Hi, Tom!" "You should've put a sign on the door," Judi said. She stared at Tom, who you know is a hunk. Tom kept close to my butt, not moving much, grinding around marking time 'til they left.

Weeks before, Diane had talked to my old friend Alice, whose dorm room was just down the hall, about what a shame Sarah's still a virgin, and isn't Tom the right one to help out? Anyway, Alice got me and Tom invited to her parents' chateau in ski country for last weekend. You can see, their fixing me up with Tom again was a setup, to get me laid. The weekend took another turn, but everybody knew it was finally going to happen that Tuesday afternoon. Then, why did Sandra and Diane and her friend walk in on us? They just forgot. It wasn't their cherries getting popped, so it was no big deal. I heard Diane's friend saying as they went down the hall, "Well, it's two in the afternoon!"

A moment later Tom came out of me and threw me on my back on the sofa and finished screwing me. A wonderful fuck! We both went at it hard and fast, so we could finish before anyone else barged in. I wound up wrapping my legs around him and humping up to him. It was marvelous feeling him come in me the regular way. Once he was done, he was dressed and out, me still apologizing for my roommates.

After that, I went wild. I'd leave my dorm room for a hamburger and not get back for four days. It was a relief getting a cock in the right place after taking it down my throat and up my ass all those years. I tried to get my other dates to screw me the normal way, but some guys were hooked on doing it whatever way we started.

The Belmont football team still wanted exotic stuff from me they couldn't get from their prom queens. I had to keep up my rep. One night in the living room at the frat house with fullback Lou Brick, I guessed what he wanted, 'cause he turned purple when I asked him. I was sitting on his lap kissing his thick neck. He fondled my rear cheeks under my skirt and trolled his broad finger up and down pushing my panties into my crack. This goose gave me the message!

Minutes later I was kneeling naked on the bed in one of the upstairs bedrooms. I pouted, "Do I have to. . . . ?" teasing him while I greased his huge sausage. He loved my grumpy look, like I hated what came next, but I'd do it for him. They all loved that! "Yeah, you do," they'd all say, 'cept Lou didn't, 'cause the big lout was too steamed up to say a word. I was getting him so hard and hot with the Vaseline I thought maybe I could goof on him and just jerk him off, but he caught on! Without a word, he grabbed me under my arms, lifted me and turned me 'round, and put my face down on the bed. I was scared, I didn't feel like tricking him anymore. I turned my gorgeous ass up, reached back and spread my creamy round cheeks, real slow, like I was terribly ashamed to show him my precious brown asshole. Well, it was humiliating. The beast held me in place with one paw, aimed his greased cock with the other, threaded the needle, grunting. Then, he was in, no mercy, grabbing my hips and ramming into me good and hard like

I deserved for trying to cheat him. The punishment turned me on. I looked between my legs at what I could see of him, his scarred knees and powerful thighs, hairy pink sack of balls jouncing and long meaty cock connecting us as he pulled it almost all the way out and then shoved it all the way back up into my bowels, and I shrieked with glee, 'cause I could take it!

A few of Lou's teammates who happened to be in the frat house heard me squawk when it hurt. I wasn't pretending, I cried a few tears. But it wasn't all hurt. *It's still a great way to be stuffed!* I thought, and hardly had to touch myself before I came. Lou went on and on, very rough, like he was having trouble coming. I didn't. I came the whole time, shuddering, squealing and groaning. I can be a noisy slut, and where can you let go if not in a frat house? Lou was rampaging out of his skull, his cock growing super hot. He didn't know or care what I was doing, just that he, ugly Lou Brick, was splitting the most voluptuous sexy cheeks on campus. He was, like, ramming closer and closer to the goal line, a yard, less than a yard, inches away, and then, touchdown! Spurting hot jets all the way up into me!

While I was in college, nothing came of Maryanne Hawkes accusing Thomas of raping me. Everybody at Belmont laughed it off. A few years later, it was big news, 'cause of the political killer video.

— 2 —

ON THE TRAIN

My agent calls this "the Thomas book," but it's not about him, it's about me, first how I got to be a Shame Artist and then practically the biggest celebrity in America for six weeks. Also, I told the editor that the title is A *Shame Artist*, 'cause I'm not the only Shame Artist. When I was still a Fifth Avenue brat, the front-running candidate for president challenged reporters to catch him with a woman who wasn't his wife, and then he kept playing around 'til they caught him. Was that Shame Art, or what? Remember the United States senator who owed his success to women's issues? Twenty women on his staff accused him of reckless kissing. He wrote about his escapades in his diary, which was subpoenaed—a shoo-in for the Sarah Moons Hall of Shame. When the Devil romps, you'd think the whole country's into Shame Art. On national TV, Congress asked a nominee to the Supreme Court about pubic hair on a soda can! If you are reading this fifty years from now, you probably think I made that up. I didn't. You could look it up in old newspapers.

Shame is about other people seeing you naked or doing tricks. Suppose, your college team's fullback comes charging out of the frat bathroom with a jar of vaseline. It's embarrassing for a moment, tipping over facedown on his bed and taking it in your ass, but when it's over, it's over, and probably only half his teammates even hear about it. Not all that shameful. Now, same act, but at your agency's Winter Solstice Orgy, you're naked on all fours with "Happy New Year!" helium balloons tied to your wrists and ankles and twenty people watch. From then on, they can be talking professionally to you face-to-face, but you know they see the balloons bobbing and your bare ass up. They remember how you squealed when the guy shoves his prick in. They can still see you sticking your tongue out when he rams you, and smiling blissfully when you feel his hot wad shooting up into you. Now, that's humiliating, and if you're into shame, you get a new tingle every time you talk to someone who was there.

When I'm bored, I look for strangers who strip me and do stuff to me in their minds. They think you can't tell. A commercial actress who worked out of a rival agency asked me if I ever sit sprawly with men, cross and uncross my legs, my skirt happens to fall open, and I just happen not to be wearing panties. Her name's

Gina and eventually I saw her do it. It's hilarious watching guys pretending to read or talk to each other while Gina's working them. I told her my favorite is adjusting my clothes "modestly" as though I'm not aware anyone can see me, but I'm really flashing some idiot who thinks he just won the lottery. Gina and I became friends.

The most outrageous mooning I ever mooned was when me and my sister Babs traveled by train to stay with Dad's relatives in Florida. Babs got into everything younger than me, 'cause she learned from me. We had a roomette to ourselves, but Babs complained she was too horny to sleep. We went to the bar in the dining car. For a few minutes we were the only customers.

Our train was coming out of a pine thicket when I saw them: a flock of winged cocks, at least nine, maybe ten or eleven, flying past the dining car window. I gasped and pointed, but Babs just said, "They're flying awfully fast to keep up with us." She thought she was looking at birds! What they were was winged pricks-and-balls, the pricks extended all the way out, like geese necks, the balls where geese bodies would be. Geese don't race trains like that! I told Babs to look again, but they caught an updraft and rose above the window.

Out of nowhere while we were distracted, a salesman sat next to Babs. My kid sister's shorter than me, but just as voluptuous. She has chestnut hair instead of blonde. "Where'd you come from?" Babs asked him. "Function Junction," he said, pointing to the little village we were passing through. He was lying. Maybe, he crept out of Babs's cunt. The Devil can come out of any crevice.

The salesman was bald, with a fringe of hair around the back from ear to ear. He wore a big diamond pinkie ring and never stopped talking. He told us a joke about two farm boys, "local yokels," who go to a whorehouse. He said one of the boys was "nervous in the service." I couldn't remember the punchline two minutes after he told it, but I can never get his stupid rhymes out of my head.

He did card tricks for us. He said store owners welcome him 'cause of his jokes and card tricks, and once he's entertaining them, he sells his line of greeting cards and gifts. He asked Babs for a tiny bit of the gum she was chewing and stuck his printed business card to his bald pate. Then, he told each of us to draw three cards without looking at them and lay them face down. He asked me if I wanted to read some writing engraved on his ring, but he was teasing me. It was in a language I had never seen before. The ring glowed like it was radioactive, and I began to feel so horny I was almost sick.

He got Babs to read the six-digit telephone number printed on the business card stuck to his head. She read his name on the card, too, but later she couldn't remember it. He asked me to turn our six cards over and read the numbers. It was his printed telephone number. Babs was impressed. I was too, but I thought, there has to be some trick to it.

"Want to play strip poker?" he said. "You deal, we might as well just go ahead and strip," Babs said and unbuttoned the top button of her blouse, which was right in her cleavage. "Babs!" I exclaimed.

"Wait, I can do better," he says. "You two sit close together and link arms, like this, that's good, and, Babs, bring your hand back and put it on your own boob. Sarah, lean closer, let her bring her arm back. Good, Babs! Make sure you feel your bra." The bartender stared at us off and on. He couldn't have heard much of this over the clack of the wheels.

"Now, both of you, the other hand! Put it down in your own lap—right in there between your sweet thighs!"

Babs looked at me sideways, like, *isn't he going too far? Aren't you going to say something?* "Come on," the salesman mocked us. "You never put your hands down there? You better hold on tight to make sure nobody snatches your panties!"

At that moment it felt as though the train were lifting off the rail. We plunged into the night sky, the whole train was a sleek silver prick, and the night a warm cunt that took it in. Faces at the windows! Babs saw them, too. We were scared, but the salesman ticked off who they were. First, celebrated sex killers the salesman called by their first names. They are turned on to their own execution, locking into eternal manic excitement. Then, writers and artists. "Margery Kempe—dear Margery!" he cried. "Your girlfriend?" I said, "Why's she dressed that way?" *"Nah,"* he said, "she claims she hates me, calls me. . . . it means, 'wise-ass.' But, I know what she wants!" He waggled his tongue at her.

"Writing a book about herself," the salesman said,

"and I'm in it." He leaned over Babs and confided to me, "You should read it." Margery is gone. "The Marquis!" chirped the salesman. The Marquis bellowed, "You won't change me!" That was in French by the way, and barely audible through the glass pane, and I can't read lips even in English, but I understood him.

Hordes of spirits appeared at the dining car window. They had their moment, they were gone. Then we were back on the rails. The salesman showed us his closed fists and asked Babs to choose one. It was her bra! "It can't be!" she wondered aloud, peeking at her bare boobs inside her blouse. I pointed to the other fist, he opened it—her panties! "I was sitting on them the whole time!" Babs shrieked. She checked under her skirt, touched herself in front and then all the way underneath. "Give them back!" she cried and lunged at her undies. But the salesman lifted them out of her reach. "You have to work for them," he said, and there was no doubt what he meant.

"Mine are still on," I said, a little miffed.

"Look at your undies later," the salesman said, "see if you notice anything."

"Tell me! What—?" I cried, but he was focusing on Babs. I thought, he might be the Devil, but then, what would he want with Babs? The Devil, a bald, middle-aged travelling salesman, putting it to my kid sister? He had a monkeyish grin when he looked at her, so I knew she was going to get what she wanted.

I planned to hang out in the bar, but something about the salesman scared Babs. She asked me, would I mind going back with them and staying in my berth, the lower one? The three of us careened through the narrow aisles back to our compartment. Babs dropped her blouse and skirt on a chair, and the salesman laid her bra and panties on them. He bargained hard, but kept his word. Babs shook her sassy hiney as she clambered up the ladder into the upper berth. He sprang up after her, I don't think his feet touched the ladder. There was a night-light, a good fucking light, it let you see everything once your eyes got used to it. Babs sucked him half the night. That's Babs, generous to a fault. I heard every slurp, gurgle, and moan. He came with a raucous scream and pounded the mattress.

I almost forgot to check my undies, but my bra felt strange. No wonder, it was insideout and upside down! The label of my panties showed in front—they were insideout and backwards! How could he get them off me, turn them inside out, and slip them on me again? I was too horny to sleep. Feeling a little guilty over leaving Babs with the demon, I went to the bar again, hoping to find someone to bring back to our compartment. Now, there were a few customers, but no one for me. The bartender was no prince, and even he was taken.

As I came back into our quarters, I couldn't help seeing the salesman eating her out. Babs wasn't shy about telling him, "Keep licking! Harder!" She's a noisy bitch when she comes. There's nothing she can do about the racket she makes, anymore than I can. And then she really went to work on him. He screeched like she was maiming him instead of giving him a good time. I did myself, thinking about all the lovely guys I could have been with in Manhattan.

Mostly, I lay on my back and listened. There was a quick struggle and Babs cried out sharply. Her little hand dangled over the edge of the upper berth. I could have touched it, but I didn't. I thought, She's not a virgin anymore, she's ahead of me. Gorilla grunts. Babs sobbing. Should I break this up? I rose up on my elbows. My mouth was a little open and about to say, "Don't you dare hurt her!" when all at once, I felt it! A feathery soft touch on my face, stroking my cheeks. My mouth fell open in awe, and a cock filled it. Long, thick, warm cock. I caught the wings in my hands. They immediately stopped beating, like, playing dead. I fondled some of the biggest balls ever. They were more than balls, there was a pulse, a churning soul in them.

You can bet I gave that cock what it wanted! It got hot as you'd ever drink a cup of coffee. The wings folded back near the balls, quivered. All at once, the wings flared out, every feather stretched out! I knew what that meant! The warm cum was delicious, like burnt coconut milk with sugar and vanilla and salt. Maybe, a little too much salt. Other pricks and balls dipped into the lower berth, like, checking on how I was doing. The moment one was done, the next presented itself at my lips. I could tell they were different men in some other life.

Babs kicked her foot out over the edge of her berth. There were rapid thrusting, churning sounds above. It was plain Babs was pinned and her legs spread and she was getting fucked silly. She panted hoarsely, then she yowled—in pleasure, I thought, but it was hard to tell. Her toes curled tight.

They shifted around. Babs drew her foot back in and turned over. She was putting her hiney up for him. I saw his foot for a moment over the edge of the berth. He had long, silky hair on his lower leg, and his toenails were long, yellow, and curved like claws. He ought to have clipped them. From Babs's squeals and shuddering groans, he was screwing her ass. I was sorry I told her about letting guys do that, but, as I said to her later, wouldn't it've been ten times worse if she had never heard of it before? All at once, she cut off in mid-squeal, gagged, and then there was silence. I knew what was stuffing her mouth.

Just after dawn, we crept through a small station in South Carolina or Georgia. My shade was open, and three men in overalls walked alongside the train looking into my berth. Without thinking, I mooned them! It felt like I was being dragged to my hands and knees on the bed and turned so my hiney was to the window. It was not the salesman, he was too small to push me around that way, and besides, I heard him in the upper berth with Babs. An invisible force made me hike my night-gown up and touch my ass to the cool window. I didn't press against the window, didn't want to flatten my round rear cheeks. The yokels got a good look at my thighs and my quim and curly blonde bush, too. I glanced around and saw them freak out. They walked fast, keeping up with the train all the way to the end of the platform, even though it was speeding up, and they leaped and stumbled off the end of the platform and ran through the weeds along the tracks 'til they couldn't keep up anymore. We passed slowly through one small town after another without stopping, and I mooned them right along. My mouth was stuffed with one winged prick or another the whole time. Whenever I even thought, "Enough, already!" I got another dose to swallow, then, another prick.

Babs and her friend were at it again, but I didn't care, 'cause I was having fun my own way. I reached back between my legs and did myself for the dozens of gawkers lining the tracks.

Before he left, I grabbed the salesman. His body felt soft, ordinary. I wanted to ask him whether it was his doing that I mooned the southeastern seaboard, but my tongue was sticky, like, gummed to the roof of my mouth by a weird taste, and I wound up bleating, "What about me?" His answer amazed me: "Babs is good for a night. You—perhaps, you'll see me again."

The train stopped at a small town just long enough for him to get off. "Wear the ring!" I cried. "That'd make it easy, wouldn't it?" he scoffed.

I kept looking for the ring, anyway.

Babs thought, maybe the whole night was a dream or hallucination and she would find she was a virgin again. But we both had that taste in our mouths, her hiney hurt, her cunt was sore, there was blood on her sheets. She'd lost it, all right. That was real. Hoping what happened would turn out not to have happened, that was the dream.

Babs had the shakes. Whatever she was doing for the salesman, the winged pricks got into her every way they could, the whole time, one after another, even two at once. The salesman brushed them aside when they were in his way, but they came right back. They even nestled into Babs's hands, like, begging for hand-jobs.

Babs thought they were the souls of men who died without getting enough loving. "Then, there must be lots of flying cunts, somewhere," I said.

Neither of us wanted breakfast, 'cause our tummies were sloshing full of pints of warm coconut-milk cum. We were both burping quietly, like, three or four soft burps in a row, and saying, "Excuse me," and then we realized we're both doing it and stopped apologizing to each other. I hugged Babs most of the morning, 'til we got to Palm Beach. She got over the shakes. Hugging her comforted me, too.

——— 3 ———

ST. DEEMS HIGH

Enough Devil stuff, back to the innocence of my early teens at St. Deems Junior High. People think from the name St. Deems that it's an all-girls' school, but it's a co-ed hot tub for rich Catholic kids. Money counted more than anything, 'cause there were Presbyterians, Methodists and Jews, an ebony girl from Paris and a cocoa Egyptian boy. A lot of the kids had celebrity parents. St. Deems was a great place to practice the art of shame. We rated boys on cuteness, kissing and touching, and dancing, and cool—meaning, who was comfortable to lose your clothes with and do stuff with. The boys were shyer than us, but showed off more. If a boy didn't just talk sexy, but knew what he was doing, the news got around.

The boys rated us on our boobs, faces, hinies, and

legs, in about that order. What we did for boys changed from one term to the next, sometimes, from one week to the next. Seventh grade, you kissed boys under the table at birthday parties. Eighth grade, when you got a boy alone for a kiss, he'd try feeling you up. The boys were tense about bras, 'cause there might be six sweet seconds when he could unhook your bra, but if he fumbled, he could lose his chance. Sometimes, I let them fumble, when I enjoyed that more than anything they were going to do, but, mostly, I unhooked for them, 'cause my nippies zinged and I couldn't wait.

We all wore bras back then. My boobs were late coming. If you didn't have boobs, you slipped foam rubber pads into your bra. The moment of truth was embarrassing, when your bra came off and what was supposed to be your boobs came off too, but you let the boy practice on your nippies, anyway.

The first time a boy touched my quim, I was an eighth grade brat. It wasn't the high point of a date, or a sex game, or anything anyone could've planned. A dozen kids from my class were in the gym before a basketball game. The lucky boy was a junior varsity player named Artie. He was half-sitting, half-standing with his butt against the coach's long table. I was wearing a leotard. Leotards turned the boys on and made the teachers nervous. They showed the little mound down in front padded by your bush. The coach Ms. Swett squinted at me down there, checking that I was wearing panties. She didn't like boys to see the outline of your quim lips and cleft.

Gabe, one of my classmates, started horsing around, twisting my arm behind my back in a way that forced me to lean back toward him and thrust my lower body 'way forward, like a limbo dancer. My knees went under the table and my pussy glided under the back of Artie's fingers where he was holding the edge of the table. I saw his knuckles in my path, but I couldn't do anything about it. Artie probably saw what was coming at him, but he didn't move his hand. The knuckle of Artie's middle finger touched my clit and the back of his middle finger sank exactly into my quim. A freak accident—a hole-in-one! For me, a jolt of lightning. Sure, I was supposed to try to get away from the thrill of that knuckle rubbing my clit. I squirmed, my quim lips twitched all over his finger. I felt my love juices flowing. It wasn't like building up to a climax when I played with myself. I was in shock and quivering down there, coming from the first touch. Artie looked at me with wonder. It went on long enough for him to feel some dampness through my panties and the leotard. Ms. Swett was away somewhere. A lot of people saw Gabe twisting my arm, but the table and our bodies blocked them from seeing how me and Artie were connecting. Artie wasn't in a hurry to get his hand away, but eventually he told Gabe, "Enough! Let go of her!" and Gabe did. I don't even think Gabe knew how he brought me and Artie together.

I went around glowing all day and did myself in the tub that evening to calm down. My whole day at school turned on whether I got to see Artie. When I saw him,

•

even at the end of a corridor with twenty kids between us, my knees wobbled so, I had to lean against a wall. I daydreamed about him fingering me again, this time on purpose! We would be kissing, he would put his hand under my skirt and peel my panties down. It was hopeless, a junior would lose face messing around with an eighth grade brat, no matter how ready to put out she was.

Not all shame is exciting. Not having boobs was no fun at all. Babs already had more than me. Luckily, there were plenty of boys who appreciated my legs and my behind. After Artie, I wanted to give more and get more, but that isn't always easy for an upper crust girl. People watch you. The best way is to find a young boy who's ready. If he's too young, he can be a waste of time. Lennie had beautiful hands and lips. He started playing with me as soon as a movie came on. His right hand went around my back and under my sweater and my padded bra and on my tit. I thought that was a great start. I snuggled up to him, and he went under my sweater with his left hand and onto my left tit. Lenny was a tweaker and a nipple pusher-puller, and after a few minutes I went nuts. I couldn't think what to do about it. He tweaked and twiddled and pushed and pulled my nippies for almost two hours, and just wrung me out. My skirt where I sat got soaked with my own sex juice. At the end of the movie I had to put my coat on before I could stand up. I smelled pretty strong, but nobody noticed 'cause the movie theater reeked of popcorn and spilled sodas that made the floor sticky.

On line for another movie, I stood real close to Lennie and the back of his hand brushed my thigh. I clamped it there. His thumb was two inches from my quim, which was tingling and making honey. When the line moved, he pried his hand away. He was perfectly happy to tweak my titties again for two hours and let me stew in my own juice. As soon as I could get rid of him, I jumped into bed and took care of myself real well. By the time I fell asleep, I came more times than a honeymoon couple.

I loved movie kisses when I was a little girl. When the hero and his girl kissed, I wanted to be up there doing it with him. I liked boys' bodies and I thought about kissing them all over before I knew anyone did that. I could see Lenny's cock was hard when he felt me up in the movies, and I wanted to touch it or lean over and kiss it, but I knew it would freak him out.

Our apartment building has windows for a quarter of a block overlooking Fifth Avenue and the south end of Central Park, and ours is the only apartment on our floor. That's how upscale the building is. The master bedroom is larger than some New York apartments. My bedroom is a good size, too. We also have a foyer, a living room, dining room, a library, small sitting rooms, the maid's room, a kitchen like a restaurant's, a laundry room, and five bathrooms—six, counting the one in the servants' quarters, which I don't know if you count. Mom tells everyone about how she scrubbed all those toilets when she couldn't afford help after Dad lost all his money in stocks. Maybe, she did bathrooms for a week. She comes off like a crazy lady when she talks about her hardship days.

With dates who were swifter than Lenny, I opened the front door quietly, just a crack, looked into the foyer to decide whether Mom was home. She was usually in her bedroom with her lover Nevil or once in a while some other guy. She used to rail at me, "You think I'm a slut, don't you?" Mom never went to a man's apartment, 'cause if it didn't work out, she'd have to leave, but if she was at home, he'd have to leave.

When Mom was out late, my date and I would sneak in and hide ourselves behind the chesterfield in the library. When she was already in, we stayed out in the little hall near the elevator. Mom put in a soft, romantic banquette you could sink into, and a lush pile carpet, and she had the walls cushioned with billowing fabric. A seashell sconce threw soft light up to the ceiling. The best part of this love nest was what you didn't see. Underneath the thick cushion seat of the banquette was a raw box, the perfect place to store towels. One thing about fooling around, it gets damp and it stains. So, I always had two piles of towels, one clean pile and one pile stiff with dried gunk to throw into our washing machine. I also hid some sexy lingerie there for quick changes. Babs wanted to use my love nest, too. I had to let her or she would have ratted. So, I told her she had to keep the place clean and kick the guy out by eleven-thirty. She kept to the minute, 'cause she knew the elevator door could open on our floor with me and a date at eleven thirty-one. When she used the nest right before me, it smelled raunchy.

By tenth grade, "going steady" was code for doing stuff below the waist. You were telling everybody you had someone to kiss you and give you a good going-over and put his finger up inside you every time you could arrange to be together in private. It was terrific, when he slid his hand under your dress up your leg and you let your thighs slip apart and he touched your quim and you got hot and bothered and your love juices flowed and you said, "I love you," and he'd say, "Yeah," and pull the damp lower strip of your panties aside, and your heart would pound and he'd finger you 'til you'd come (*Yay!*) or he'd get bored (*Boo!*). This got to be standard, and then you didn't have to go steady to do it. Lots of girls went steady for six weeks and then switched. Boys fingered you all different ways. I was crazy for it. I heard one boy say to another boy about me, in a corridor at St. Deems, "She loves the finger."

Boys always took you to movies where the girl blew the hero, once you understood that's where she was going when she kissed his chest and sank lower on him while the camera wandered around the room. I doubted I'd ever get a boy to let me do that to him, but I knew if one did, I'd love him forever. I practiced by licking my thumb and thinking of Artie or some other cute boy. I blew on my thumb, trying to figure out exactly what you did when you did a "blow-job." I wondered what cum tasted like and how much there was. Cathy's older sister told us all about it. She said I should give my first love, Billy, a hand-job and taste his cum. Before I got a chance, Billy gave me my first mouthful. It was after we played duets on the piano at Cathy's party. Cathy and I have almost the same birthday, so it was my party too. Billy was going to be a pianist and I was almost as good as him. I kissed him on the piano bench and he said, "Where can we go?" We sneaked into a closet.

Billy exclaimed, "God, you're passionate!" What he meant was, I was hot and wet and quivery down there. Billy had one hand on my bare butt and he was swirling two fingers in me and his thumb was on my clit.

All at once, I came, leaning against him and biting his shoulder to gag myself so I wouldn't scream. He wanted to lay me right on the closet floor, but I wasn't ready for that. He'd never done it, either, but he was dying to begin. I rubbed his cock through his pants. It felt like it was two feet long! He said he'd go crazy if I didn't do something, so I said okay, and sucked his earlobe to let him know what I was going to do for him. I pushed his hand out of me and pulled my panties up. He didn't get it! He was frantic that I was just going to leave! I whispered in his ear, "Idiot! I'm going to suck-you-off!" and he got so excited he knocked a half dozen of Cathy's dresses off the rack. I picked them up. He opened the closet door a crack to let some air in, a good idea, 'cause we used up all the air in the closet a while back. We were afraid somebody'd see the closet door open and make a scene, but Cathy was guarding the door for us. Billy unzipped and took his cock out. It was marvelous to touch, huge and silky smooth and very sensitive. I made him sit bare-ass on the floor. I slid to my knees and started licking. I didn't try to swallow his cock, which Cathy and me had heard about from her older sister, 'cause I didn't want to gag.

Billy had been hinting he wanted this for weeks. It was his first time, too. I was afraid he wouldn't ever come, just keep groaning and pushing my head down. We were running out of air again. Then he got red hot and cried, "Sta-a-ay on m-me," so I guessed this was it, and a moment later I got my reward, a big salty sweet slimy glop that I bet was doing two hundred miles an hour when it splattered at the back of my mouth. I loved the taste, but there was so much spurting into my mouth so fast I didn't have time to enjoy it. I never dreamed there'd be so much. I gulped and gulped and more kept coming. Nobody warned me about how slimy it was. I wasn't sure I liked the slimy texture, but I guessed I'd better learn to like it if I was going to be doing much of this. I didn't dare slow down gulping until I sensed I was getting ahead of the flood.

By the second time I blew Billy, a few days later, I decided I loved slimy. It was part of what made the taste so special. After that I sucked Billy off every chance we got, sometimes twice or three times in a row. But we never went steady. Billy didn't want that to ruin our friendship when we would eventually break up. He was sure I'd leave him for some older guy. Like, I couldn't be attracted enough to him, 'cause we were friends? Billy looked nerdy back then, scrawny with glasses and brush haircut, so he didn't think I would stay with him.

When we went out together, guys would hit on me right in front of him, like they couldn't see him as my boy-friend. But now it's ten years later, he's just sent me a publicity photo of him, and he's incredibly handsome.

Cathy hadn't sucked anyone off yet. Boys were thrilled to play with her big boobs and they agreed she gave major league hand-jobs. I was proud of myself for being first in our class to blow anyone. It turned out that there was no shortage of boys happy to let me lick their cocks and balls 'til they came in my mouth. A few boys didn't call back after I sucked them off! I'd have a little cry, but there was always another one scratching at my door.

I was always looking for someone who appealed to me as much as Lenny, but who knew what to do. Doug was a new boy at St. Deems. He had gray eyes, black curly hair and an intense, lone wolf look. He wore a biker jacket and took drags on hand-rolled joints in school. When a teacher came by, he'd drop the joint, still lit, into his pocket. I was impressed. The first time Doug kissed me, in Central Park in broad daylight, he held me to him by my butt. A dozen people watched us from 'way off. I couldn't breathe and my heart pounded. I took him to my love nest in the middle of the afternoon. Mom was in with the flu. I reached under the banquette for a couple of towels. Doug took advan-tage of my bending over groping under the banquette for the towels to pull my panties down. "I didn't say you could do that!" I protested softly. I stayed bending over, looking away from him, resting my head on the seat of the banquette. I loved that he was looking at my ass and cunt from ten inches away!

Just then we heard the elevator pass and the muffled voices of people talking. This almost never happened in the evening, 'cause we're on the eleventh floor, right below the penthouse apartment. We froze. He didn't touch me. We waited until the elevator went down again. Somehow, we went back to kissing. We were both aware my panties were below my knees. Knowing my quim was moist and twitchy and my knees were spread for him and he deliberately wasn't touching me drove me nuts. A moment later he did, though. I stripped off and lay down. He tried to fuck me, and I was almost ready to lose my cherry. I wanted Doug to get in me, but I couldn't help wiggling to give him a hard time. I guess I was scared, too. I thought he'd get in somehow. Instead, he came on my thigh and belly and cursed me, calling me a "fucking tease." I decided right then I would definitely lay for him, but I didn't tell him. The next day, Doug started acting as though he owned me and I wasn't allowed to see other boys. I told him I didn't love him and I would see anyone I wanted. He cooled off, like, he'd show me. And that was that.

On Cathy's advice that stimulating your boobs makes them grow, I rubbed and tweaked my titties like mad. I told Billy if he wanted more blow-jobs, he had to pet my tits during lunch hour. We were supposed to be in the cafeteria during lunch hour, but there was a corner in the science room where we could be alone. Billy would eat a couple of cookies while he fondled me.

Sometimes he got careless and rubbed my tits with Oreos, and I made him lick them off.

My plan was to get my boobs petted at least fifteen minutes every day, but I couldn't take more than two minutes without needing something below. I'd slip my panties down below my butt and Billy would do me. He had great hands. Then, I'd unbutton and unzip him and suck him off. He'd feel my little boobs for all the time left until the bell rang for one o'clock classes. After a couple of weeks, I got him to eat me. He was the first who really did it. He said I tasted delicious. His face was a total mess. Luckily, there was a big lab sink where he could put his whole head under the tap, and lots of paper towels. After that, we were both horny as hell every day 'til lunch hour, and still horny afterward, but feeling a lot better.

Boys always think they're getting away with something, like you're supposed to be too dumb to know what they're thinking. I asked them what they thought about when I blew them, but they said they didn't think anything. Billy was the only one who was honest with me. He admitted sometimes he thought, *I love you, Sarah,* but other times he thought, *Now you're going to swallow my cum, you slut!* I said, "Why don't you say those things to me while I'm doing it?" So, he did. Guess what? He came better than ever, and I was thrilled whatever he said. It was the same for me, sometimes I was full of love for Billy, sometimes all I could think was *Here it comes, slut, glub it all down!* But Billy's parents moved to Kansas City, and I didn't see him again for ten years. He wrote me sweet letters and I called him when I was blue.

Cathy's theory about boobs growing when they're fondled enough turned out to be true. All at once, in a few glorious weeks, mine went from lemons to cantaloupes. I had a great body, long legs, hips, round butt, slender waist, narrow wrists and ankles, and at last— boobs! Big creamy white boobs with longish pink nippies that drove guys wild! Yes!

After Billy, I was desperate to get someone to eat me, but high school boys didn't know what to do. The jocks didn't have a clue and they were too satisfied with themselves to ask a girl what she likes. I used to daydream that Mom's boyfriend Nevil would make love to me. He would know what to do. We were already intimate in a way. Ever since I was too big for Mom to punish, she made Nevil do it. It was routine. She would send me to my room. Nevil would come in, put me across his knees and spank me with his hand. For the longest time he didn't take my panties down, but I made sure they were sexy—tiny or see-through, so my hiney was bare, or nearly.

In classes I would often cover my mouth, which would be open wide like I was yawning, but I'd be day-dreaming about sucking Nevil off. When the teacher called on me, I couldn't say a word 'cause my mind was somewhere else and my mouth was stuffed with cock! If they gave me enough time to recover, sometimes I could play back my mental tape of the question and answer it.

Every night I played with myself 'til I came thinking of Nevil eating me. That's how I got to sleep. I didn't know how to seduce Nevil. I paraded around in T-shirts without a bra so he could see my nippies. He was already seeing my bare legs and backside when he punished me. When he wrestled me across his knees for a spanking, my boobs would brush against his forearm and his left thigh. One spring day I was supposed to be showing Mom my new bathing suits, but she was in the library on the phone with a lawyer or somebody. I was in her dressing room, the door was open, Nevil was sitting on an ottoman in Mom's bedroom watching me in three mirrors that showed me from every angle. I stripped slow, so he knew I knew. When I was nude, I watched him. He had a bulge in his pants in all three mirrors! I tried on the suits, striking fashion poses. When I heard Mom on the way back I closed the door to the dressing room. I heard Nevil say matter-of-factly, "Sarah's in there waiting for you."

I found Dennis, a boy who'd never have figured he'd have a chance with me, and I told him I'd give him love lessons. He ate me out at least once a week for three months in our love nest at my front door. His reward was, when I was wrung-out coming, I sucked him off. Sometimes, I blew him first while he played with me, and then he ate me.

When Mom was inside the apartment, it felt safer for me to make out in my cozy love nest. Nevil never left before dawn. I covered the pinhole viewer with a bit of black tape as soon as me and a date got off the elevator at my floor. It sounds like I had it all worked out, but one night I got caught kissing Dennis good-night a half hour after we settled into the nest.

It was worse than just kissing. Mom harped on where I was kissing him, one of my favorite places on a man, underneath, where you can mouth the root of the prick growing out of the sack of balls. Also, my blouse was open and my bra down and my skirt up and my tiny panties around my knees. We were so into each other, the door was wide open before I could get my face out from under him and push his face out from under me. I held my bra up to cover my tits with one hand and yanked my panties up with the other. I was blushing down to my boobs. Dennis went into a daze huddling over his pole. His face was coated with my love gravy. Mom and Nevil dragged me inside. Mom ordered Nevil to spank me with his belt right there in the foyer.

I couldn't believe it when Nevil took his belt off. I was too turned on to be scared. Nevil being a gigolo and all, you'd think he'd understand about a girl blowing a date goodnight. But he acted as indignant as Mom. I was still trying to button my blouse when he put me across his knees and raised my skirt in back. I was sure he would take my panties down, but he didn't. They were my cutest, in back just a ribbon with a frilly border that was supposed to cover an inch of cheek on either side, but now was twisted into my crack. Nevil got an eyeful of round creamy ass cheeks, as always when he punished me. I couldn't protest 'cause my cunt was steamy damp and twitchy, and the crotch of my panties sopping wet.

My panties were famous. Me having classy "come-and-get-it" panties like Mom's drove her nuts. She called me "a slut and a thief," 'cause I lifted lingerie from department stores.

Dennis must have heard the smacks of the belt on my hiney and me bawling. He was on the other side of our front door and it would have taken him awhile to clean his face with the towels under the banquette and get himself together. I didn't hear the elevator come for him at all. Maybe, I was too distracted, or maybe he listened at our door the whole time.

Nevil's belt made my fanny bounce. I kicked my heels up and howled. Actually, I felt more like laughing, and would have if it hadn't hurt so much. There was something hilarious about lying across Mom's gigolo's lap, skirt up showing my gorgeous ass, being punished for the awful sin of licking my date's balls and cock. Dennis had me on the verge of coming, and the whipping didn't wipe that out, it added to my excitement.

But it was all too sudden, being yanked from Dennis's tender touch to suffering Nevil's belt. I couldn't enjoy myself across Nevil's knees as much as I might've with more time to stew about how I deserved it and get ready for it. Nevil made my cheeks bounce. This was the first time he really hurt my hiney. I guess he had to be strict so Mom wouldn't catch on that for us, it was sex.

Nevil's cock was trapped in his pants, but I felt it hard

against my thigh. Tell me that giving me a red ass didn't turn him on! I was turned on to him, too. If we could've just made Mom go away, we could've had something delicious together.

Then we did! It just happened. I was squirming from the terrific sting in my butt when the front of my quim nestled onto Nevil's left knee. It rubbed me exactly at the right spot at the right time, and I let go! I humped his knee and yowled! They thought it was just hiney pain. Nevil kept whipping my ass, I kept humping his knee and coming and screaming. Mom said, "Serves you right, slut!"

The irony was, before this evening, when I was so horny I felt brutal to myself, I used to imagine Nevil spanking me with his belt! Usually, it'd be for trying to seduce him. He'd catch me showing myself like I did in Mom's dressing room. He'd say, "Come here, little slut!" I'd picture him doing it lots of different ways, like, making me lie across Mom's ottoman or bend over holding my ankles. Once, when Mom was out, I pretended I was Nevil. I dragged myself by my bare titties to her ottoman and flung myself across it and took my panties down. Then I was me, imagining Nevil behind me raising his belt way back for the first smack. I kicked up my heels when he lashed me and made crying faces. I tried to feel how much it would hurt, but I couldn't get into it. I spread my knees and stuck my hiney up at him raunchy as I could and that made him whip me faster and fiercer, all-out, merciless, and then I could imagine the pain a little. Maybe my problem was, I was also reaching my right hand 'round back and through my thighs and underneath myself, the palm of my hand pressing hard against my hot, damp, churning cunt and two fingers rolling my clit. When I was exhausted with Nevil flogging me, and all, I knew he'd want me to blow him. Then he'd hug me and blow on my hot rear cheeks and kiss my tits and lick my clit and eat me out. Oh, well.

After Nevil really spanked me with his belt for the Dennis affair, I always imagined him whipping me more like it happened, across his knees, except Mom wouldn't be there and afterward I'd blow Nevil and he'd make love to me. I thought about giving Nevil my cherry, but that scared me, 'cause then he would have too much power over me. I knew he wouldn't leave Mom and her money.

Considering I got a red hiney for Dennis, I expected him to be extra nice to me the next day in school, but what happened was, he dumped me! What a fink! It was partly 'cause his family never liked me. Afterward, he looked like he regretted it.

In the couple of months while Dennis and I took turns kneeling on the pile rug in front of my door, it changed for all us girls from what we let boys do to us, to what we did for them. Sometime that winter, "going steady" meant you were taking care of him, too, one way or another. We were all "hanky girls" or "sucky girls." "Hanky girls" give hand-jobs and caught the stuff in the boy's handkerchief. I was definitely a "sucky girl." I loved the slimy salty taste and I couldn't understand wasting a drop. They told me I had great hands, but I loved the power it gave me over guys to munch their pricks down. Size didn't matter that much, they all looked beautiful to me. And I wouldn't quit when I got a mouthful. I licked them stiff again and sucked them off again. I got under their balls and mouthed them. I sucked boys off until they went totally limp and could hardly stand up. I wrecked them.

I didn't go steady with anyone, and I was very popular. Cathy sucked a guy off, at long last, and walked around school with a worldly look, long red hair piled up on her head and her tits high. Sex at St. Deems was like money in a runaway inflation. Suddenly, all of us were sucking, and some of us were screwing, and we talked to each other every day about what we were doing.

Alice, the coolest girl in our clique, announced her rule was: Once she let a date get his hands on her bare boobs or her thigh, he could do whatever he wanted. "Even fuck you?" Cathy asked. "Especially fuck me," Alice said, looking at Cathy like she was a child. That marked the end of an era for most of the other girls, who had been wrestling with every new guy for ten breathless minutes after he went up their skirts and took their panties down. A few kicked and scratched 'til they were pinned on their backs and their legs spread. A friend of ours said she didn't stop fighting even when a guy pinned her. She wriggled her pelvis so he couldn't get in (just like me with Doug). But he threatened to smack her face hard. She just lay there scared and five seconds later he was in her all the way and she couldn't remember why she was resisting.

That Easter vacation, me and Babs took the Devil Train to Florida. Afterward, once she was together enough to go out again, even Babs screwed. I had my own way of pleasing guys. I didn't wrestle, I didn't say no a lot, but I also wouldn't screw. I started off pure oral. At least I didn't have to worry about getting knocked up. I checked my upper lip when I was gulping cum all the time, but it isn't true about growing a mustache.

—— 4 ——

JOKES AND GAMES

Here's the stuff everybody wanted to know about the St. Deems crowd, once it got around that vice presidential candidate Tom Thomas took a turn with Cathy one evening in our game *Guess*. When Tom was just a college smoothie, me and Cathy shared him for a while.

There was jokey sex all over, even after we were doing real stuff. Some girls put out more in games, when it didn't count, than they did on dates. You found out how stuff felt, but you didn't get tied up with anybody you didn't like. Boys didn't have to figure out what to do if you liked them. Games and jokey sex rang my bell, 'cause they're all about shame.

One of the boy's big jokes was "whooshing" a girl. A lot of boys crowded around and held you so you couldn't move, and a boy went under your skirt and, whoosh! pulled your panties down to your ankles! Sometimes, that's all there was to it, they let you go and you pulled 'em up. Sometimes, another boy would throw your skirt up and they would singsong. "We saw your pus-sy!"

I didn't always mind being whooshed, but when I was in a bad mood, I hated it. It was better not to fight, 'cause they would drag you off your feet, pin your arms and legs and take your panties down, anyway, and toss them around, and you'd have to run from one boy to another trying to catch them. If the bell rang, everybody'd run to class and you might never see those panties again. You might have to go the rest of the day without panties, unless you kept extras in your locker for natural and boy-made emergencies. Boys kept your panties to jerk off into, and me and some other girls got our panties back all bunched up with dried cum.

There were tit-games, like *Names*. You're surrounded, they pin your wrists, and a boy holds his hands over your eyes. When they can, they bare your boobs. It depends where they catch you, whether they can get away with that. A boy tells you to name the pitchers with the best ERA's or the batters with the most RBI's, or the presidents since Franklin Roosevelt, and he starts tweaking your tits. You do it fast to get it over with. If you get flustered and make mistakes, your nippies are in for a lot of tweaking. Paula (before she became Alan's girl) learned batting averages and ERA's, state capitols and presidents, but some nerd asked her the first ten chemical elements. She looked pathetic, standing there with her boobs out, crying, and naming the same common ones over and over. "Beryllium and boron," I called out, and then she could do it. The guys chased me, but I was out of there.

At parties, we played *Guess*. The idea was, five or six boys picked a girl to be "It." Being "It" first was a smart move, 'cause *Guess* got wilder in later rounds. The boys blindfolded "It," and one of them did something, anything he wanted, almost, for about twenty seconds, and she had to guess who he was from his technique. If "It" guessed wrong, the boy got to do something else to her. That was it, he got two turns at most with her. If she guessed wrong again, he had to sit down and another boy got to do whatever he wanted to her for twenty seconds. If she guessed right, the boy was "It." He was blindfolded, and a girl got to do whatever she wanted to him.

Stripping an item of clothes off "It" was one thing you could do. Three girls could drop a boy's underpants: Step One, undo belt; Step Two, unbutton his pants; Step Three (next girl), unzip; Step Four, take pants down, Step Five (next girl), take underpants down. That would leave her with twenty seconds to play with the boy's cock. We didn't play *Guess* much 'cause boys didn't like standing around, blindfolded and naked below their shirt tails with balls and pricks on view, even when they were a good size. Some boys got terrific hard-ons when you took their underpants down, some sort of halfies that stuck out instead of up. If you weren't shy, it was neat to squeeze and pull their hot pricks. Some girls pinched boys' butts or smacked them. One girl, Dee, when she got her turn, whispered she was going to do something she'd never done before. It happened that the boy with his pants around his ankles, Dave, was a special friend of hers. Dee kneeled and licked Dave for her first turn and she held his stiff cock in her mouth and bobbed her head for her second turn. Everybody cheered. Both turns, we let her go 'way over twenty seconds. Since she'd never done this for Dave when they were alone, he didn't have a clue who it was. One of his wrong guesses was "Sarah!" For some reason that made Dee mad at me, but the others convinced her it was a terrific compliment.

I liked cradling a boy's balls and playing with his rear end, but they would've known my touch. So, what I did depended on how much I wanted to risk being "It." Girls who had little boobs, like I used to have, hated to stand around blindfolded with our bras off.

The more you remembered how boys did stuff on dates, the better for you. Like, no two boys touched your nippies the same way. I usually got off after one or two tricks. I could name ten boys before they even touched me from how they smelled and the way they breathed.

My friend Cathy was wild, but she couldn't remember how boys did stuff and she had lousy luck. She always guessed wrong. One evening Tom Thomas, who fooled around with Cathy and me and other St. Deems girls, turned up at a party in a brownstone. He was much older than us. None of the parents who guarded the front door saw him come in or leave. He took off his tweed sports jacket and touched it to the wall, where it stayed like it was on a hanger, loosened his tie and rolled up his sleeves to join the action.

Cathy was already naked, with guys doing practically everything to her. Fucking was understood to be out (since everybody but "It" had to stay dressed), even when a boy claimed he could shoot the works in twenty seconds. Cathy had full breasts and the boys gave them lots of attention while she guessed one wrong name after another. They fingered her, too, but she kept guessing wrong, as though every guy didn't have his own way of doing that! I wanted to yell "You dumb slut!" 'cause I felt bad for her.

Out of nowhere, Tom was at the front of the line. Somehow, he "MRG'd" into our Game, like into the famous video I did with him years later: He wasn't in the picture with me, then he was. You know how a stage magician appears or disappears in a puff of smoke? It was like that: the air puffed him out of itself. I'm not saying Tom is the Devil, Cathy and me and lots of other girls know him too well for that. Besides, would the Devil run for vice president and let himself be creamed at the polls? But, maybe the Devil edits Tom in wherever he wants him!

Tom bent Cathy 'way over, so her long red hair piled up on the carpet, and clamped her against his left hip and leg. I would've known that was Tom anywhere. Cathy didn't know he was at the party and she didn't think of him. On his second turn, Tom spanked her bare hiney—three typical Tom spanks, crisp, loud, meaty, all in exactly twenty seconds. Cathy's rear cheeks turned pink and she cried, *"Owww!—Owww!— OWWW!"* Again, she guessed wrong! Now, she was supposed to stay bending over 'til someone put her another way. The next guy, Sam, fondled her butt on his first turn. Her soft white and blotchy pink cheeks wobbled in Sam's hand. She guessed wrong, again. On his second turn Sam reached his hand well into her crack, and cupped her asshole. Cathy said later he gave her a gentle goose, not a let's-see-how-far-up thrust. She was already about to cry and all it took was a fingertip poking into her tail pipe to make her go to pieces. Everyone wanted to let her off, so we stage whispered, "Sam!" which was against the rules. But Cathy was whirling after being stripped, tweaked, petted, fingered, spanked, and goosed, and she didn't get it. Finally, she heard us stage-whisper the name of the next boy, who was innocently rolling her ass cheeks. He quit in protest when she repeated his name, and the game ended.

A few months later Cathy and me had a sophisticated party at my place. Cathy celebrated her birthday the same week. By now everyone was into blowing. Cathy was as crazy about it as me. We slow-danced with one boy after another, with lots of kissing and nuzzling, and when we got hot with a boy, we dragged him off to a bedroom. Dave (Dee's ex-) showed me "69" that night. We came together. Terrific!

All the boys raved about the party, 'cause they got sucked off three or four times. I blew five boys, and

Cathy did four, and the other girls did their share. High school boys make so much cum, three doses would have been plenty. I gulped five to keep up my rep. If a girl had big tits and was pretty, she got the cute boys, and sometimes put out less, too, if she wanted to hold back. Me and my friends didn't want to hold back, we wanted guys who made us go forward. Putting out made a girl popular, but then she had to keep doing more and more and more guys, to stay ahead of the pack. I'm not sure you can understand all this unless you went to St. Deems.

—— 5 ——

CREAM OF THE CROP

I goof on men when I can get away with it, but with guys I really like, I often wind up bending over bare-ass for punishment. I love dominating men and driving them nuts, but when I can't, I love to be humiliated, punished, and used like a sheik's sex slave. It's all deliciously shameful. Either way, shame turns me on.

For a Shame Artist, it's sexy to mess around in public. Like, the first time Tom Thomas touched me, about eight of us were hanging out on a deep-pile rug in Cathy's living room. We all had our shoes off and Tom was barefoot. Whoever wanted to pair off was already in one of the bedrooms. Tom was on a sofa behind me, not quite part of our group, but close enough to join in when he wanted to. I squeezed his calf without looking at him when he told a good raunchy story. A few minutes later he brought his shin up into my armpit and started petting my left boob with his toes, right in front of everyone. I was wearing a blouse and a filmy bra. It was so insulting! Not even his hand, his foot! I could've clamped his leg, I could've said, "Stop that!" and he would've, but then where would we be? I ignored him, everybody ignored him as well as they could. He extended his big toe, got me right on the nippie, my nippie was hard and burning through my blouse, I was going nuts, but I kept talking to everybody else. After a while he took his toe back. I won! The next day he called me. I admitted my other nippie, the one that didn't get toed, felt jealous, and we went out.

As a Shame Artist I created my masterpiece the day I graduated from high school. My senior year, guys I'd been going with were in college or seeing the world. A boy in our class named Alan Darshow was after me. He was a rich nerd totally programmed by his Daddy to take over the family sports car franchise. He got a new Porsche the day he was accepted by a business college for kids like him.

Alan was always the first boy to get to the gym pool for boys' swimming and this time I was the last girl to leave girls' swimming. He was ten minutes early just to gawk at us in our 1940s tank suits. So, I gave him more. Normally, you go from the pool into the girls' locker room, pulling your suit off when you get to your own locker. But here the two of us are in the pool area, no one but Alan and me. He's by the diving board, I'm across a deep corner of the pool, maybe twenty feet away. Pretending I don't know he's there, I peel my suit down, letting my boobs bounce out. My nippies are hard and longish from knowing what this is going to do to Alan. I push my hair back, wringing water out of it. Of course, I'm also posing, elbows way back, showing off my tits. I slowly push my tank suit down over my hips and let it slide to the tiles. Then, I bend over, deliberately pointing my ass at him, pick my suit up, and walk naked to the girls' locker room. No way could he get his hard-on down in time for class. I suppose I could've gotten reprimanded for strolling into the locker room naked, but nobody noticed.

This just shows how bored I was. It doesn't mean I wanted to go out with Alan. To put it bluntly, I didn't care to finish an evening by sucking Alan off or taking his prick any other way. Even my Mom wanted me to go out with him. He was extra polite to her. What did she think "going out" with him would get me? A diamond ring? A low-slung convertible roadster with bucket seats? No, it just meant, one way or another, Alan would get to pump his load into me. Maybe she knew that, and it was OK with her 'cause he was rich. *Hey,* Mom, you suck him off.

I couldn't get rid of Alan. He'd heard what I was doing for guys and he wanted his piece of the pie. It didn't matter to him that I couldn't stand him! Watching his Dad sell cars, he learned to take "No" to mean, *Throw in something to cinch the deal.* Alan trapped me in the corridors at school and offered me bribes, like, he'd take me to rock concerts no one could get tickets to. I considered going to a concert with him, letting him think I was going to blow him afterward, and then slipping away. But it would have been too much trouble.

Finally, I got even on graduation day. His Dad and Mom were sitting front and center in the auditorium. We were all waiting backstage to march out for our diplomas. Alan was standing off to one side by a stage flat. He was wearing a blue-silk suit, a white dress shirt, and an executive silk tie. He might even have been wearing silk underpants, too, for all I know, 'cause when I came up close behind him and played with his rear end, there wasn't much between his butt and my fingers. Hardly anybody could see what I was doing. We were way off to one side and partly behind the flat. One girl asked me about it at the party that evening.

"Don't move," I whispered in Alan's ear. He knew I wouldn't want a guy who wasn't wild like me. He even bribed Paula, his steady, to tell me he was great in bed. That's what a snake he was. Paula told me about the bribe. She also said she wasn't screwing for him and doubted she ever would. Paula was glad to have someone to talk to about Alan. She confessed she let him feel her up, and looked to see how that grabbed me. I shrugged, sure, if anybody's ever going to tweak your tits, it's your high school steady. She admitted that on special occasions, if he treated her OK and forgot to hurt her feelings the whole evening, she'd let him put his hand up her dress. She said he wasn't bad at fingering, just kind of mechanical, which is what I had guessed.

Paula told me why Alan was such a horny freak. He drove himself crazy by not jerking off, trying to be more mature than the other boys. The other boys couldn't keep their hands out of their pockets in math class when me or Cathy went to the board. But Alan not only couldn't score with Paula, he couldn't score with himself! Meanwhile, he let everyone know he was screwing Paula all the time, which made the rest of us even less interested in him. Paula swore she never touched Alan's prick, and that's why he broke up with her every couple of weeks, but when he couldn't get anywhere with anyone else, either, he'd call her again.

Now, ten minutes before graduation, Alan has a big problem. The Darshows, all the other parents out in front, the place crawling with teachers, him in his silk duds, and me fondling his butt like I bet nobody ever did before or since. His cock is hard as a rock, there's no chance he'll get it down before we're called to march out. I trace a finger down the crack of his ass and he breathes hard. This isn't the way he'd planned it, but he's not about to turn it down. His scheme would be, take me out some Saturday night, spend lots of money on me, get me drinking champagne, drive me somewhere he can kiss me and turn me on with his expert tit-twiddling, and, then, when I'm drunk and helpless with lust and too compromised to argue, fuck me, or make me do any of the other things he's heard I do. Well, surprise!

I teased behind his balls. He gasped, "Please, Sarah, stop." Delightful to hear a boy say that for a change—and just laugh at him! See what a bitch I was? I had him right where I wanted him. He was like a virgin who's gone too far—maybe it started with some nice kisses, and now her bra is off and her panties are down, and the guy's ripping his pants and underpants down and all at once it dawns on her she's going to get fucked! I mean, a virgin who doesn't know all the tricks I do! Anyway, she's on her back and the guy's kneeling between her thighs and pinning her wrists down by her shoulders. The tip of his hard prick's just poking into her cunt when she pipes up, "Please, don't." That's how Alan sounded.

I cradle Alan's balls in my right hand. They're heavy, loaded with bustling eager executive sperm. At the same time I lean against him so my hot tits bore into his back, and I mouth the back of his neck. I slip my left hand around to the shaft of his prick and murmur how big it is. It's average. I give him an extra-loving hand-job.

"I'd love to fuck you," I blow my hot breath in his ear, "fuck you, fuck you, fuck you." Of course, I was thinking, *Fuck you, asshole!*

"Please, please," he whimpers. It's too late for mercy. His cock's red hot and throbbing in my left hand. I knead it harder. A little squeeze and slide on the shaft, squeeze and jerk on the top knob. All the while I fondle his balls with my right hand.

He turns purple, moans, and fights coming. *"Oh, what a lovely prick you have, Alan,"* I croon in his ear. I suck his earlobe. "I'd adore to lick your cock all up and down. Bet you'd like to come in my mouth, wouldn't you? Make me gulp down every drop?"

[59]

No question he would, from the way he's breathing. His eyes bulge more than usual. I slip my right hand back off his balls and find his asshole. I glide a fingertip around the rim. "Maybe, you'd like to fuck me in my rear end," I whisper, in my lowest, dirtiest voice, "make me kneel with my backside up and spread my cheeks, shove your big cock all the way up my ass." I goose him slowly to go with what I'm saying. "I'd squirm on your big prick and you'd give it to me good."

Now, the weird part was, I started this to pay him back, but talking as sexy as I could and being so close to him, rubbing his cock and balls and butt, and feeling him go all to pieces, I turned on myself!

"Hold it—!" he begged. I felt the instant he caved. I'd won, but I didn't let up. I sped the hand-job in front, and behind, my right middle finger stuffed a little blue silk suit fabric straight up. He came, twitching like a fish on a hook. Of course, he couldn't cry out. I reached up with my left hand to feel the flooding damp. The cream oozed through the whole front of his pants and the belly of his pretty shirt. It stained the back and the edges of his silk tie and the inside front of his jacket and one jacket sleeve from his elbow to his cuff. His alligator belt and its gold clasp dripped white. I went back to rubbing his cock with my left hand, so he'd have the longest and best orgasm of his life, except that he was completely disgracing himself.

Jets of cream keep coming. I goose Alan like I own his asshole, which I do for awhile, and I squeeze his balls lovingly to make sure every last drop comes out.

Then, so he knows it's no accident, that I'm deliberately fucking him over, I wipe the cream oozing through his pants into my hand back onto the chest of his shirt.

Graduation music blared over the loudspeaker. They were lining us up to march in. "What do I do now?" he wailed. I could've left him to die. But I'd got what I wanted. "Walk close behind me," I said, "I'll put you in a taxi, you go home." He takes off his jacket, turns it inside out so it covers most of the mess. "I'll tell everybody it was an emergency—something you ate—we couldn't take time to get your parents—I put you in a taxi to the hospital—but, you say you threw up and by the time you got to the emergency room, you were feeling better, so you just went home to rest."

"Thanks," he said, dazed. "Don't mention it," I grinned.

I'll bet he threw out the suit, the shirt, and the tie. My left hand smelled fishy and my right middle finger stinky, so I made a quick detour to the girls' washroom. I joined my class onstage, waved to Mom, and then went down the front row and told Alan's agitated parents about the food poisoning. I guess St. Deems mailed Alan his diploma. He didn't make it to our graduation party later that evening, where I was still so horny I misbehaved with three guys one after another, and in between Paula and I got off in a corner and had a giggle.

— 6 —

AT THE ARTISTS' BEACH HOUSE

The old charges of date rape against Tom Thomas might never have turned up again, except I got involved with Sofi and Francis. That story began at the four artists' beach house, where Sofi saw me the first time and I met Silas Hardon.

Dad lost all his money in the stock market in the spring of my freshman year at Belmont College. Mom declared she was broke too, and wouldn't pay for me to screw around three more years. When rich people say they've lost all their money, they don't count assets less than a million. If Mom would've sold the Fifth Avenue apartment and paid off her mortgage, she'd still have had a crummy six hundred thousand, but that didn't seem like real money to her, 'cause she couldn't live in high style on the interest.

Anyway, Mom said get a job, and warned me I better marry rich. I worked as a receptionist. Bor-r-r-ing! However, the first week a guy from the office and his two pals took me and two friends of mine to a club where girls came out on the dance floor and stripped. One was OK, three in a row were awful. When my friends and me went to the ladies', I showed them what a strip could be. I didn't plan it, it just came to me.

"My impression of a girl letting a boy take her panties down for the first time," I announced. I played both roles, the boy not believing he's getting to do this, the girl putting up a coy struggle. The boy drags 'em down inch by inch 'til her butt's bare (mine was!) and she covers her face with her hands. When he does stuff to her, at first her knees lock and her toes point in, then her legs turn to jelly and she humps and groans. A sharp old lady watched my act in the large mirror over the sinks.

"Auditioning for me, Sarah?" she said, picking up my name from my friends. The funny thing was, I could see her in the mirror, but I couldn't figure out where she was.

"No," I said, "should I be?"

"That depends," she said, "I'm one of the owners. The one who hires the talent."

"You want me to be a stripper here?" I said. I kept turning around and around trying to spot her.

"You could be a star," she said. "You got looks and class."

"Where are you? How much would I make?"

"Tuesday through Saturday, you're on twelve minutes at nine, eleven, and one in the A.M. Three different outfits and acts. They don't have to be clever, but keep 'em raunchy. Five hundred a week, plus tips." I agreed. She said, "Be here 8:30 Tuesday evening in your stage clothes." At the time I didn't actually meet the Queen of the Night, who appeared in this dive as boss lady Ethyl, but I was under her protection ever afterward. The pay worked out to thirty-three bucks a strip plus scads of twenties guys tucked into my G-string. I spent too much on "stage lingerie" at a place the girls told me about.

The other owners of the nightclub were three middle-aged hoods. They got me to strip for them when Ethyl wasn't around, not even in a mirror. New strippers had to give these guys freebies, basically, blow them to show you're a good sport. They let you know lots of women want your job.

It was after my eleven o'clock strip the first Friday. I was skipping off the stage naked, but before I pick my bathrobe off its hook, two of the hoods lifted me by my armpits and put me down on the stairs to the cellar. It was walk down the stairs ahead of them or get shoved down.

You could hear the bump-and-grind music above for a girl stripping. I knew what was happening, one of the other strippers told me it would. She said she cried, but she had to do it, anyway. I promised myself I wouldn't cry. I danced for the three of them, adding a trick that was my way of telling them how sleazy they were. I had

Jack hold up his middle finger, and crouching over his palm, I took his finger in my snatch and humped it. I meant to fake coming, but I got carried away with how low and revolting all this was, and I actually came. "Jeez!" Jack wheezed, "she's squeezing my finger!"

I'd just as soon have left then, but they passed me around, pawed me, and set me on my knees in front of Jack, who dropped his pants and whipped it out in my face. The other two unbuckled, unbuttoned, unzipped. I didn't have a lot of choice with their stiff pricks out and waggling for attention.

The three pricks looked vulnerable, like three baby birds in a nest with mouths gaping open waiting to be fed. I started off contemptuous, but the truth is, I love sucking, and in no time I got into it. It was thrilling having to do this to keep my job and get out of there in one piece. I went from one to the other on my knees on the cruddy linoleum floor. First, I rubbed each prick between my boobs. Then, I licked each prick 'til it was almost ready to shoot. Then, I teased Jack over the top, and while I was gulping the last of his cum, I smiled up to number two. I totally wiped those pricks out, demolished them, one two three. Afterward, my nerves were shot, I was edgy and horny, but I pulled myself together for my one o'clock show.

My performances on stage were class acts, steaming with hot shame. The exotic dancers me and my friends saw were low-class. They never learned about shame growing up, 'cause it was all around them. It takes parents with class and a school like St. Deems to make a Shame Artist.

Stripping was great the first six nights or so, and then it was like any other routine, boring. Luckily, I met Larry and his three friends. They were artists who had a house in the Hamptons. Larry asked me to work for them, modeling and entertaining their clients, in return for a place to flop and all I could eat. I figured I'd scrounge off them for the summer and look for work in the fall. I was thinking about fashion modeling and getting into TV commercials. Larry was rugged and handsome. He had scars on his face and he limped.

July, anyway, I flopped in the famous party house on the beach rented by the four artists. One day it dawned on me that these four had more in common than sharing a house, a mistress, and art. They all had major scars. They always hung out together as though they were afraid to go anywhere alone.

At their weekend parties a Thai cook prepared trays of hors-d'oeuvres that I took around to the guests, gallery owners and wealthy clients. Did I say I was nearly naked? Before my first party, Larry said, "Take everything off." I pretended I had to do whatever he said. That can be easier than figuring out how much you can say no to. Larry tied a micro black silky apron on me that barely covered me in front and left my behind bare. I found black bikini panties that went with the apron. He didn't plan on the panties, but he wasn't disappointed. The rear strip supposed to cover my crack sank into it. For my top, he gave me a butler's vest with black and yellow stripes, like a bee. No buttons, no button-holes. A little brass chain dangled down on one side, but whatever it was to fasten to was missing, torn out. The vest covered my tits when I kept my arms at my sides. As soon as I raised an arm, a tit popped out. That was it. Almost bare ass and peek-a-boo boobs. The chef handed me a tray of hot hors-d'oeuvres and Larry pushed me out among the guests.

I let my tits rest on the rim of the tray, the vest hanging alongside them. The jokers reached across the tray, hovered over the baked bite-sized shrimp pies, and said, "I'll take one of these," tweaked one of my nippies, "and one of these," tweaked the other one. I was pretty turned on by the time I worked the room. Some women gave me a hooded look, *You hang around my man, I'll scratch your eyes out.* Carrying a tray made it easier. The guys started off too cool to pinch my behind as I passed by, but after they got bombed at the marguerita bar, it seemed like the thing to do. It would've been rude for me to walk away from a pinch, so I stood there blushing and gave each paw its moment. There were sweet pinches and sensual ones and a few greedy grabs. Some were witty. There were tiny tweaks, butt-rollers, cheek-shakers, double pinches (one on each cheek), and goosey pinches.

A guest tugged at the bow of the ribbon behind me. I tried to pin the apron to me with the tray, but it slipped to my ankles. I set the tray down to pick the apron up. "Panties!" a man called out. OK. He didn't know he was daring a pro stripper! I flipped my panties down, like, inside out, and pirouetted, showing it all to everybody. Then, I flipped the panties up, picked up my apron, tied it on, grabbed the tray, and exited with dignity, amid cheers. It was my way of turning the tables.

The idea of having a beautiful almost-nude hostess was to make sure everybody understood this was the "in" place to be. The first party night Larry pointed out a little gent staring at me with a terrific bulge in his pants, and said, "Sarah, that's Silas Hardon, a connoisseur of beauty. Jolly him up, will you?" He wanted Mr. Hardon to want to hang out at the house. So, I stood as close to him as I could get without rubbing up against the bulge in his pants. OK, we rubbed once, my thigh against the little guy's hose. I was intrigued. It was as long as my thigh! That's poetic license, what I mean is, it felt like it was that long.

No one told me who Mr. Hardon was. His face was never on the news, and his real name was never mentioned when the poop hit the fan. Silas Hardon was very generous to me and asked me not to use his real name in my book, even though I was using Tom Thomas's name and President Edwin Chase's name. When I asked him what he did, he said he worked for a media firm, like, you would think maybe he filed videocassettes and went for coffee. But, then, Larry wouldn't have cared whether I cozied up to him or not. So, I knew he was somebody.

But, also, Mr. Hardon was a mouse! I planted myself in front of him with my hands on my hips, sweeping my vest open. My bare tits were a quarter of an inch from his chest. If he took a deep breath, they'd burn two holes in him. He was shorter than me, even though I was barefoot and his shoes were built up. He wanted to take me away, but, I told him, "Can't, honey, I'm on duty." He wanted us to find a bedroom that wasn't being used, but I told him, "Sweetie, they're all reserved." He begged me not to be cross with him for suggesting that, so I said, "You're very naughty." I ordered him to come back to the house. Every time he came back, one of the artists sold him something. One time I was modeling nude. He was afraid to come too close. Another time I was just walking around the house in my bikini bottoms, but he didn't dare approach me. He didn't know whether it would have been OK with the guys and he didn't want to lose his drop-in privileges.

Late one Monday afternoon, Mr. Hardon came by when the artists were out. I was sunbathing nude in a canvas chair on the deck. I was glad to see him because it had been a perfectly boring day. The truth is, I was forbidden to wear a stitch for two days. Going naked was part of my punishment for something I'd done with a local stud, Carl the Goat Man, toward the end of our Saturday night bash.

I said, "Silas, take off your clothes!" Out came a long hard skinny prick, twitching like a twig in a hurricane. He was a soft little man with sparse sandy hair and a long cock. Never exercised a day in his life, I bet. Any sun at all was too much for him. His face was boiled pink and skin was peeling off his nose. His backside, and his belly and thighs where the swimsuit covered them were chalk white.

"What do you want?" I said. He couldn't speak. I took one of his rear cheeks in my hand and pulled him close. I licked up from his big pink balls to the crown of his cock and took it in my mouth. I gave his balls a squeeze and let him feel my fingernails, just the right mix of caress and terror for him, and he swiveled about a minute and came down my throat. Little son of a bitch pumped a lot of cum into me. "Sarah, you're the greatest!" he said. I went back to sunbathing. He dressed and split.

I made that story up to please the guys in the house. Later, when I met Sofi, I told her what I really did to Mr. Hardon. She knew him well, in fact, she came to the artists' parties with him. Silas Hardon was her client as well as ours. I gathered he ran a big business by telephone and fax from the Hamptons.

I'd sold enough paintings. I wanted to have fun. Mr. Hardon did whatever I said. I sat up in the deck chair and declared, "You're a dog—Down on all fours!" "Bark, Silas!" "Roll over!" "Give me your paw!" I let him chew my tits a while. Then, I ordered him to eat me out. I clamped his face hard to my quim and tried to drown him. Once I started coming, I wouldn't let the little wimp get away. His face was coated and dripping. But, he was so excited he had to have something. He thought he deserved it! He begged me to blow him.

I reminded him he was a dog. I let the back of the

chair all the way down and stretched out on my belly. I made him lick my ass. He kneeled on the deck, his paws on my butt, licking up and down in my crack. Sofi loved to hear me tell this part.

Mr. Hardon wanted to fuck me, but he was worried the flimsy chair would collapse. I told him that was the least of his worries. I yelled, "Down, boy!" and made him sit at my feet and play with himself. He got unhappy, his cock drooped. "I can do this at home," he said. "How dare you!" I screamed at him. I sounded like Mom! I raised my hand like I was going to slap him. He was scared of me. I jumped up and took him by the back of the neck. "Get up!" I yelled, and marched him over to the railing. On the way I picked up a paddle that was lying on the deck. We had a set of four of them and a ball for the beach.

The last time one of these paddles was used, two days before, was on a gorgeous, round female butt—guess whose! I started getting into trouble about one-thirty Saturday morning. The party went on to about three-thirty, but the couples left around midnight, and by one-thirty more singles were leaving than coming. Anyway, I'd had too many margueritas. I was at the rail out on the deck for fresh air when Carl came up behind me. Carl was a big lug, hairy as a goat, with little white curved horns, too, and cloven hooves. If you go by images, you jump on that and think, *Aha! Horns! Cloven hooves! Carl's the Devil!*

No, he was just part of the beach scene in the Hamptons. Why should the Devil look like a goat, anyway? A goat's harmless unless you annoy it. A long time ago, one ate my picnic, not just the sandwiches, the basket and part of the blanket, too.

Anyway, Carl came up behind me at the deck rail. I was looking out over the ocean. My blonde hair streamed in the breeze. By now, the deck lights were out, we were alone, not counting a few other couples smooching in deck chairs. The Goat Man stood close behind me, massaged my boobs. I was wearing the open butler's vest that made them easy to get to. My nippies are longish anyway, and right at that moment they were pointing to England. They weren't the only thing that was hard. I felt Carl's cock sawing up and down my crack. I loved that. I shimmied against it.

The problem was, Larry had let everybody know I was his screw after the party. I wasn't sure what to say to Carl when he took my tiny black panties off and ate them. I sailed out over the ocean right into the stars where the Queen of the Night waited for me combing her hair out on the crescent moon, each stroke streaking silver over the crests of waves far at sea to our shore.

When my senses came back to me, my feet were off the deck. My legs were spread wide, Carl was between them. His hands were under my rear cheeks, lifting me up, and he was screwing me from behind with long, sensuous thrusts. I was leaning forward holding the railing for dear life. I was still wearing the micro black apron and the vest. Then, the deck lights came on. Larry was there, fuming, and lots of other people. I couldn't see back of me, the Goat Man Carl was in the way. I had all I could do to hold onto the railing. I looked out over the dark beach to the white breaking waves. Carl rooted around in me and lifted my butt all the way up and down on his cock, giving me a good bump up as I came down. He was showing off and showing me off, but he was passionate, too, stamping the deck with his right hoof, slashing my vest with his horns. A woman said, "Some ride!" in a sarcastic voice. I thought she might be jealous. I sure hoped so!

Up, down, up, down! I couldn't help moaning with pleasure. Everybody knew I had just wandered out to the deck and a few minutes later I was letting the big hairy goat fuck me. What made it more delicious was, everybody knew I was supposed to be Larry's piece of ass this evening, and now all he could do was watch me churn on Carl's wonderful prick. It was my way of zapping Larry for acting too high-handed with me. He limped away mad as hell. I never saw anyone limp that fast.

The lights went off again. After a moment Carl lifted me off and laid me on my back on the deck and got on top of me. I wrapped my arms and legs around his hairy body. He was heavy, but as long as he kept fucking me like this, I didn't care. Carl had a rep for fucking until women cry "uncle," which got him laid all up and down the beach. I came again and again, and then the Goat Man exploded and machine-gunned me, and I was worn out coming.

I thought, how romantic and dangerous this is, with

Larry stewing in the house. I hoped he'd just go to sleep, but he was up, ragged, and pissed. Carl knew he was not welcome at the house just now, so he left. It was a quarter to three, and there were only about a dozen people in the living room and three in the kitchen.

What was Larry to do, fuck me better than Carl? He couldn't. Instead, he told me to bring him a paddle. A few people saw me go out to the deck and get the paddle and smuggle it back half hidden under my butler's vest. My apron was backless, so they could see my rear end on all these trips, if they looked. When I was crossing the living room with the paddle, I put it behind me for modesty, but, then, I thought, that doesn't matter anymore. Shifting the paddle up and back, I dropped it and it clattered. Now, everybody was looking! I heard snickers. I picked the paddle up and scooted into Larry's room, blushing down to my nippies.

Larry was sitting on the edge of his bed. I handed him the paddle. I was a mess, Carl was gone, and I didn't know if we'd ever get together again. Larry was offering me a way to get this caper behind me, so to speak. I stripped off my vest. Larry croaked, "Over," and I went across his knees. I didn't bother to take off my tiny black apron, which wasn't going to get in the way of anything he wanted to do to me.

"You left the fucking door open!" Larry snarled. "Would you fucking mind—?" I hadn't meant to. From the instant I came into his room and he took the paddle from me, all I saw was his knees waiting for me to lie across them, all I thought about was how much my rear end was going to hurt. But once across his knees, when he said that, I turned my head up toward the door and I saw two or three people in the living room gawking at us. One of them was a huge jolly fat woman. All evening she kept planting her elephant body in my way to get more than her share of hors-d'oeuvres. She wore a loose tent of a dress, but it was plain she had six times as much boob as a woman needs and more meat on her ass than there is on a whole hog. I got myself up, shut the door on her, lay back across Larry's knees.

I admit bringing Larry a paddle and presenting my backside prettily turned me on. It's not that I'm crazy about suffering hiney pain, but the more humiliating it is, the sexier I get. Hurting back there is part of it, and when my hiney's on fire, when it hurts more than I can stand, I go into a sex frenzy. I put my ass up a bit for Larry and whimpered, "Please, don't hurt me." You'd have to be a Shame Artist to understand.

Everybody, the couples in the bedrooms, everyone in the living room and kitchen, heard five terrific smacks of the paddle and me crying, *"OWWW!"* and begging for mercy in my teasing brat voice that makes a man want to give it to me three times as bad. Larry spanked me hard, on and on, like Carl fucked. That was his idea of paying me back, and he loved seeing my buttocks bounce. At first, the whole house was quiet except for the loud meaty smacks and me yowling how sorry I was for misbehaving. Then, it hurt too much to say anything. I could feel the hurt spread all through me, into my fingertips and toes, even into my titties jiggling over his knee. I pumped my hiney, kicked up my heels, and bawled. Phil and his girl for the evening snickered in the bedroom next to ours.

You can hear everything in those beach houses. Every move made our bedsprings sing—Larry's fast hard spanks, me pumping my ass and kicking my heels up. Me and Larry heard the party in the living room shift to outside our door. The door didn't come all the way down to the floor or up to the ceiling. A dozen people were breathing on the other side of the door, maybe eight feet away. At each spank, I cried, *"WAHHHN!"* and sobbed louder, and a woman laughed *"Ha-ha-ha!"* it was the fat woman who saw me over Larry's knees before I got up and closed the door! What's so funny, I wanted to ask her, about me getting paddled?

SMACK! *"OWWW-WAHHHN!"*

"Ha-ha-ha a-ha hee-hee-hee!"

Fat bitch! It amuses her to picture my rear cheeks bouncing and turning red?

SMACK! *"OWWW-WAHHHN-AHHHN!"*

"Ha-ha-ha-ha hee-hee-hee-hee!"

It's my bawling, isn't it? That's what tickles you! Cunt! I was so mad at her, I almost forgot how bad my hiney hurt.

SMACK! *"WAHHHN! WAHHHN! WAHHHN!"*

"Ha-ha-ha-ha a-ha a-hee a-hee!"

Was it funny 'cause I misbehaved and was getting what I deserved? I promised myself I'd take whatever Larry decided was the right punishment. But after eight across my crack, three on my right cheek, three on my left cheek, two on the back of each thigh, six low mean ones on the sensitive curve of the cheeks right over my asshole . . . I lost count, my ass burned, I couldn't take any more. I wanted Larry in me, but I was bawling so hard I couldn't tell him. I tried to wriggle off his knees. Larry tossed the paddle down on the bed, dragged me around, fixed me across his left thigh so my head and shoulders were behind him, and spanked me with his hand. I love a few hand-spanks on my tender red bottom to finish. I prayed he was finishing.

Outside our door they probably caught on he was using his hand, but they couldn't hear him spread my thighs wide apart, and they didn't know he was slapping down in there so his palm wapped the tenderest part of my cheeks near my asshole, and his long bony fingers lashed my pussy, like saying, "What a naughty pussy you were out there on the deck!" So, I got an extra mean hand-spanking on top of a terrific paddling.

The way I was lying, facing backward, I could twist back toward Larry and almost kiss his backside above where he was sitting on it. "She's offering to do whatever he wants," a woman said, I think another woman, not the obese laughing cunt. After a few more smacks, he slid me down his left thigh to the floor and lay back, propping himself up on a pillow. For the last few minutes I'd felt it wasn't fair, he was punishing me too much. But once he stopped, I realized it might be about right for what I'd done. I began to feel how much I loved Larry. I licked his balls, which I knew drove him wild. My face was wet with tears. I couldn't even touch myself back there, that's how bad it hurt. Larry told me to lick lower, behind his balls. I did. It's just about my favorite place on a man to kiss. Then, I whispered to him to turn over. He repeated real loud, "Turn over?" and a guy outside the door said, "Is he telling her to turn over?" and then the laughing cunt said, "No, *she's* telling *him* to turn over! *Ha-ha!*" Now, that was clear to everyone.

Larry lay on his cock, like, presenting his handsome behind. I'm crazy about men's backsides. I love to smooch them when guys appeal to me as much as Larry. That's considered far out, so I do it less than I'd like. But at this moment the best way to make up was to give Larry exotic kisses beyond anything I gave Carl out on the deck. Anybody who heard Larry's shrieks of pleasure might have guessed what I did for him. Larry practically fucked his bed. I could tell when he was about to come before he could, 'cause my nose was close to the action! I told him to roll back over, and he did, and I got my mouth on his cock just in time for a spurt to slap hot and salty 'way back in my throat. It was gulp fast or drown. I could hear my friends from college saying, "Poor Sarah, she went to the shore last summer and drowned."

See how I stayed in charge, even, when I was paying for my indiscretion? I told Larry when to turn over and when to turn back over. Unfortunately for me, the punishment was not complete just because Larry was satisfied. Next morning, before I was completely awake, Phil told me for all of them that for the next two days I was under House Punishment, which meant I was grounded, not allowed to wear any clothes at all, and that I had no privacy. I was not permitted to close myself in a room, not even a bathroom, or go into a closet. No one particularly wanted to see me on the pot, but it was humiliating to have to leave the door open. I found myself wistfully eyeing my swimsuits and summer dresses. I was afraid even to touch them, 'cause my hiney was still rosy and tender from Larry's spanking and didn't need any more attention.

Lounging about or wandering around the house in the buff, I was subject to more than the usual twiddling and tweaking, patting and pinching. I was supposed to come when called and obey with a smile. Sometimes, "obey" meant bring tea, sometimes it meant going to my knees and licking, or lying on my back and spreading, or bending over holding my ankles. I was sternly warned not to whine about any of this. Nevertheless, after Sunday brunch I showed them how puffy my quim-lips were from Larry's finger-lashing. Bravely, I faced the four of them, stamped my foot and told them I wouldn't stand for any more corporal punishment except on my well-cushioned rear end. "If you don't keep control, you can't say what you're doing is art." So said Ethyl, the Queen of the Night.

─── 7 ───

WHAT GOES AROUND, COMES
AROUND

The next day I marched pale, naked Mr. Hardon to the same railing where the Goat Man Carl gave me a thrilling ride. Holding Mr. Hardon by the back of his neck, I forced him to bend over the railing and smacked his pudgy white butt with a paddle. WHACK! WHACK! WHACK! I love being on the handle end! His balls swung up and back and he howled at each spank. He was semi-hard. I called him naughty wimp and asshole, and paddled him hard as I could. WHACK! *"OWWW!"* "Whining creep!" WHACK! *"OWWW!"* "Nasty boy!" WHACK! *"OWWW!"* "Ass-licking dog!" WHACK! He whimpered, "Please, Sarah, that's enough!" and tried to raise his head, but I was too strong for him. I could hold his head down with half my strength. "Sarah, please!" he moaned. I smacked his ass 'til my arm wore out. I took it out on Mr. Hardon for the flaming red backside Larry gave me, the quim-lashing, and even having to go naked for two days. Mr. Hardon didn't need to know that.

"Now, jerk yourself off!" I yelled. He jerked off for more than two minutes, but didn't come. "You want more?" I asked, showing him the paddle. He begged for more time, and then he realized he was succeeding and smiled. He shot his wad across the deck. Didn't harm the deck, mostly, it sank into the wooden planks. Probably good for the planks. Mr. Hardon never came back to the house.

What actually happened was, the paddle got heavy. Mr. Hardon yowled, his eyes leaked tears, he held his red behind, but he still begged for sex. Amazing. I made him lie on his tender ass and I squatted over him, put his long skinny cock in me. Ms. Quimmy was almost back to herself again, and I guessed normal use wouldn't do her any harm. "You have sixty seconds to come, puppy-face," I scowled, "or, you go over the railing again, and this time I won't take it easy on you." I knew how to talk strict.

I learned from Tom Thomas. He used to strap me soundly for five minutes 'til I bawled and my hiney hurt so much, it was unreal. Then, while I sucked him—and he could see my ass was on fire—he would say, "Next time, I won't take it easy on you."

I hovered on Mr. Hardon's prick and did a slow, clutching grind. It felt good enough. He was out his gourd with pleasure. "Now!" I said. "I'm trying, Sarah," he cried. I slapped his face. He humped up triple-fast and exploded in me. Lucky for him.

He raved, "Sarah, you're the greatest!" Pity, should've made him jerk himself off. Two minutes after he was done, he dressed and excused himself. He never came back. Which I regret. I love spanking a male behind, even when the man's a pathetic wimp like Silas Hardon. Too bad I don't get to do it more.

In high school, one of my favorite daydreams was spanking the football team when they lost. I don't remember how the coach happened to pick me for this terrific job, but I'm strict. When they win, they get to do whatever they want to me. Something like the last part actually happened! But, I bet if St. Deems had really put me in charge of rewards and penalties, the football team would've finished first in the league instead of seventh.

Mr. Hardon couldn't stay away from me. He didn't drop in anymore, but called every day to check whether I was alone. I wouldn't go to his house. Fuck him. When I was alone and bored, I ordered him to come over immediately. I greeted him naked from my deck chair. The paddle was within easy reach, where he could see it. I enjoyed telling him to strip. I liked the way he sucked my toes. He would do it all day if I said to, but I could only take so much, and then I'd tell him to lick his way up my legs. I twirled the paddle while he licked my clit and plunged his snout into my hot wet cunt.

Then I make him lick everything down under and up to my tailbone deep in my crack. I lay on my tummy so he could smooch my asshole. He was real affectionate about it. I even put my ass in the air and wiggled it, to give him a challenge. He burrowed in between my wiggly cheeks. The perfect slave! I called him, "filthy dog," but there are men who are less fun.

Another day I demanded whether he wanted to fuck me, but he denied it. He was too scared to know there was no right answer, he got punished whatever he said. I grabbed him by the back of the neck and marched him over to the rail. I told him I was going to spank him twice as hard for lying. He yowled out over the beach at each smack. It was a long way to the next house or the water's edge, so it was rare anyone heard him. When I let him up, he had a hot-red ass. What he loved to do then was suck my nippies. I let him comfort himself crying on my boobs. I'm not heartless. Then, I'd make him sit on his tender ass and I posted on him. I give him one minute to come. He went into a humping, swiveling frenzy trying to.

One day, Mr. Hardon got his courage up, asked me to blow him. I was indignant. I made him stand in front of me. I unbuckled his belt, pulled it out through the loops, and told him to drop his pants and underpants. His dick was dancing around semi-hard, excited but terrified I'd smack it with the belt. I made him hold his ankles and I strapped his ass 'til he apologized. He never dared ask to get on top of me, or do me from the rear, which I knew he'd love, from the rapturous kisses he planted on my behind. He was so grateful for whatever I gave him, you'd think it was his first sex ever.

As the summer wore on, I got lazy and just put Mr. Hardon across my knees instead of marching him to the rail. He claimed to like it better across my knees. He thought it was more "intimate." His hot, hard cock rubbed against my thighs the whole time. I decided I didn't like him crying my name, like, begging, "Sarah, please!" when I was giving him a red ass, so I told him, from now on address me as "Ma'm." Also, I told him not to use words like "intimate" or bother me with what he liked. I whacked his rear end 'til he blubbered, "I won't, Ma'm," and, at the same moment, he came! It shot out onto the deck, but there was plenty on my thigh. "*Ugh!* What's that?" I demanded. He said he couldn't help it. "Now, you're going to get it," I yelled. I whacked him another dozen good ones, as hard and fast as I could.

I let him cry himself out sucking my tits. After a while he got hard again. What the hell, I lay on my back on the deck and let him get on top, "just this once," and I allowed him to take his time, so long as he kept stroking manfully in and out and swiveling. I was curious about how well he could do it. I told him if he paused, he was going to get the reddest ass in the history of the Hamptons. He didn't dare stop and he was good for five, six minutes, maybe, ten, I lost my sense of time. I admit, it was a super fuck. You can't tell anything from a man's build. Afterward, he looked so happy, it was amusing. I told him, "Get out, go home! Don't think anything's changed!"

I didn't have my own room at the artists' beach house. I had some clothes in Larry's closet and some in Phil's. They said it was a house rule that nobody slept in the living room; but they made the rule up for me. If I couldn't sleep in the living room, I would wind up sacking with Phil or Larry, depending on who was more interested. I'd say, "Eat your heart out," to the other one, but he'd get me the next night or the night after that. They were cool. Not knowing who I was going to spread for 'til the end of the evening drove me wild. I didn't get to choose, and they warned me I was in big trouble if I angled for one or the other. The last thing they needed when they were trying to paint was to fight over me. And there was more to it than that.

They never fought, and the others weren't jealous when Larry diddled me in front of them. It took me a couple of weeks to get the real scoop. It was a multiple-body story. You see stuff like that in TV movies. It's more common than people know.

Five years ago these guys were just beginning to sell. They were coming back from a patron's party where they had coke and downers, not to mention social weed and champagne. Phil drove 'cause he was sober compared to the others, but a cop chased them. Phil tried to outrun the cop, but he couldn't, so he cut across the highway. His U-turn was too tight and the car flipped over and over till it hit a tree. Now, they were all dying and they knew it. Phil was demolished worse than the car, Ben passed out, he thought for the last time, Ivan was cursing, Larry's bones were all broken, but he saw himself climbing out of the car!

The four souls negotiated desperately. The most alarming part was, Ivan and Larry saw their souls unravel as they bickered, white vapors like from dry ice rising from the souls and vanishing into the night sky. The souls agreed, if any of their bodies survived, whatever remnants of the souls were left would be shared among them. Then, three souls were gone, used up, leaving dribs and drabs behind them, a few talents, thoughts, feelings clinging to the mangled bodies.

Luckily, they were ten minutes from the only hospital this far out on Long Island. The medics and the emergency room did a great job, and all four bodies survived. They looked and acted somewhat like they always did 'cause they had sticky gobs of their former souls, though now they were all sharing and living off the soul that was originally Larry's.

Here's one way they acted differently: When Larry was interested, he'd pull me to his room by a tit or push me ahead of him with a hand under my rear end, goosing me along. Phil pointed to his room and I'd scoot in. Ben cuddled with me. Ivan hated me.

One evening I was just getting down with Larry. We were naked in bed, he was sitting up against the wall finishing a beer, and I was sucking him. Two soft lamps, muted jazz on Larry's radio. Outside our door, Phil said, "Larry?" I expected Larry to say, "Not now!" but instead he said, "Yes?" Phil opened the door and said, "Want a beer?" "I'm OK," Larry said, waving his bottle. Phil thought Larry was waving him in! He sat in an armchair a few feet from us and drank his beer. I stopped sucking. I was offended 'cause Larry didn't say "Hi!" to me or offer me a beer.

They talked about a run into Manhattan for painting supplies. Larry guided my head down. I went back to it. I had to raise my butt in Phil's direction, but he knew me pretty well from that angle. It occurred to me that maybe they'd agreed on a threesome, but they just talked about how the Thai cook was driving them crazy. He not only insisted on authentic ingredients, he wanted to know exactly how many people he was preparing for and when they would arrive. I kept sucking Larry and showing Phil my gorgeous naked rear end, and he could get into it or not, *fuck him!*

Phil said, "Sarah gives great head." I thought, *That's it, that's the best he can do.* It was more a report card than a compliment. He said it like I'm not here!

Larry said, "I agree, totally. Last night was great!"

Last night? I was with Phil the last two nights! What about the great head I was giving him right now? I have never felt so much like biting a cock. Instead, I bobbed up and down more vigorously and used my tongue my special way—men say I should patent it.

"Wasn't I with Sarah last night?" Phil said, "I think it's your turn tonight."

"I'd like that," Larry said.

I came off Larry's prick and said, "I'm hee-eere!"

"Sarah's a great all-around lay," Phil said, with his one-sided smile. His head's still misshapen from the accident. One eye and the bony brow above it are pushed a half inch low. He can't smile on that side of his face.

Well, he just lost his chance tonight! I straddled Larry where he was sitting against the wall, guided his hard prick into my cunt, and posted on him.

Phil pushed himself up out of his chair, took a step toward the door. "Phil," Larry said, "if you see Sarah, would you tell her I'm waiting for her?"

"Sure," Phil said. I humped Larry hard, swiveled down, squeezed up. He held my butt in his hands.

"Tell Sarah I have something for her," Larry said slyly.

"I'm coming!" I gasped, *Uhhh-uhhh-ooo-ooo-ah-ooo! Ooo-ahhh-ahhh-ahhh!*

Phil chuckled and left. " 'Night, Larry."

" 'Night, Phil," Larry said.

I kept moaning a while, the way I do. As soon as I could speak, I poked Larry and demanded, "What was that about?"

"It's between us," he said. Then, he came, and I milked him. He flipped his head side-to-side and shrieked, like he was way over the edge.

I wanted to talk about it, but he said he needed to rest—'cause Phil was going to send Sarah!

"I'm Sarah! Look at me!" I cried. I was still straddling him.

He looked at me. "You're beautiful," he said, "now, can we get some sleep?"

Ben liked it in the morning. While Phil and Larry jogged along the beach, I went to Ben's room and got in bed with him. Sometimes, I'd suck him, but he'd sleep right on, dreaming I was sucking him. He wouldn't wake up till he was about to come in my mouth. Sometimes, when he was awake enough, Ben rolled me over on my back and screwed me. The joggers would come back, and we'd all have breakfast together.

Ivan acted like he wasn't interested. The last time he fucked me, near the end of July, was the most humiliating fuck of the month. Everybody came through the living room and saw me kneeling in the wicker armchair and Ivan behind me, and they saw how we were hooked up. Everybody was Larry, Phil, and Ben, two girls from the beach and a couple of house guests—who did sleep in the living room, despite the "house rule,"—and Silas Hardon. People think it's perfectly OK to stroll over and ogle if you're taking it some way they think is exotic.

We started out fooling around in the living room about eleven one morning. When I ran into Ivan, I was carrying my toothbrush in one hand and a tube of toothpaste in the other. All I was wearing was Ben's pajama top. Ivan was in a swim suit. After ignoring me all week, he decided on the spot he'd like to kiss me, but I turned my face away 'cause I needed to brush my teeth first. I didn't even want to open my mouth to tell

[89]

Ivan to get out of my way. Okay, it happened I sucked Ben off just before. They could shoot a toothpaste commercial with this true story line. Anyway, with Ivan, I was more annoyed than blushing.

Ivan didn't give up! He kissed my neck, which I usually love, but I tried to get away. I also needed to bathe after spending the night with Phil, before giving Ben his morning treat. Ivan got under the pajama top and gave me a good hard pinch on both nippies and rolled them in his fingertips. That always rings my bell. I was already horny. Phil was okay, I came with him, but a whole feast for him was like half a shrimp for me. And sucking Ben off was sweet, but it left me horny. So, when Ivan started on my nippies, I went from an edgy bitch thinking, *Get the fuck out of my way*, to totally melting in ten seconds. He kept kneading my tits as hard as he could, and I just closed my eyes and dropped the toothbrush and tube. I expected we'd go to his room, but Ivan wanted to do me where we were. I unbuttoned my pajama top. I never got it all the way off. Ivan dropped his swim suit. He whispered something lovely in my ear. All I heard clearly was the last part, "Sarah, turn around!"

I knelt on the cushion in the cane chair like he wanted. Ivan stroked in and almost out of my cunt about a dozen times, and I was starting to love him a little, and that very instant he came out all the way, which I thought maybe he had to do to slow himself down. Then, he put the tip of his prick at my asshole, and I clenched up. Once upon a time, taking it in the ass was a specialty of mine. But you don't just do that to a lady, you ask her first.

Ivan couldn't get in there with me clenching, so he started saying—a bit late—what a gorgeous ass I had, how round and silky and smooth it was, all the time fooling with it and trolling his prick up and down in my crack, and probably figuring whether he could get away with saying how pretty my asshole was. I've heard that, can you believe what guys will say? Just thinking about that loosened me up! Well, it may not be pretty, but it is sensitive, and by now I was so horny I was almost sick, and I needed his cock back in me, it didn't matter so much where. He almost said, "Please." I could feel how much he wanted this. Then, he was gimletting in, I didn't clench for an instant and he got the head of his prick in where he wanted it. I squawked 'cause it was a tight fit. That's when everybody started filing into the living room and gathering 'round.

Damned prick would be all the way up my ass when he got good and ready. When I realized I was taking it in my ass, after all, without being asked, I pulled forward in the wicker arm chair, but he held me by the hips and thrust into me deeper and deeper, till his groin pushed against my rear end. He didn't need my permission anymore, I could clench all I wanted, and it would just give him a treat. Now that we had an audience, he gave it to me good—all the way in, almost all the way out, pause, all the way in. Everybody except Mr. Hardon drifted over till they were sitting and standing practically on top of us. They forgot their manners, 'cause of where I was taking it.

Picture this, I'm still wearing Ben's pajama top, unbuttoned, and my boobs are hanging down, jouncing. I put on a show, bumping and grinding, squealing with delight, so it wouldn't look like I was a dumb broad letting herself get fucked in the ass to please Ivan, but more like, it's what I wanted.

Most of the time, when I put on a show, I'm coming, but faking that I'm faking it. It's easy for me to come, the hard thing is not to come, and that's what I'm really faking—not coming—when I fake I'm coming while I really am coming.

Ivan goes under my arms and pinches my nippies, pulls me back and forth by my tits. His balls slap my cunt. I reach under and hold his balls to my cunt to make sure he doesn't get too frisky. That tames him. I also flick my clit a few times, enough to get off. What with all the delicious shame of everybody watching me take it in my ass, I come, and it's marvelous! I don't mind that it hurt some getting there, not at all! I deserve a little hurt for being such a slut, it feeds into my pleasure. I only cover up that I'm coming by putting on a show of coming. I hope all this makes sense.

It felt like Ivan was punishing me, I didn't know for what. It was like a public spanking, that kind of thrill, shame flooding me and turning me on all over. Ivan went on and on, I came again and again, but he didn't come. Some punishment! People drifted away and back. Ivan rammed in and out and wanked his cock around with his hand. A lot of men want ass-fucking to hurt you, and if you enjoy yourself too much, they do it rougher till they're sure it hurts. After a minute, Ivan pried off my hand that was holding his balls to my cunt. He screwed my butt wilder and wilder. I was tender back there, but I didn't mind, 'cause I was coming all over again, wave on wave of pleasure that washed out the hurt.

I thought, if I cry, maybe he'll come, and that's what happened. I sobbed out loud, and he gave me jets of hot cum, an enema all the way up, and whooped like a game show winner. When he pulled out, he gave me a parting slap across my rear cheeks, so I was right about it being a kind of spanking. Then, he said, "Have a nice day," and ran off, leaving my messy, fucked behind waving in the air.

It was awkward stepping down backward out of the wicker chair toward my audience. I didn't look at anyone directly. I didn't bother to button Ben's pajama top over my tits. I had to keep my asshole tight and get to a toilet fast, 'cause I was holding a hot cum enema in me. I forgot my toothbrush and toothpaste till lunchtime.

Ben cued me in that the day before Ivan overheard me say when I was looking at his paintings, "What is this shit?" So, the rump fuck was his way of getting even. The other guys were extra polite to me for the rest of the day, which means they thought Ivan had gone too far, and I'd leave. But when I didn't, everything settled down to normal, except that over the next few days they all had to fuck me in the ass, too.

The guys weren't wrong about me thinking of leaving. I hate to admit it, but you can get shamed so bad there's no art left in it. It wasn't just that they all took turns screwing me in my ass, but Larry and Ivan joked about it. It reminded me of people making fun of me at St. Deems. I got cranky for a few days. None of the guys could talk to me and I wouldn't do anything for any of them, either. Finally, at dinner one night, Larry wondered out loud whether a paddling wouldn't improve my disposition. Phil said I should have one last chance to stop sulking and put out all around. "Or else, what?" I said. Or else, get spanked and put out all around! I told him, "Up yours!" and they looked shocked. I wasn't allowed to talk like that.

Ben told me I was going to be punished after dinner. I could sense they were all getting hard around the table. I wasn't wearing much and I was out in the middle of nowhere, my lover had eight hands to hold me and spank me and four stiff pricks to put into me. I said, "Fuck you, too," but softer, 'cause I felt close to Ben. He'd have been the last of the four to give me a red backside. But he looked right at me, a little sad, and said, "Drop your panties." A sensitive, rueful son of a bitch! If Larry or Phil had said it, maybe I'd have refused.

I was reduced to sticking my tongue out spitefully at Ben, the way little girls do. I knew it was silly. He nodded gravely yes, like, I'd have plenty to lick. I wasn't ready to look for another place to stay. I stood up, hooked my thumbs into my panties and pushed them down, all the way down and off as I sat. All I was wearing now was a summer frock that was too short to tuck under me. I was barefoot. I petted my panties under the table with my toes, *nice panties*.

I began to like these guys again. They were looking at my tits. My frock was scooped out low in front and sleeveless, with big arm holes, so they could see lots of creamy boob. Also, my nippies were stiff from all the attention and poking through the thin fabric.

I felt like talking. I was light-headed, what I was saying didn't make sense, but I couldn't stop. One moment I told them the cane of the chair seat tickled my bare bottom, and the next moment I was reminiscing about when I first come to live with them, I was here only three days, nothing much had happened, when I got incredibly horny and changed for supper into a see-through blouse and a short wraparound skirt and no underwear. After dessert I circled the table sitting awhile bare-bottom on everybody's lap and kissed them and they fondled me and I wound up blowing all four of them. We all fell asleep together in a heap on a deep pile area rug in the living room, legs, arms, bodies all touching, someone's head nestled against my butt. Sweet! I wanted to do it all again the same way, but nobody let me sit on his lap. I was in big trouble.

I didn't realize dinner was over till Ivan told me to clear the table. We shared cooking during the week, but I cleared and loaded the dishwasher. One of them slipped out to the deck and brought back the paddles. The last time I came out of the kitchen, there was nothing to clear and they were twirling the paddles.

Larry and Phil marched me down to the area rug in the living room. They held me under my elbows. I was scared, my feet barely touched the floor. Phil told me to bend over and hold my ankles. That raised the frock in back mostly above my round cheeks, maybe just the top inch of my crack was covered, but they all cried in one voice, "Take it off!" I let the frock slither down my body to my shoulders and shook it off over my head onto the floor. I was naked. Shame thrilled through me. I spread my legs to brace myself and stuck my ass up. I tried to get over my panic and be cute and sexy.

They took turns—who could make my rear cheeks bounce and my tits jiggle the most? Who could get the loudest yelps out of me? After three smacks from each of them, I danced away, rubbing my rosy behind. Enough! But Phil came after me, dragged me by my tits to a sofa, put me across his knees. He waited till the others brought chairs and sat in a tight circle with him. My ass was stinging. Phil, busy organizing, forgot where he left his paddle. Someone handed it to him. He spanked me sternly, like he knew this would be the last time I was going to be across his knees, gorgeous round cheeks where he liked them, he had to make each smack count. He paused after each one while I screeched, kicked my heels up, and humped his thigh.

Phil warned me not to carry on too long. As soon as I could, I stopped moaning and squirming, bit my lip and raised my rear end a few inches, turned it up for the paddle. They passed me from lap to lap, two hands under my armpits, two supporting my boobs, a hand cupping my crotch, wrist jammed down between my hot ass cheeks, a couple or three hands under my thighs. Even with all the help, my boobs got bruised bumping against their thighs and over them. They were all horny out of their minds, so they didn't notice. I was horny, too. The awful pain in my hiney flowed into my cunt. Ms. Quimmy didn't hurt the same way, but ached for a good cock to soothe her. My nippies zinged. Ben played with my tits when I was across Larry's knees. He said the way my tits jiggled at each spank turned him on. The second time I clambered across Ben's lap, he laid his paddle down and spanked me with his hand. I can't say it hurt a whole lot less, 'cause I was so raw back there everything hurt, and Ben made my cheeks bounce to show he was one of the boys.

My bottom was on fire and I was bawling. I stuck my ass right up in their faces, no matter how much it hurt. It made all the difference between just lying there with a quivering tail, crying my eyes out till they decided they'd punished me enough, or being, well, the star of the show. I didn't notice when they took their pants down. I was still suffering across Ben's knees, Ivan's prick was out and he swiveled so it was in my face. I was supposed to lick it. Everybody thought I was turned on to Ivan, but that he despised me since I let him fuck me in my ass one morning last week with whomever was around watching. When I'd say, "I hate Ivan," they'd just say, "Sure," like I didn't mean it and I'd bend over for him anytime. That made it extra brutal and humiliating when he pushed my head down. I was in no position to explain that I didn't care to lick Ivan's cock. So, I did.

After Ivan spanked me the third time 'round, he spread my thighs wide and jibed about my steamy wet cunt, poked two fingers into me and diddled me, and said, "What a slut!" I couldn't help my quim lips twitching all over his hand. It wasn't fair Ivan calling me a slut, but I couldn't protest, 'cause my head was in Phil's lap. All I could do was lick Phil's cock fast and furious.

All the pants and underpants were down and all four cocks out, waving in the air. I crawled 'round the circle quicker, goosed along, my hot hiney poked and pinched, my boobs absolutely mauled. My tongue was hanging out, I was sobbing and sucking at the same time. A Shame Artist uses her sobs to suck better! More sucking now, less spanking. Still, a well-aimed terrific smack across my burning ass every once in awhile encouraged me to suck with all my heart and not be surly anymore.

As soon as they let me off their laps, I took the guys one after another, this way, that way, I came and came and came, my switch stuck at CLIMAX, any way they gave me a hose, I opened up for it, clasped it inside me, even two at once for double pumping, till I didn't know which end of me was which, and I reeked from their brilliant artist jism.

A Shame Artist craves change, even from the most

humiliating setup when it gets to be routine. Anyway, a few days later, I was still recovering from too much of a good thing, when I met Sofi on the beach, and her offer sounded great.

— 8 —

OUT OF THE FRYING PAN

I helped Sofi keep her husband at home and mellow. Sofi picked me for the job when I was serving hors-d'oeuvres at the artists' house the evening I met Mr. Hardon. At Sofi's, I got my own room, a salary that was less than my allowance when I was a kid, and dreams of TV ads in the fall.

Here's how I met Sofi. Late one afternoon, I was walking along the beach directly down from her house. I spotted a guy up on the deck watching me. He turned out to be her husband Francis. He looked cuddly. Hairy chest, weathered face, crooked grin, black hair graying at the temples. I sat on the sand with my back to him and took off my top. He could see my bare back, dimples, the north slope of my butt. I twisted and gazed along the shore, giving him a profile view of full young tit pointing toward Montauk. He had to come down and check me out.

Nothing. After a while I rolled the back of my bikini bottom down. Then, he was off the deck. That's what it takes, I decided, show guys rear cleavage down to where I sit on it, and they're mine. *Oops*, he didn't come, Sofi did.

Sofi was slender, elegant, a former fashion model, in fact. She was wearing a bikini, too. At first I thought she was coming to tell me to cover up or move on. No, she sat a few feet away facing me, and after a moment, took her top off. Sexy tits, how mine would look in fifteen years, if I was lucky. Dark hair with a red bronze glint to it. The sun brought out the red.

We were both topless, no names yet. Sofi told me all about me and men. She said men ask me about my love life, but never understand what I tell them. They always try to fit me to their idea of what life must be like for a beautiful golden blonde with creamy white skin, blue eyes, full lips, big buoyant boobs with inviting slightly long, stand-up pink nippies, a small waist, prominent flaring hipbones, long legs, slender wrists and ankles, and a super round ass, who adores taking hard hot cocks in me and milking them.

Sofi said I humiliate men when I can get away with it, and when I can't, I let them humiliate me, and that turns me on, too. She said I tease men, lie to them, and make fun of them every chance I get, and they never catch on. (Wrong, sometimes they do.) When men come on to me with compliments and theater tickets, Sofi said, it bores me, but when they order me to lick their balls, I love it. That's part of what she meant when she said I was a Shame Artist. She told me I like kinky sex, threesomes or, even, an audience. She got me to admit tricks I never told anyone about.

Sofi made me blush by saying I'm a slut who can't get enough. She had a way of tearing you down casually, like, we both know it, let's see where we go from here.

I felt helpless with Sofi. I wanted her to say I was a good bitch. Like I wanted Sister Martin in seventh grade to approve of me. Sister Martin's body was so sexy she was always on guard lest it lead her to sin. Her legs were lean from walking and climbing stairs swifter than anyone. She had a pretty Irish face, white skin and freckles, light red hair and green eyes, but she was beginning to show tight lines from trying to have only pious thoughts. One day she called me a little slut and said she would teach me a lesson. She gave the rest of the class an open-book math test. She pulled me by my ear into the girls' room, clutching her spanking ruler. The class snickered. Everybody knew what I was going to get. The girls' was across the corridor, ten steps away. A boy would open the classroom door a few inches and everybody would listen. The other nuns at St. Deems Middle School sent you to the Principal, Father Archibald, who would frown at you and say things like, "Sarah, you have let me down and I am very sad." That was a hoot. But Sister Martin was a law unto herself. Everyone agreed the seventh grade was the school's last-ditch chance to teach us morals. The parents didn't mind, 'cause if any of them had complained to Father Archy, he would've had to transfer Sister Martin out of St. Deems. Probably, most of the parents didn't even know, 'cause when Sister Martin spanked you, you'd done something so bad you didn't run home and talk about it.

All I did was show Dennis my quim. He was the same boy I gave love lessons to a few years later in front of our apartment. I always got caught with him!

In the seventh grade everybody knew Dennis dropped his pencil on purpose, so he could scramble around and look up our skirts. Why didn't Sister Martin spank him? 'Cause, "Boys will be boys," so, for decency's sake, girls have to behave proper! One day when Dennis dropped his pencil, I slid forward to the edge of my chair and slipped my panties down. I was Dennis's favorite 'cause I had sexy panties I lifted from B. Altman's and Lord & Taylor's lingerie counters. I loved to wear sexy panties, even though I had only a promise of a bush then, a few wispy blonde curls down there.

Dennis looked my way, as usual, and I lay back in my chair and spread. *Whoopee!* He saw the works, maybe even a peek into the pink folds of my pussy. I thought Sister Martin was too busy correcting papers to notice, but when my quim freaked Dennis out, she spotted him pointing like a bird dog. A second later she saw me pulling up my panties and smoothing down my skirt.

Sister Martin dragged me into a stall with her, put down the lid of the kid-sized toilet and sat down. The stall was too small for both of us to be in there, and too narrow for me to lie across her knees, but that didn't stop her. She made me take my panties all the way down to my ankles and crawl along her left thigh, so my head was 'way behind her between the back of the toilet bowl and the metal partition, and my feet stuck out under the half-door of the stall. I had to clasp her hard lean thigh with both my thighs, and my left hand reached around her body to whatever it could grab, to keep myself from falling off. I was clinging to her hip, the top of her butt, really, which was more intimate than anything you'd think she'd allow, but she didn't bat my hand away. I braced myself against the side wall with my right hand, which couldn't reach anything to hold onto. The heat of our thigh-clasp was marvelous. I could feel her thigh through my thin dress against my quim. No question, it was a thigh-job, like some boys give you in slow dancing. Maybe, she was so into chastising me that she didn't realize.

Sister Martin plucked my dress up in back and tapped my bare cheeks with the ruler and gloated, *"Now* you'll squirm, you nasty slut!" Sister Martin was always telling me not to squirm in class. She was very strict about the boys keeping their hands out of their pockets and us girls sitting up straight like little ladies, which meant not rubbing our butts against our seats.

I could tell she was raising the ruler all the way up. Then she slammed it down. I heard myself yowl like it was someone else. My hiney burned! I wanted to bolt, but my ankles were entangled in my panties, and I couldn't even kick my heels up, 'cause they hit the bottom edge of the metal door. I tried to shield my hiney with my right hand. She yanked my wrist up my back almost to my shoulder blades. I got maybe twenty seconds, a long wait, to accept that my ass was where it was, and it was going to stay there till Sister Martin was satisfied. Again, a tap on my rear end right alongside the burning strip, to let me know exactly where I was going to suffer the next smack. Terrified, I looked the other way, glancing up behind the toilet seat and behind her back. For an instant I saw the ruler raised so high in her fist it reached back over her shoulder! Then the ruler was on the way! She spanked my ass hard as she could, I think till her arm needed a rest. She was right about me squirming. I pressed my clit hard against her thigh and squirmed like mad! The delicious sensations down there helped a little against the awful stinging pain when the ruler smacked my hiney. The pleasure and the pain shot through each other inches apart and all mixed up.

Sister Martin held me in an iron grip and waited till I stopped bawling. She described what the Devil does to little sluts who open their legs and show off their private parts. The Devil's punishments are a lot worse than spanking. You would choose a spanking by Sister Martin anytime.

She tapped my raw flaming bottom with the ruler, again. I begged for mercy. At the same time I couldn't help glancing the other way, up behind her back. I saw the ruler way up, reaching back over her shoulder. She spanked away as fierce as before to give me a taste of what eternal torment was going to be like if I didn't mend my ways. I hugged her hips, slid up and back, squirmed on her thigh, and humped like a male dog! At some point in the frenzy my dress hiked itself up in front, too, and my naked pussy rubbed against her thigh. My quim sucked at her thigh! At least, it felt like it did. I was beyond caring whether she would catch onto that. Waves of delight and agony washed through me, one swelling the other to higher crests.

I didn't know what was happening to me. Sister Martin must have felt my quim sliding and squirming against her thigh, but I doubt she knew she gave me one of the most splendid orgasms of my whole childhood. When she was done, she jerked me to my feet, made me stand with my back to the mirror and hold my skirt up in back. My panties were still down. She told me to "See what a naughty little slut's behind looks like!" as if I didn't know that my usually creamy, adorable cheeks (everybody said so, even back then) were a mess, crimson, swollen and puffy. She marched me back into the classroom and stood me in the corner for the hour till school was out. My quim was still jumping.

I reached down carefully so no one could see and felt Miss Quimmy twitch in my fingertips. Slowly, gently, I comforted myself, kept the sweet feelings streaming through me. Sister Martin repeated to the class some of what she told me across her thigh about indecent behavior, and about the Devil. It felt like everybody could see my red hiney glowing right through my panties and the back of my skirt.

Afterward, I was afraid of Sister Martin, I cringed when she was behind me, but I also got a crush on her. I tried harder on my homework for her. I lost any interest for years in showing boys my pussy. I wanted to be a virgin nun like Sister Martin when I grew up and spank the asses of little sluts like me.

Sofi's pitch wasn't only for her husband. The way she sat with her legs spread was an order, *Go down on me, chew my bikini off, eat me out!* I'm not making this up, I can hear things people don't say, especially when it's about sex. Or when they're mad at me, which they are a lot.

Before Sofi I had only one affair with a woman—a classmate at college, Alice, my friend from St. Deems. Sofi asked me back to the house for a soak in the hot tub on their deck and dinner with them when her husband came home. I said I had to go back to the artists' house to change. Sofi vetoed that. She said there was no time, but she'd find something for me to wear.

I got seduced in the wooden hot tub right away. We were both naked. A few light kisses and then Sofi lay out along the rim, one knee raised so I could get at her. Kneeling on the underwater bench, I kissed the inside of her thighs and licked her clit. After a minute I pulled back and studied her quim affectionately. I had a rush, like, I knew I'd be spending a lot of time with my face between Sofi's thighs. I must've sucked a hundred cocks, but this was only my second quim, and I guessed it could be a major one in my life. I wanted to do a good job. I raved about her beautiful auburn bush. She smiled, but she was edgy, like, she wanted kisses, not compliments.

I planted a hard kiss on Sofi's squishy lower lips to show I meant it. When my nose was rolling her clit and my tongue tasting just inside her cunt, she trolled one hand in the hot tub and reached under me. She played with me casually, like petting a dog you aren't crazy about, but you want to show you like dogs. She came so hard I had to grab her backside to keep my place. She stopped petting me, all she could do was hang onto the rim of the tub. Then, the storm passed, she was still coming quietly, but she put two fingers in me and petted my clit with her thumb.

I was getting feverish myself. A car pulled up their driveway and into their garage. Sofi rested her other hand on the back of my head, signalling she wanted me to keep going, finish her off. I licked earnestly. I figured if we kept on, the husband would join in. Sure enough, a few minutes later I felt someone else in the tub behind me. I didn't hear him 'cause of the noisy water jets, but I knew he was there. Sofi was tense again, she threw her head back, stopped doing me altogether. She clamped my head between her thighs, her fingernails digging into my shoulders.

The instant Francis touched me, I swung my butt up for him. He played with me a moment, the way men do, fixing you for screwing. It doesn't matter how prettily you put your tail up for them, they aren't going right in, they've got to fuss over it. A moment later, he rammed in, and, WOW! He felt terrific, thick, long, hot, hard. He stroked in fast, out slo-o-owly, and in! stuffing me with pleasure. If my cunt were my mouth, I'd be biting into a perfect pear. I squeezed him hard as I could and he fucked me like a horse. He was a horse, the longest and broadest cock I've ever had! He drove my face right into Sofi's quim. I wanted to look back, but Sofi ordered me to keep licking, and clamped my face where she wanted it. I resented that for a moment, but then I was thrilled! It was humiliating not to be allowed to look back! I had a good mind to say to Sofi, what do you think I am, your sex slave? But I couldn't say anything, 'cause my face was clamped to her quim and I was getting smashed into it every few seconds by a huge cock. I loved it!

I reached back to check out what I felt filling my cunt all the way up to my shoulder blades. I was cautious, thinking, a man I haven't met mightn't want me touching his cock. See the irony? But Francis pulled out a little and put my hand on it. I felt the right side of the shaft and the undercurve, and the top curve. It was a real monster. Then, he pried my hand off and shoved all the way in, and I groaned—right into Sofi's cunt. "Now, you know why I need help," she laughed. A jolly, rumbling laugh, trying to catch her breath, winding up in a snicker, *"Ha-ha-a-ha-a-ha hee-hee-hee!"*

That laugh—I knew that laugh! I wanted to come up for air, but Sofi trapped me with her thighs, which all at once were stout walls of flesh. They'd gone from slender, toned thighs to circus-lady fat. Her buttocks, and all I could see were the bottom rolls, were enormous pillows. Her cunt was bigger, too, my head could fit into it!

They were going to kill me! That's why Sofi lured me here! They'd suffocate me under Sofi's mountains of flesh! They'd drown me in her cunt! They worked for the Devil! They'd sell my soul to the Devil and my body parts to medical labs!

I prayed to the Queen of the Night. I saw a vision: First, a blank mirror, then Ethyl in the mirror putting on eyeliner and remarking that my best chance was to please them. Her words calmed me. I reached around Sofi's hips, sank my nails into tons of buttery ass and licked my heart out.

Sofi became her trim self again. She let me come up for air. I got over my terror enough to relate to the terrific, swiveling fuck I was getting from behind. A few marvelous minutes later I said, "I'm coming!" and Sofi nodded, like, granting me approval. It was strange going all to pieces in front of her, riding her husband's cock. Then, Francis came, ramming me like a pile driver, each thrust delivering a generous hot jet.

I finally got to turn around and meet Francis face to face. I told him he made a new Olympic mark for the javelin toss. He had swabbed somewhere deeper inside me than anyone ever touched before. I was glad he wasn't jealous about me licking his wife.

* * *

Most of this actually happened later in August. It could have been like that the first time, if Francis hadn't been such a jealous maniac. "You slut!" he ranted as I scrambled out of the tub, "Eating—my wife in—my hot tub!" He was red in the face and his eyes were squinty and his jaw jutted out. He looked like he was going to punch me. I was afraid. Sofi threw me two towels. I didn't know whether to blot myself dry or cover up with them. I did a little of both. "What are you going to do to me?" I said.

He simmered down as he looked me over. I tied a towel around my hips and draped the other one loosely in front of my boobs. "You've been naughty with my wife," he chided, and then I knew he wasn't going to punch me or throw me out. He was going to punish me in the usual place and make me be twice as naughty with him. I blushed and admitted I'd been naughty, and he grinned that great crooked grin I saw from the beach.

"Inside," he said, hooking his thumbs in his belt. It would've been hard to argue 'cause I was nearly naked and wet and my hair was stringy and my face messy with Sofi's sex juices. He was going to use the belt! My ass, my poor ass! Men who think giving you a red bottom is great fun don't care how much you suffer.

I was acutely aware of my ass cheeks. They were so scared of whipping, they wobbled against each other under the towel. It's not fair, having to carry two tender white globes of blubber behind me to be punished! Anywhere I go, whether I'm caught fucking a stranger, giving a messy blow job, or eating out someone's wife in a hot tub, I always wind up presenting my bare buns and suffering back there.

Sofi slid a glass door open and I followed her into what would have been a living room, except that there was nothing, no furniture at all. Just a bare wood floor, like a dance studio. A telephone on the floor. All along one wall, about a foot from the wall, small heaps of books and fashion magazines where they were dumped out of a bookcase.

"There's no furn—" I started to say, but Francis was behind me unbuckling his belt and slipping it out of the loops. I forgot what I was saying. It was a narrow leather belt dyed an awful pastel blue, an ugly match with his blue bermuda shorts.

And he was wearing the pinkie ring. Okay, if you think of the Devil as the power that makes you sin and who's in charge where you get punished for your sins, Francis fit the bill. He also happened to look more like a decadent Spanish grandee, the way people picture the Devil, than anyone I ever met. There's no reason why the Devil shouldn't favor pastel blue at the shore over black and flame red, or use a leather belt instead of a pitchfork.

I was still dripping. I dropped my boob towel to take care of the little puddle I was making on his floor. I swept the towel with my toes, blotting up the water. I counted on the beauty of my bare titties to soften him a little.

"Turn around, bend over!" Francis barked. See what I mean about always paying with my ass? I knew that was coming. But his voice was harsher than I expected.

"Better do what he says," Sofi put in. She had put on a beach robe. Sofi sounded detached, but maybe she was trying to help, letting me know it could be a lot worse for me if I didn't do as I was told.

I leaned half-way over, sliding my hands forward to my knees, sticking my behind out. I was distracted by the absence of furniture, like, do they live here or what? In another moment I would've been there—legs spread, grabbing my ankles, behind turned up. But I wasn't quick enough. "Like this!" Sofi sang out, taking me by the waist and bending me all the way over. I protested, I knew very well how to put my ass up without her help! Francis shut me up. The shame turned me on. Not being allowed to say a word made my cunt churn. I wanted to cry. I wanted him to fuck me.

I wound up with my legs splayed, bending all the way over, Sofi jamming me against her hip so I couldn't move, my face two inches from the floor. My hair drooped to the floor in wet ropes. The tuck in my towel was loosening. The towel just covered my butt and the top of my thighs in back. "Shall I?" Sofi said, and Francis grunted. She drew up the bottom of the towel to the small of my back.

Clamped in place, I waited for the strap. My rear cheeks were still damp. Looking through my legs, I noticed a single drop of pool water on each golden curl of my bush. I could feel a trickle of drops down my crack.

Ever notice how much shame has to do with behinds? Kissing someone's behind? Showing yours? Having it pinched, goosed, screwed? And spanked? Spanking's sex that hurts. I count on sex right after, 'cause it turns guys on, and getting a warm red butt makes me want cock. When I was growing up, I got spanked for being sexy, which just made me sexier.

"Gorgeous ass," Sofi says. She's a connoisseur. Francis is standing 'way to one side of me, measuring the distance so the first smack of the belt will land where it's supposed to. The belt is stiff, still curled from being around his waist. He straightens it out. He's going to use it full length, which can hurt more than when they double it.

"How many?" I say, trembling. "Wouldn't you like to know?" Sofi says, and at the same time, Francis answers, "Twelve." She's meaner than he is. He sees me looking at him and he smiles. I smile back. Try smiling when you're turning your hiney up and you're scared. Sofi's over my back, she doesn't catch this. Francis can see my damp blonde bush and my quim smiling at him, too (I feel all open and ever so screwable), and I know he wants what I want. His pinkie ring's glowing! I bet I can pry him away from Sofi, if I get a chance!

The belt! Oh, no! WAP! *"Ylll!"* I scream. A good one! Droplets of water spray off my rear end. I was right, the full-length stiff belt stings awfully. But I can take it. I think I can. Sofi holds me so I can't move. I shimmy in her grip.

WAP! I scream again. That hurts too much! The wetness makes it worse! I reach back gingerly with my free hand to touch my rear end, but Francis says, "Hold your ankles." I do. He's masterful, all right. I wish he would just step up to my rear end and fuck me.

The third one! *"YlllEEE!"* The ugly belt smacks mostly my left cheek and the tip of it tickles my crack. It stings too much in the crack! I jump, but don't get anywhere, except to press up an inch into Sofi's fat. She's grotesquely obese again, her knees are almost as big as my head. She uses her weight to keep me bent over.

The towel falls down, damp and cool across my ass. Oh, I need that! But Sofi lifts the towel off my fanny again. WAP! The fourth one! It catches me real low across both cheeks. It hurts too much to scream. I'm breathless. I pant like a bitch. WAP! I cry, *"WAHHH!"* My eyes are full of tears. They know I'm crying. I wiggle my butt. My rear cheeks are on fire. The flames spread to my cunt and turn me on more. The jolt when the strap lands makes my boobs swing forward and jounce around, brushing Sofi's forearm that is holding me under my ribs. My nippies are swollen and hard as though they've been petted. My body's a war between hurt and lust.

After the sixth smack, the hurt wins. I cringe. I try to tuck my tail in, like, away from the strap. "No," Sofi says, pushing the small of my back down, "this goes down, and this"—she cups her hand under my ass— "goes up." I wince, because her hand holds me in a raw red place.

I'd like to please Francis on my own, if she'd give me a chance! I turn my ass all the way up for the strap. I can feel my rump glowing red.

WAP! I scream and scream. Francis remarks when I quiet down, "It would be better to take your punishment without making such a racket."

I whimper. "What?" Francis snaps, annoyed. I hate whimpering myself, but I can't stop. I bite my lip. I want to obey, but it's hopeless. The very next lash catches me by surprise across the backs of my thighs, and I scream louder. The next one tickles my crack again and I bolt upright, almost out of Sofi's grip. My towel falls again, partly covering my ass, one cheek, anyway.

"Back off, Sofi," Francis says. I bend way over, sticking my hiney out at him. The only way I can win is to offer my ass better than Sofi makes me do it. Slowly, I roll the towel up in back. Through my legs I see Francis enjoys the tease. I grind in a little circle for him.

"Face forward," he says.

The last three whacks whip my cheeks where they're already on fire, and I yowl continuously and cry my eyes out. The fanny pain and the glory of submitting turn me on. Francis can see my cunt quiver. Sofi knows I'm turned on, too. After the ninth smack, I can't take anymore, and I offer bribes, like, I'll be extra naughty for them, I'll do whatever they want. Sofi, a mountain of flesh, reminds me that anytime a slut gets a good spanking, it always reaches a point where she thinks she can't take anymore and offers to kiss ass. So, I get my twelve lashes, and I skip all over the empty living room, up and back, holding my backside, and a few minutes later I have to do everything, anyway.

* * *

That's almost the way it went, except that Francis wanted the treats I offered right away. I figured I could get him so deep into me that he'd forget the last three smacks. He dropped his bermudas, and his prick stuck a mile up out of his briefs. It looked powerful, long and thick with an impressive crown on it, and goofy at the same time, like it was a dumb happy prince. I wanted to kiss that prince! I scooted over on my knees, tugged his briefs to his knees, and licked the big oaf up and down. When I'd worked up to the challenge, I took the sweet lovable crown into my mouth and sucked hard, tonguing all-out, no subtlety, just going for it. I was eager and turned on. At the same time I lifted his heavy balls with my fingers, getting to know them.

He didn't come. I licked down his warm meaty cock and mouthed his balls. He was standing right over me, still holding the belt. I love to be under a man's balls looking up to see the glee in his face when he thinks you're his slave. From this angle his prick looked two feet long. He twiddled my nippies viciously, testing me. The edge of the belt dug into one nippie. It was all exciting. My cunt went crazy.

I couldn't tell how Sofi liked me being with her man, but she set it up, so I guessed it was alright with her. Couldn't worry about her now. I worked the shaft of Francis's cock with one hand and explored his butt with the other. He turned around, offered me his ass. I smooched his cheeks warmly, burrowed a little into his crack, and then out again, teasing him. I liked keeping him waiting for what he wanted. I licked a little deeper at each dip into his crack, a little lower and naughtier. I love rimming, when I'm attracted and totally dominated, and the guy's reasonably clean, all of which fit Francis. But I backed off this time, didn't go the whole way. We all knew it. "Thanks ever so much," I said, still on my knees, as though he'd given me a treat, and now it was over. Sofi snorted.

Francis discovered he was still holding the belt. "Right there for the last three," he said, meaning stay on my knees, "face down, ass up!" As Sister Martin used to say, "It's not smart to be clever." I crossed my arms on the floor and laid my face on them, and put my behind up. My boobs were on the floor, too. My towel had fallen off. I hurt plenty back there, but the worst sting had gone away while I smooched Francis's backside. I hoped Francis was softened up by my kissing.

No! The last three licks of the belt were extra strict. I howled. The sting was outrageous, I jumped out of my skin, but I kept my ass turned up. Maybe, the last three wouldn't have been as wicked if I'd gone the whole way. The dumbest thing a Shame Artist can do is hold back, even to save something to give later. The moment it was over, Francis didn't give me a moment to feel sorry for myself, he took me by the hips from the rear, and shoved his enormous meaty cock into me before I could raise my face off the floor. He said, "I like it hot," meaning the heat from my flaming ass. I was sloppy wet, so he went right in. He fucked me hard and fast at first, and then settled into slow, long strokes. His groin stung when it touched my raw rear cheeks, but it felt good, too.

Whenever I remember that day, say, anytime I see a wet towel on the floor, I think about how Sofi's gross arms held me down for the whipping and how I skipped up and down the big room without any furniture, boobs bouncing, clutching my backside but just making it worse 'cause it was too raw to touch. I also remember skipping around a couch and chairs. That must have been another time.

I see Francis stripping off, me staring at his lovely cock sticking a mile up out of his briefs, and Sofi clearing her throat and offering me a tour of the upstairs. They let me look into my room where I was to stay that August. Then, they took me to their bedroom with the playground bed. Sofi turned the white cotton bedspread down. I pressed the mattress, like testing whether it was firm enough. I must have decided it was, 'cause the next thing I remember was Francis screwing the daylights out of me.

As I said, a lot of this happened later that August. What really happened the first time I met Francis was that Sofi decided we should have dinner first, before anything else.

——— 9 ———

WHEN FRANCIS CAME HOME

"**Y**ou've been naughty with my wife," Francis said, looking me up and down. Less cuddly than he appeared from the beach. Sofi and me were wrapping ourselves in bath towels. I was trembling.

"What about her?" I protested. "She seduced me!" I wiped her sex gravy off my face with my towel.

"She knows what she'll get," he said, still staring at me. There was a huge bulge in his pants. This was going to be easier than I thought.

Sofi mimed, "what she'll get." Dropping her towel, she went up against the white plank siding of the house as though manacled to it, spread-eagle, arms up, legs wide apart. She had a rear end a man could love, a perfect trim upside-down heart. She jerked her bottom and shimmied like she was getting whipped. This performance was just to remind Francis she existed, 'cause he was obviously smitten with me.

Sofi had such a superior air about her, I'd have crawled to Southampton to watch Francis whip her, to see how she took it.

One day after Sister Martin spanked me, I happened by when her hair was caught in the hinge of a foot locker. She was kneeling, head in the locker, butt up, calling for help, but there was nobody left in the school. I lifted her long gray dress up onto her back and took her coarse white bloomers down. Curly light red bush, virtuous cunt, firm athletic buns. "Who are you?" she cried. "A rapist," I told her in a fake deep voice. I announced I was going to do such sinful sex things to her that if she liked them even a teensy-weensy bit, she would go to Hell. I played roughly with her backside like I thought a man would and pinched the cheeks hard. I stroked her inner thighs, cupped her quim, grazed her clit with my thumb. She said, "Don't stop, I love you!" Then, I tapped her shapely muscular backside with her spanking ruler. She suspected it was one of us, and she threatened every terrible revenge she could think of. At that, I smacked her with her ruler till her butt was red as a stoplight. Another time, after I spanked her, I took her cherry with a blackboard eraser. A trickle of blood down the inside of her thigh. I left her with the bloody eraser stuck all the way up her cunt.

Most of the time, these lovely daydreams blew up in

my face, like, she got her hair free, snatched the ruler away from me, dragged me to the girls' and spanked my hiney worse than when I helped Dennis with his quim problem.

Sofi came off the wall and wrapped herself in her towel. She led me to the shower. When I stepped out, she handed me two pieces of pink linen underwear that she said were part of a Victorian "modesty arrangement." The top had a frilly pouch supporting each breast, but it was low-cut, so the top of each boob was bare almost to the nippie. "It does something nice for your titties," Sofi said, tying a bow around the back of my neck, which lifted my boobs a bit.

I put on the loose bloomers and tied the ribbon at the waist. Victorian ladies must've been fatter and shorter than me. The holes for the thighs were enormous, and there was no elastic at all, so it was all open. A man could reach in and touch whatever he wanted.

"This is it?" I wondered. Sofi explained that a Victorian lady would wear it with four or five more undergarments, and outer garments, but that it was my outfit for the evening. Stupid size and all, I liked it! It said, *Here's a sex slave who doesn't even deserve lingerie that fits.* Sofi wore an elegant negligee and robe.

In the living room I modeled my outfit for Francis, who lounged in an easy chair. Sofi went to get dinner. After a moment I became aware of someone else in the room. Silas Hardon sat quietly in a deep sling chair over by a wall of windows that looked out on the pool and beyond, to the beach. How long was he there? Francis asked him to join us. Mr. Hardon waved broadly no, like, *Don't land that plane here*, to tell Francis he was grateful for being asked. His hand left a faint glow in the air. "Is that from a pinkie ring?" I asked. Sofi went over to Mr. Hardon, whispered to him, came back with the ring. She didn't show it to me, she put it on Francis's left pinkie. It was no longer glowing, but it was also not an ordinary ring. If I could get closer I'd look for an inscription in weird letters.

I sat sprawly with one knee raised, maybe six feet from Francis, my heel pressed modestly back against my cunt. Francis could see the back of my thigh and some curly blonde bush and maybe a little quim. A sea breeze passed through the room and I felt it down there. Not knowing how much of my twat the loose bloomers showed turned me on. I sensed my ankle didn't hide the twitching of my cunt lips. Francis stared at my cunt and nodded, like, agreeing with something it was saying. Then, he raised his eyes to mine. What was he staring at? Trying to hypnotize me. Well, you can't hypnotize a person to do something she doesn't want to do. That's what I've always heard. I stood up and shuffled toward him. Like, a man can't just hypnotize a strange woman to drop her panties and spread for him. I'm sure I read that in a magazine. I leaned over Francis, kissed him on the neck. Also, a man can't just hypnotize his date to suck his cock, unless that's what she really wants to do. Francis played with my hiney. I had an incredible letch to strip for him, suck him and fuck him.

The next moment, I was practically sitting in the palm of his hand. I was opened up, my cunt twitching like mad and flooding. I needed something bad. I remember wanting to get a closer look at the ring, and then I felt it under me. It was hopeless. I was sitting on the Devil's fucking ring. Francis's fingers played in and out of my hot humid swamp. The lower strip of my bloomers, sopping wet with my slippery sex grease, drooped below his hand. I might have apologized for gushing if Mr. Hardon wasn't watching all this. I wanted him to think I was in control, the way I was with him!

"Whatever you want, Sir," I panted in Francis's ear. Sofi told me that in their house I was to call her "Ma'am," and him, "Sir." Even when we were alone, no matter what was going on, "Ma'am," and "Sir," although outside, or back in New York, they would be Sofi and Francis.

I wanted Francis to say something nice, like, how gorgeous my ass was, or, how I turned him on. Nothing. I decided to lose my damp bloomers. I fumbled with the bow. The ribbon I pulled didn't do anything. The bloomers were loose, I could have just pushed them down, but I was trapped in the idea that I had to undo the bow. "This is all making me horny, Sir," I blurted out. Men love to hear a piece of ass say she's horny, she has to have it, blah, blah.

Francis nodded out toward the hot tub, like, that's why I was horny. "No, you," I gasped, clamping the hand with the pinkie ring between my thighs. I couldn't take teasing another second! When this bitchy feeling comes over me, I do have to get laid. Anything goes, a whipping is okay, so long as I get a good screwing afterward. "Fuck me!" I moaned.

At the same moment Sofi rolled in a cart with dinner. To Mr. Hardon first, obviously he was the guest of honor. I scrambled off Francis's lap as Sofi wheeled the cart toward us. We each took a plate, like, dining was the only thing on our minds. I was so horny, I felt sick. I went back to my chair. I didn't feel hungry, but I pigged out. Maybe, I was hungry.

"You and Silas know each other," Sofi announced. I had been sitting on his face for a month. Sofi hadn't been clairvoyant when she seduced me on the beach. She saw me playing nude hostess at the artists' and she knew what I did to Mr. Hardon, some of it, anyway.

"How long's he been here?" I demanded. I wondered whether he saw me lick Sofi in the hot tub.

"A while," Sofi said.

"Know what B and D stands for?" Francis said. They're offering me, "breakfast and dinner" if I stay with them, I thought. Then, it came to me, *bondage and discipline,* but my mouth was full, so I just smiled. Did Francis really manacle Sofi to the wall? What would I be getting into here?

Sofi's sausage and peppers and her salad were delicious. Francis was warming up to me. He saw my nippies poking through the Victorian lingerie. My nippies were longish and swollen. His cock was up and swollen, too, the head of it coming out of his bermudas when he unbuckled his leather belt. I was stunned, like, it was big and stiff and came to a lovely crown. It was the biggest! I was excited and scared. My cunt was grasping for it!

But I wasn't sure what he was planning. He was fingering the belt buckle. The belt was a sick pastel blue leather to go with his bermuda shorts. I hate leather dyed weird colors. I said to myself, *Slut, now you're going to get it for kissing Sofi's twat.* Silas Hardon would get to watch, I supposed, that was why he was here. No, that's why I was here! I was supposed to put on a show for him!

I imagined Francis giving me a vicious pastel blue spanking. I tried to guess how bad my ass was going to sting, to get ready for it. Then, Francis and Sofi would do me so many ways I wouldn't know whether I was coming or going. Mr. Hardon would look on, maybe play with himself. I couldn't tell what they were saying from what I was thinking. Sofi was the most dominating woman I had ever met, and she danced around trying to please Francis. He must be something. It was that huge lovable prick of his. I could please him. I was more scared of her. She could slap your face or tear you apart with words.

"Sofi and Silas tell me you're a Shame Artist," Francis said. "What's that about?"

"Tell Francis how you humiliate men," Sofi said. I gave her a blank look. She reminded me, "You were telling me about mooning the Sports Car Prince at the swimming pool?"

I told them about creaming Alan on graduation day.

Sofi loved that, at least she had a glint in her eye the whole time, but as soon as I was done, Francis snapped at me, "Stand up!"

Maybe he didn't think my story was all that clever. He unbuckled his leather belt. My knees felt weak. He was staring at my sagging bloomers. The underneath panel and inside thighs were sopping wet, and the whole seat was damp gray. I was wetter than poor Alan, one minute before graduation. Odor of horny slut rose from the bloomers. "I can't help it," I wailed. It was so unfair! I knew I was going to get whipped worse for being sloppy-excited. A dry bitch would get off easier.

Sofi chuckled. Francis said, "Drop them!"

The bloomers slithered down to my ankles. I was barefoot. The floor was wood planks with a shiny waterproof varnish. Francis could see my blonde bush and twitchy, drooly quim. So could Sofi and Mr. Hardon.

"Come here!" Francis said.

But I took only half a step toward him. All at once, I was more afraid than turned on. His prick was playing peek-a-boo behind his sport shirt. I looked back sorrowfully at my bare round hiney. I make it sound like I'm always itching for the strap, but that's just shame art. At that moment I would much rather have talked my way out of being punished. I offered to wash the bloomers around my ankles.

"Yes, you will," Sofi snapped. *Oops!* Was it wrong to say that?

"Come here, darling," Francis said softly. It was the first lovey thing he said to me. It was what I wanted to hear. Pretending my ankles were bound by the bloomers, I took little jumps over to him. I glanced at Sofi, who was smirking, Now you're going to get it, slut.

I wanted to say to her, "*Hey,* I took care of you," but I didn't dare. It would just have made Francis madder.

"Your tits are beautiful," Francis sweet-talked, "show them to me." I lifted them out of their pouches, showed them one at a time, tucked them back in and petted them, to tease him. Then, I took the pink linen top off over my head. Naked. Screw Sofi!

"Come here, Sarah," Francis crooned, "you charming storyteller."

He might not punish me at all, I thought. Maybe, all he wants is me to kiss my way down, yes, that's why he unbuckled, to give his swollen cock headroom. He wants me to give him what I gave Sofi. I'll unbutton his shorts and lick that sweetheart prince of a cock. I'll suck him out of his chair! And I'll get an extra charge out of that wimp Silas Hardon watching what I do for a real man.

I leaned down for a kiss. Francis took my nippies in his wonderful strong hands, kneaded and pulled them out the way I love. His ring gave off a cozy glow, like the yellow lights of a home you see from out in the snow.

I came close to a mouth-on-mouth, but I couldn't quite reach his lips, 'cause the way he wanked my nippies held me off. I was breathing heavily and tingling all over and my cunt was writhing.

Just when I brushed his lips with mine and my eyes closed and my lips parted, he tugged one tit to lead me and swept my legs out from under me with one knee, spilling me in slow motion over his knees. It was as smooth as any face-down across-the-knees flop I'd ever taken. He certainly was strong. I knew in mid-tumble where I was headed. My tits jiggled down over his left knee and I was lying hiney up across his thighs. I found myself clasping his left shin, all I could reach of him.

"Bastard!" I cried. Sofi gasped.

I was aware of my bare voluptuous ass and how much it could hurt. Practically in his face, two creamy white round cheeks—that close, my rear end has to look too big. But, everyone says it's gorgeous. People who see famous, box-office asses all the time rave about mine. When it comes to putting it up for punishment, though, it hurts like any ordinary backside. Maybe more, 'cause I'm awfully sensitive back there, although nobody believes me. Like, nobody believes a weightlifter can catch cold.

Francis rolled my rear cheeks and pushed them together, plumped them up like pillows. Still hadn't said he was going to spank me, or did he? Maybe he just liked to play with asses set up for spanking. Except, now he drew the narrow blue belt out, a slapping sound, loop by loop. The shaft of his hard cock pressed into my side. I was outrageously turned on. I sneaked my left hand back along my side to touch his prick. He caught my hand and pinned my wrist to the small of my back. Then, he waited to see if I had any more bright ideas. I guess he liked looking at my steamy, churning cunt. I spread my thighs a few more inches for him.

Delicious shame spread over me, not just all over my

hiney and through my quim, but all the way to my tits plopping over his left knee. My nippies perked up—they were blushing! My face, too, I could feel it change colors. Sofi sat on the floor in front of Francis's chair, closer to my face than my fanny. I had this flash, she wanted to see me cry.

I couldn't see Mr. Hardon. I sensed he was heaving himself out of his seat to his feet. There, moving his chair in for a good look.

I knew Francis was doubling the belt. When you've been face down, across-the-knees, as much as I've been, you don't have to see what's going on behind you. I rubbed his left calf desperately with my free hand, like offering, *I'll be nice to you, don't be mean to me.*

I sensed Francis flip the belt back way above my hiney, picking where he'd land the first smack. I turned my tail up for it like a good bitch and held my breath, when all at once Francis cried, "The chair's on fire!" and flung the belt down. I thought for a moment he was going to dump me off his lap. No such luck. He kept me in place while he poked frantically beneath himself. No one had been smoking. Then, we all realized what it was, Sofi first, actually. She pointed, laughing helplessly, "It's her cunt!" Francis was sitting in a pool of my hot sex juice. When I'm turned on, my vagina pumps out a flood. I love the word vagina. It sounds like it is, open and warm, you know? My love juices were so hot Francis thought his ass was on fire! I scorched and scared the Devil or one of his minions! Imagine that!

Francis was relieved there was no fire, but agitated over his messed-up bermudas. "I'll wash your shorts, Sir," I called back up to him over my shoulder. Was that okay to say? I was facing his ankles, couldn't see how he took it. I was afraid I was ruining his chair, too.

"You'll do all our laundry," Sofi said crisply. As it turned out, the chair covers were washable—I washed them—and they didn't own the furniture, they rented it.

My blood rushed to my head 'cause of the angle I was lying at. Do men think of that when they put you across their knees? I don't think so. All they're interested in is your ass and thighs and your quim. I wiggled my ass, like saying, *Remember me? Going to whip me today, or when?*

Sofi handed Francis the belt doubled up. I felt him raise it, and WAP!

"OWWWI" I felt the sting right across both my cheeks. WAP! That hurt! I couldn't help flinging my leg out, 'way off his lap. It must have been a raunchy sight for him, looking down at my crack, my blonde bush matted with sex goo, my trembling, open cunt. He hauled my wayward leg back. "So, you're ready to climb off," he laughed.

"Yes, Sir," I whimpered.

WAP! WAP! WAP!

I screamed, pumped my ass furiously, kicked my heels up. The three fast smacks cut into my backside. It hurt too much, and at the same time, it excited me over the top, 'cause I deserved it. Still, I couldn't help trying to shield my bottom with my free hand. Two seconds later, it wasn't free anymore. Francis pinned both my wrists against the small of my back. Sofi calling my vigorous kicking-up "unmannerly," and Francis forbade me to kick my heels all the way up. He strapped the back of my thighs to show me the penalty for that.

Sofi smirked, obviously enjoying watching me squirm. That hurt more—no, that's stupid, the spanking hurt more—but it made my heart sink, it was so unfair, that I ate her out and now she was getting off on me suffering for it.

WAP! WAP! WAP! across my cheeks. "Crimson!" Mr Hardon croaked. He must have loved the show. I wanted to scream at him, "You could never get me like this, you worm!" but, then, WAP! WAP! Two strict spanks, low down, catching the undercurve of my rear cheeks, where I'm so tender a lick of a belt hurts un-bearably. I screeched and flutter-kicked real fast, but well-behaved, heels a few inches up.

WAP! My tender spot again, the undercurve close to my asshole! He did that on purpose! I lost it. Usually, I hold together longer. I begged Francis to stop. I said I'd do anything he wanted. Anything any of them wanted. You know what's really humiliating? When you offer to do anything, *anything,* and they ignore you.

The blue leather belt was raised above my fanny, again. I sobbed helplessly.

"I'll give you something to cry about," Francis said. I'd heard that one before.

—— 10 ——

GROWING UP HORNY

When Mom called me a little slut and I cried, she'd say, "Wait till Nevil gets here! He'll give you something to cry about!" Nevil was fifteen years younger than Mom, thin and wiry, sun-tanned, a sailor. He worked in a travel agency, but lived high off Mom.

Dad left when he came home in the afternoon and caught Nevil putting his pants on in the bedroom. Mom was in her bathroom. Mom came out wearing a robe, surprised to see Dad there scowling at Nevil.

Mom immediately saw how to explain everything. Nevil was ill, left work in the middle of the day, but on his way home brought us the airline tickets for our family vacation. A maid let Nevil in. He went looking for Mom 'cause he wanted to explain the reservations he'd made for us. He found her bedroom, but she was in the bath. After a few moments wondering whether to call out, knock, or leave the tickets, Nevil became woozy and lay down on the bed. Mom said all he remembered was shucking off his loafers. His head was spinning. Mom said he felt chilled, and no longer aware he was not at home, he threw off his clothes, got under the covers, and fell into a deep, sweaty sleep.

It was amazing that Mom grasped all this from the bathroom. Dad threw back the covers and found a damp, pungent spot in the middle of the bed. Nevil admitted he occasionally had wet dreams when he ran a high fever. He apologized for the mess, but as he began to see the logic of Mom's story, he got sore at Dad for his accusatory tone. Mom insisted Dad apologize to Nevil.

Despite Mom's terrific story, Dad moved out. Mom sued Dad for divorce on the grounds of desertion. Dad thought he'd win in court. More surprises for Dad: Mom didn't tell the same story in court. Mom and Nevil denied everything. Two doormen forgot they ever saw Nevil. Dad's lawyer kept mixing up hours and dates, and he couldn't ask a witness two questions in a row. After the trial, Dad's lawyer admitted that he was better in the law library than trying cases in court. He expected Dad to congratulate him for his mature acceptance of his limitations. Meanwhile, Mom won the apartment and alimony, child support, and me and Babs. I was eleven. Dad had to pay for our high school, my piano lessons, Babs's sculpture classes, college, medical bills, and more.

Dad told me that Nevil's face was curiously familiar. He began to recall he had passed Nevil in the lobby of our building a dozen times, Nevil coming in as he left, Nevil going out as he came home. Nevil had even been along on our vacations.

After Dad left, Mom felt she was giving up everything for me and Babs, and on top of that we were disobedient sluts and fresh to her. She yelled at us all the time. Before we got too big, she spanked us at bedtime with her back brush. She was afraid of us mocking her, so she was extra strict. We had to drop our pajama bottoms and go across her knees. When we were both bad, I waited with my bottoms down while Babs got it. Mom dumped Babs off her lap, blubbering and rubbing her red hiney, and I got mine.

They sent my older brother Roy to military school and sports camps, but whenever he was home was too much. He jerked off all day long and nothing happened to him, except his underpants were stained and in the summer there were always flies around him. I hate flies. I'm not afraid of mice, I like them. I don't mind bees, wasps, or yellow jackets. They hang around me when I wear flowery perfume, but they never sting me. I don't mind spiders, 'cause they catch flies.

I was saying about Roy. He did stuff to me, like tweaking my nippies. Telling him to stop didn't work. Once, I was naked in the bathroom leaning over the sink brushing my teeth and he burst in and grabbed my hiney cheeks with both hands. Also, Roy let his friend Johnny feel me up. One day I was lying on my bed in my panties and a polo shirt reading a grown-up novel. As the heroine gave herself to her true love, I tweaked my nippies through my polo shirt and slipped a hand inside my panties. I imagined her true love looking like Artie, the boy in the gym with the golden knuckle.

A horsefly from Central Park buzzed at my window screen. That was unusual 'cause our apartment was on the eleventh floor, but it happened. I suspected the horsefly liked my smell just now and wanted to nibble you know where. I shut the window just to make sure, and also so I wouldn't hear it. A moment later Roy barged into my room without knocking. I rolled over on my belly, casually slipping my hand out of my panties. "Get out of my room!" I yelled, but instead he went to the window.

"Why don't you open the window?" he said, "it's a great day." I told him, "Go out and play, then!" He opened the window, jostling the screen like it was an accident. The horsefly whizzed past me, buzzed at the other window, and flew off into the rest of the apartment. Roy slammed my door shut. When I turned around, Johnny was with him. They both just stood there, staring at my backside. I was wearing ordinary panties, but even then I filled them well. "Get out, I'm not dressed!" I yelled. The boys teased me about a damp spot in the crotch of my panties. I slid my legs together, put a pillow behind me to cover up, and pretended to read.

Johnny was so excited he rubbed his hands together, like, frantically washing them, and he scratched one lower leg with the other. Roy gave him the go-ahead. Johnny darted in under the pillow and played with my hiney. I couldn't say no, 'cause now the whole crotch on my panties was wet. Johnny's hands on my butt felt good, but when he touched me underneath, I threatened to scream. Roy said I could scream all I wanted, he'd shut three doors between us and the rest of the house. Besides, Roy said, if anyone heard me, he'd say I was showing Johnny my ass and he was trying to get me to cover up. Roy was really a criminal type. I believed he could get away with it, 'cause I got into trouble the year before mooning the St. Deems baseball team.

Johnny plucked at the sopping wet strip. I rolled over onto my back to defend myself. Roy grabbed my arms and held me down. Johnny played with my hard nippies through the polo shirt. Then, he lunged into my panties from above and hooked his middle finger into me, a first, not counting my own finger, which I'm sure you don't. I bit Roy's forearm and he let go. I flipped on my side away from Johnny and doubled over. It worked, I got him out of me. He complained to Roy that I had sprained his finger, and held it out for sympathy, sniffed it, called it a "stinkfinger," and made a face.

Johnny was like a big horsefly. I don't mean only the mustache bristles he was so proud of he wouldn't shave or the big glasses that made his eyes big like a fly's. I mean, you can't bargain with a horsefly, you can't scare it off, you can't beg it to stop. It doesn't care what you want, it keeps at you. Two seconds after I wrecked his finger, Johnny was sitting on the bed behind me pulling my panties down below my hiney. I elbowed and kicked back at him. I tried to stuff the pillow behind me to cover my crack, but all at once he hauled me into his lap, grabbing my ass in one hand and working his other hand between my thighs. I felt a couple of fingers poke all the way up in me. The pad of his thumb was on my clit. I collapsed on his chest, horny and sick. This wasn't like with Artie. I hit Johnny on the back and shoulders. He kissed me. I thought of biting him, but I was whirling. Roy started off smirking, but he was amazed at how I shook all over when I came.

They both had bulges in their pants. I was sitting on Johnny's lap, really on his hand, and leaning against his chest. He put my hand on his bulge. Seemed fair, I got to feel his hard-on, but it made him crazy. He said he was going to screw me and dumped me on my back on the bed. Roy wasn't sure that was a good idea and tried to talk Johnny out of it. Johnny stared at my twitchy quim like he'd never seen one before, which I bet he hadn't. He decided he liked it well enough, and took his pants and underpants off. Roy ran out of my room, ran back in and out again two or three times. Johnny's pole looked enormous. I wanted to faint, but I couldn't. Johnny lay on top of me and I thought, *this is it*, but he didn't know how to put it in. He kept sliding it over my cunt, which was exciting and scary. Then, he pried my quim open with one hand and held his prick in his other hand, but he couldn't bring them together. When he got close, I wiggled a bit and he was way off. "Stop moving!" he shouted. I took his prick in my hand, also a first! and pretended to guide it to my cunt, but it was too late, 'cause his hot jism hit my belly. Spurt after spurt plopped on my belly and soaked my polo shirt. As soon as Johnny was finished, he ran out and Roy ran after him. The fly was back, buzzing the inside of the window. Now, it wanted out. While I looked for a shoe to swat it, it got away.

I threw the shirt in the back of the closet and washed my belly. For weeks I was afraid that the cum in my navel could make me pregnant, even though I also know it couldn't. I called the stain in the shirt Original Sin, 'cause it never came out completely. I showed Original Sin to my friend Cathy, and she sniffed it. Roy and his friends got away with everything. Only girls had to be nice and not do sex stuff.

Mostly, I didn't do sex stuff! I thought about it and talked about it with Cathy. Mom called me a slut 'cause she thought sex was on my mind all the time. She listened in on the phone when me and Cathy talked about boys. When I was almost twelve years old, I shot up three inches and all at once I was too big for Mom to yank me across her knees. The last time she tried to, I punched her in the belly and knocked her wind out.

Awhile after I shook Mom up with that shot, she called Nevil at his travel office and said, "Sarah's behaving like a tramp," and he snarled right back, "I'll take care of her,"—I heard his nasal twang—and she told me so Nevil could hear, "Now, you're going to get it, you little slut!" She sent me to my room, gloating over me 'cause I knew it was all set up. I hadn't done anything wrong, just talked sexy with boys on the phone and let them feel me up. I hated Mom. I never blamed Nevil for spanking me. Mom made him spank me and Babs till we got too curvy.

In my room I thought about ways to kill her and make it look like an accident. Sometimes I imagined getting arrested, but then I would make a brilliant speech at my trial and get off. When it got closer to spanking time, I put on a skirt and my sexiest panties for Nevil. He liked me in skirts better than jeans. I lay on my bed pretending I was already across Nevil's knees. I reached behind me and felt my butt, which was smaller then, but round and cute as a young girl's butt can be. I'd lift my skirt in back the way he did, and imagined his strong right hand smacking my hiney. I even winced and kicked my heels up!

And I felt sexy. Rich little girls aren't supposed to feel sexy, but I always did. I patted my ass with one hand (spank! spank!) and with the other I rolled my secret button till I could hardly breathe and I felt like I was going to explode. I got all wound up like a wind-up toy dog, and then I wound down all at once. I shook all over and yelped into my pillow. It felt wonderful. I played with my nippies some more, my secret button, and my quim and my behind, and I got all wound up again. I was in a frenzy by the time Nevil came.

Nevil knocked but didn't wait for me to say it was okay to come in. Lots of times I let him catch me playing with myself. I was giving him a message. He would say, "You sassed your mother," or, "Gloria (Mom) says you promised a boy you'd jerk him off under a blanket at a football game—Are you doing that?"

I'd protest, "She's crazy!" or "It's my blanket!" but Nevil never saw it my way. He sat on my bed and put me across his knees, lifted my skirt up in back and spanked me with his wiry hand. My favorite panties were tiny in back, or sheer, so my rear cheeks were mostly bare. Nevil's spankings didn't hurt all that much—he wasn't serious about punishing me—but they excited me out of my mind. I told him, "Really do it! Hurt me!" Nothing I did with boys turned me on as much!

I wanted Nevil to use his belt. I wanted him to hurt me so much I couldn't help bawling. Also, I was dying for him to take my panties down just for the feeling of being exposed that way. I told him it would be okay, if he felt he had to take my panties down to punish me as I deserved, he could do that. He didn't. I think, for a long time, we both had the feeling Mom was going to barge into the room. But she only did that once, when she remembered something additional she wanted Nevil to punish me for. Mom stayed away 'cause she knew it was wrong to have her gigolo get that intimate with me, even if it was meant to improve my morals. Once or twice every time, Nevil would "accidentally" brush the damp spot on the crotch of my panties. I wanted that touch right on my quim! I could swear those touches were getting longer! Yes, and he was brushing me in both directions! I wanted more! One day I begged him to finger me. I grabbed his wrist behind me and tried to guide his hand where I wanted it. For that he gave me a dozen extra spanks, strict as he could, but he didn't tell Mom, 'cause she didn't get on me about it. So, me and Nevil had something together, after all!

The next time I was face down across Nevil's knees and he lifted my skirt, I had a surprise for him—no panties! That spanking hurt more, alright, and it was super sexy! I knew he was watching my wet, twitchy quim! He gave me a little, too, not everything I wanted, but enough to keep me from feeling ignored. He rubbed my red rear cheeks and cupped me underneath with his hand. That was all it took. I came to his touch. We never mentioned it afterward, and it never happened quite the same way again. It was wonderful.

Nevil spanked me bare-ass from then on. Mom sent me to my room to wait for Nevil every few days. It was part of our household routine. Like the silver got polished, the parquet floors got buffed, and Sarah got her bottom warmed—all by Mom's servants. Also, it was part of her and Nevil's sex life. She probably enjoyed Nevil being hard as a rock after he spanked me. She didn't catch on it wasn't all bad for me. One time, a week went by without any discipline. I missed it. When Nevil was on the way over, I "talked filthy" to Mom, something about "wasn't it fun to feel a boy's ass when he kissed you?" She sent me to my room. By the time I got there my panties needed a rinse! I threw them in my sink. Twenty minutes later I was showing my bare hiney to my own personal Master of Discipline.

After a few weeks I tested Nevil by wearing panties,

and he took them down with a vengeance, as though that wasn't what I wanted all along. A while later Mom and Nevil caught me cuddled up with Dennis in my love nest in front of our door, and she ordered Nevil to use his belt. That didn't go exactly the way I would've wanted it, 'cause she was there. He couldn't make love to me. He couldn't acknowledge me as a secret lover at all. However, the Dennis affair was a turning point. Before, when Nevil was done spanking me, he'd make me stand facing the corner to think about what I'd done. After Dennis, as soon as Nevil gave me the last spank, I'd throw my arms around his neck and kiss him. He'd exclaim, "You're being punished! Stand in the corner!" But I knew he was pleased. I breathed warm air into his ear, licked his neck with my mouth wide open, plucked at his lips with my tongue. I played with his butt, too. I knew I was winning, 'cause he let me do all that. He held my warm red backside in his hands while I kissed him. At last, he kissed back.

One day Nevil was as horny as always after he spanked me. He had just used his hand. We kissed. I squirmed in his lap, fondled his cock through his pants and murmured, "I want to suck you off." I knew what I was saying, 'cause I was already sucking Billy off. That was different. Billy was a classmate and a friend. He didn't spank me and he didn't screw Mom.

Nevil grinned and cupped my red bottom to feel the heat it gave off. Maybe he was the Devil, 'cause any normal man would've just unzipped. "Please, *Oh*, please, Nevil," I said, "let me do it!" He unbuckled his belt, pulled it off, and ordered me facedown, back across his knees! I couldn't believe it! This time he really hurt me. "I hate you!" I bawled. But I was so turned on I didn't care what he did to me. I was molten mush and twitching underneath, he could see it and touch it, and he did. "I'll never forgive you as long as I live," I pouted when he was done, "unless you come in my mouth."

Nevil had given reforming me his best shot and failed. I won! He caved in, agreed it would be lovely. But, there was no time. Mom was waiting for him in her room. I refrained from saying that I could've taken care of him in the time he'd wasted whipping me.

Two days later, we got together in one of the sitting rooms, which are small extra living rooms. The servants never went into the sitting rooms except to vacuum according to a schedule posted in the laundry. Mom was out when Nevil came. He was early on purpose. I led him into a sitting room before he could change his mind. For him, it was a sitting room, for me, a kneeling room—you get the idea! His cum was as slimy as Billy's, and much saltier, not nearly as sweet. I decided Nevil's taste was more sophisticated, but I liked Billy's sweetness better.

I took care of Nevil a couple of times a week before Mom got home. Also, once we were lovers, we always messed around in my room after he spanked me. I figured I was paying Mom back. I loved the way Nevil kissed my tits. I never forgot that he assured me, when I was younger and had minor-league boobs, that size didn't matter. Aside from being Mom's gigolo and debauching me, Nevil wasn't a bad guy.

The way Nevil knew how to touch me made me feel he had the right to. I got hot and wet and lost control and punched him in the chest. It was ironic, Nevil helping me stay virgin for Mom's sake, 'cause if she had any idea I was licking his balls in every corner of her apartment, she wouldn't have been at all pleased.

Nevil made me beg all the time, kneeling naked between his thighs, lips parted, showing my tongue, eyes pleading. I gave him the idea. What's more humiliating than begging for a mouthful, especially from a man who just gave you a stinging red hiney? And then he'd croon insults while I did stuff for him. He purred, "Keep licking, bitch, keep licking . . ." Maybe, I told Nevil about Billy doing that? I don't remember. The whole time I gulped Nevil's cum, he chanted, "Swallow it all, little slut, every drop, that's right, you little bitch, swallow . . ." What a coincidence! Both Billy and Nevil giving me that extra thrill of shame.

It finally dawned on Mom that I loved every smack of Nevil's hand. Also, that my rear end was as round as hers and twenty-five years younger. My thighs were perfect, which nobody'd say about hers anymore, and my skin was silky smooth. Nobody told me or Babs not to expect any more Nevil spankings. He just stopped.

I never told Babs about me and Nevil. I warned Nevil, if he let Babs blow him or do anything else for him, I'd tell Mom and maybe Dad, too. But Nevil never showed any interest that way in Babs.

Nevil spanked Mom once in a while, though she ran the show. When Mom drove Nevil crazy enough, he'd ask her, even in front of us, whether she wanted a spanking. She countered by calling him names that made me and Babs wince. He'd twist her arm and they'd agree to continue the discussion in her bedroom. Mom banged doors closed along the way. The doors bounced open, or we'd open them. There was a brief struggle in her bedroom—Nevil taking her across his knees and baring her bottom. Her curses faded after a few sensationally loud, meaty smacks. Nevil walloped her voluptuous bottom good and strict! She'd grunt for the first few smacks, and then she'd just bawl helplessly like a baby, *"WAHNNN!"* I was always touched when Mom cried like that. Me and Babs were too thrilled to count spanks, though we always said we would next time.

One evening when I was out, Babs heard Mom yelling at Nevil, "I'll call the doorman and have you removed from the apartment!" Babs crept into Mom's dressing room and saw it all: Nevil dragging Mom in a negligee across his knees, lifting the negligee baring her round soft backside, her cursing and hitting at him, his pinning her wrists behind her, his stern spanks, her threatening whatever, SMACK! her threatening something else, SMACK! right through to Mom crying and begging for mercy, more smacks, and Nevil letting her down, and her sucking him, kneeling on the carpet and wiggling her blotchy pink ass. Babs was stuck in a closet in the dressing room until Nevil and Mom both fell asleep. Interesting about the blow job, 'cause of the incredibly hard time Mom gave me and Babs when she caught on that we were blowing guys.

One morning Mom cracked a joke that didn't make sense—'cept if she thought the boys sniffing around me were content with fondling my boobs. My sexpot Mom was always on me to stay virgin. For a while, 'til she and Nevil caught me blowing Dennis in front of our door, she didn't have a clue how I managed that.

I loved the look in a boy's eyes when I smiled and unbuttoned and unzipped him and licked my parted lips, 'specially with a new date who didn't know he was going to get anything. As for Mom, even after Dennis, she never accepted that whatever else might happen on my dates, one thing sure to happen was that I would suck cock 'til I got a mouthful of hot salty cum. It was like Mom was shocked all over again every time she pictured me taking a prick in my mouth. She said it was her fault for not being strict enough. Sometimes, she said it was St. Deems's fault, and sometimes my father's fault for leaving us. I said, no, it was her and Nevil's fault, meaning I knew she blew him. But she couldn't take a joke.

— 11 —

How I Became Promiscuous

I missed Nevil warming my hiney every time Mom worried I was as sexy as she was. Each time it was a frolic across my lover's knees. He used his hand and it was more exciting than painful. But Mom could never leave well enough alone. After my double date with Alice one Saturday night, Mom had Nevil cane me.

Alice was stunning. Her body was too elegant for the St. Deems boys. Her guy Mark was in graduate school at Yale. They fixed me up with Josh, Mark's best friend. Josh had a big chest and belly, like a hog, and a sly, amiable grin. I liked him, but he kept away from me all evening. Josh liked me, too, but he was shy. It felt like Mark wanted me more than his big pal, 'cause Mark stared at my tits and talked to me more than to Alice.

The four of us were on the way back from Newport.

I thought it'd be fun to tease Mark by making out with Josh in the back seat. I got hot thinking about how we could drive Mark crazy, like the grosser we made out, the better. I'd be paying Mark back for neglecting Alice. Alice wouldn't mind, so long as I didn't actually give Mark anything. But Josh didn't try to kiss me, even when I nestled up to him. He didn't say much either. I rubbed my neck against his, a good trick. You learn a lot watching horses. I could tell he liked that. After a while I put his hand on my blouse in front. His jaw dropped. He massaged my right tit 'til it was hard and burning through my bra. I tweaked his nipples through his shirt, like saying, *I get to do the same to you*, and he breathed like he was going to have a heart attack. He unbuttoned my blouse, but took forever to get me unhooked in back, even though I pulled my blouse out of my skirt and turned away from him, looked out the side window. Then, he got the bra unhooked, I turned back to him, my boobs plopped out—and Mark caught the moment in the rearview mirror just as I hoped he would. I let Josh maul my tits awhile. He squooshed them through his fingers and pulled my nippies like he was milking a cow. I even said, *"Mooo!"* Not sure he got it. A nice guy, but an idiot. I unbuttoned a few buttons of his shirt and showed him. He didn't catch on I was teaching him how to touch me.

Josh chewed my tits. It drove me wild, Mark and Alice seeing him do it. I rubbed Josh's thighs, grazing his cock, which was hard as the gear shift. All at once, Josh shoved his monster paw under my skirt between my thighs. I went up on my knees and gave him a little spread to work in. He tweaked one of my cunt lips and then the other through my panties. He kept doing that, like he wasn't sure what to do next! My turn! I unzipped him and pulled on his prick through his underpants, and when the head of it poked out over the top of his shorts, I fondled it. I was actually in his pants before he was in mine. Now, he got so excited about what I was doing for him, he was almost useless. I slipped my panties down to remind him it was his turn, and he put his middle finger in me.

We kept rolling on top of each other. "Watch out—you almost hit the gear shift!" Mark cried, exhaling noisily through clenched teeth. Mark kept glancing back, pretending he was checking out the traffic through the rear window. Alice knew he couldn't help looking. She just watched the way you'd watch puppies rolling around nipping each other. My bare behind was pointing toward Mark when I straddled Josh with my panties half-way down my thighs. Josh held my beautiful round butt with one hand and worked a thumb up my cunt. "I love that," I whispered in his ear and licked his neck, and I came, and he gave me a good hard thumb-fucking. I went crazy. I didn't care if he broke my cherry, but he didn't. His thumb was goopy, but not bloody.

Mark parked on a nearly empty street just down from the Central Park Zoo. The street was empty because it was in the wee hours Sunday morning in the summer and the whole world was at their country homes, except

Mom, 'cause Dad had to sell ours to pay his debts, and Alice's parents, who were in New York this weekend on their way to Europe with Alice. Mark still had to drop Alice off at her parents' hotel and drive two hours to get home. Alice kissed Mark for half a minute and went down on him. That was her way. She screwed him silly before we left Newport, but she knew that after watching me and Josh, Mark needed another round.

Alice was cool. She never wore makeup, and she could take a guy into a bedroom at a party and come out twenty minutes later with not a hair out of place. The guy would be a happy wreck, so relaxed he couldn't stand up, a goofy smile all over his face. But I didn't have the knack of hiding anything. I was playing with Josh's balls and pulling the shaft of his cock in a nice teasing way, with a little twisting squeeze, when, all at once, it's on the way! I start to go down, but we're too close to each other, I can't get my mouth on it in time. Splat! I get some cum in my hair and on my cheek and in my ear, some on the shoulder of my blouse and on my bra strap, and only the last jet in my mouth.

Josh apologized, but he was still hard, and I could tell he wanted me to keep going, 'cause he held my head down, so I kept sucking.

I wanted to finish Josh off in the car. I didn't want to ask him in. Anyway, this Saturday, since I knew I'd be late, I let Babs have the love nest outside our front door 'til 3 A.M. My big round rear end was up, bare, almost in the front seat. Alice said, "Sarah!" softly, like, chiding, and cleared her throat, twice, but I couldn't stop and figure out how to cover my tail and I didn't care if Mark got an eyeful. My ass was in his face when he turned his head, his friend's hand held my wet cunt two feet from his nose. I heard footfalls of people passing by the car. They stopped and watched for awhile, but there was nothing I could do, so I kept sucking. Alice had sucked Mark off in no time flat and was sitting up for quite a while. Mark swung the car door open and the walkers remember they were on their way home. In maybe six, seven minutes Josh came again. It seemed a long time to suck a guy with two friends waiting for you to finish in a small car on a city street. This time, I was able to swallow it all.

Mark called me a month later. I wasn't seeing Josh anymore, and Alice was in Europe. "Aren't you Alice's friend?" I said vaguely. Not only wouldn't I forget anybody who saw me in action, but Alice called me from Cap d'Antibes last night to say she was dumping him. "We're breaking up," he announced. "It's too soon— call me in a couple of months," I told him. I guess I was the booby prize 'cause Alice was booting him! But, maybe, who knows?

The three of them dropped me off around the corner at my Fifth Avenue apartment building. Josh didn't get out of the car. I didn't want him to, anyway. He was dazed and somehow hadn't covered his prick. It was semi-hard and beads of cum kept bubbling up. I leaned over and licked a few times to finish him off, but he got harder and more beads oozed out, so I gave up.

I didn't know or care how gross I looked. Why did

Alice let me go in that way? I never asked, but I think she accepted that I was hopeless. She probably assumed the doorman and the elevator man saw me like that all the time. Mom and Nevil were in the breakfast room. I streaked for the guest bathroom, but Mom was right in behind me. "If you don't mind!" I cried. It was no use. She pointed at my chin and shrieked. Then, I saw the beads of cum on my chin in the mirror, a generous dollop in my hair, a streak on my blouse, and another on my skirt. Mom made a haughty face as though she never blew anyone! She screamed at me to strip off my stained clothes. I didn't think anything would be showing below, but when I took my skirt off, my panties weren't pulled up right. The crotch was sopping, and Josh had smeared my own juices all over my behind and thighs. I smelled pretty strong.

Mom said I was grounded and I'd be punished. I felt ashamed. She shrieked, "Wash every inch of you and go to bed!" The next day, Sunday, she and Nevil were gone most of the day, but the one time she saw me, she said, "You're going to get it!"

Monday evening, there was no chance to be alone with Nevil. Mom couldn't wait to tell me Nevil would give me a good caning. *Caning?* Nevil got caned in an English boarding school or maybe he saw it in a movie. It was hard to know what to believe about Nevil. I deserved punishment for arriving home dappled with cum, but the more I thought about caning, the more gruesome it sounded.

I wasn't allowed to see the cane. It was made of a

wood that grew in India and treated some special way that made it pliant and firm. It was guaranteed to hurt worse than anything. Mom wanted me bending over my desk in my bra and panties. Then, she got so hopped up, she began to talk about having me naked. She sounded like she didn't care that Nevil would see everything! Nevil had a wicked grin except when Mom looked at him. Then, he was sober and concerned for my welfare. He had a hard-on. The one time he had a chance to say something to me, he harped on my blowing my date and said he was going to enjoy whipping me, but I already knew that, 'cause, discipline aside, he'd smacked my bare butt lots of times for the sport of it.

There was something extra humiliating about Nevil caning me to please Mom that turned me on. Since she didn't know Nevil was giving it to me in the mouth every few days, the joke was on her. But I was scared the cane would hurt too much.

Mom had second thoughts about Nevil seeing my gorgeous ass and my cunt and all. She knew she shouldn't make me bare my ass for her gigolo! She toyed with the idea of letting me keep my panties on. I suggested I wear my vanilla ice cream summer pajamas, and she went for it. These pajamas were from my sexpot Aunt Deedee, who said when she gave them to me that they were for my honeymoon. They were made out of the lightest stuff, see-through, like plastic wrap for food. I was the food. Mom wasn't aware how I'd filled out. When I put the pajamas on and looked between my legs in the full-length mirror, my rear cheeks looked naked, with a vanilla-tint. Below, I could see cunt lips and blonde bush. Mom wouldn't be happy about Nevil seeing me that way. That's why I wanted him to.

Mom sent me to my room to put on my vanilla pajamas and "think about what you did." I put the pajamas on, but instead of sitting around stewing, I called Cathy, who thought it was funny. She was the only one who knew all about Nevil. "You deserve it, you slut," she said. I called her slut, too. She kept rubbing it in, like, "*Oh*, my god, with a *cane*?" Cathy said my voice was muffled. The drawstring was loose and my pajama bottoms drooped a bit. I held the phone between my chin and my shoulder, tweaking my tits with one hand and playing below with the other. She picked up on my breathing and guessed what I was doing. We had a little joke, talking about boys on the phone and doing ourselves. Cathy said she wished she could watch me get red stripes on my ass. I said she could imagine it and play with herself. She said, "Are you still going to love him after this?" I said, "Well, it'll be a test, won't it?"

I heard the caning party on the way to my room. I dabbed my cunt and the inside of my thighs with a towel, wiped my fingers, and threw the towel under my bed. Cathy called out cheerfully, "Keep your ass up!" which didn't register till I hung up. I pulled my vanilla bottoms up, tied the bow in front and bent over my desk, face and palms down, ass up, just as Mom opened the door with Nevil in tow.

Mom looked Nevil over nervously. He was cool, like

this was an everyday chore. Even though he saw my bare butt pretty often, he admitted later that it was exciting all over again in the sheer pajamas. He carried the cane in a slender black case, like a billiard stick. I put my hiney up as sexy as I could to spite Mom. Nevil took the cane out, stood behind me to my left and swished the cane in the air. I glanced back at the cane. It was dark brown, almost black, with a dull finish. I was scared. I pretended I was pointing my asshole at Nevil, like offering him what he talked to me about all last week. If he thought he had any chance of getting that, maybe he'd go easier.

Nevil was rarin' to go, but Mom had to be in control, so she told him, wait, and made me say what I did wrong, like, "Giving Josh a hand job, a blow job ... whatever."

"What kind of a girl does things like that?" Mom demanded. If I said, a girl like her, it would be worse for me. I knew what she expected me to say. She told me at least twice a week.

"A bad girl, a slut," I said.

Finally, she let Nevil get on with it. He checked the arc of the cane across my rear cheeks, drew back— *THWICK!*

"OWWW!" I cried. The cane dug in! Amazing how it stung! I touched the burning flesh gingerly through the sheer pajamas.

"Put your hands back on the desk, slut!" Mom yelled. I shook my head, no. My eyes were wet with tears. They were going too far.

"Bend over," Nevil said sweetly, actually, meanly, 'cause the sweet was a tease.

I hated him. No, I loved him. This was a way to show him how much. I bent over, but my hands rushed back to shield my hiney!

"Hands on the desk!" Nevil snapped. I obeyed, but that was really hard! My ass wiggled in protest. He drew the cane back, waited. She nodded to him. *THWICK!*

"YAllllEEE!" I screamed and bolted straight up, grabbing my tail. It was beyond fire. I jumped up and down, which made the tears in my eyes run down my cheeks. Nevil watched my boobs bounce in my pajamas.

"Bend over, hands on the desk!" Nevil barked.

"It hurts too much," I cried.

"Good," Mom said. "Put your hiney up."

"I learned my lesson," I whimpered. "I won't do stuff with boys anymore."

"Nevil," Mom said.

"Bend over right now," Nevil told me. He was much stronger than me. He could bend me over or twist my arm five different ways so I'd bend over.

There's a lot I wanted to yell at him, but I realized I better not. The safe thing was to bend over.

"Backside up!" Mom said. My tail tucked in, like a whipped dog's. I thought of Cathy's parting shot, "Keep your ass up!" Gingerly, I turned my ass up for Nevil.

He was drawing the cane back! I covered my butt with my hands, palms out. He took both my hands and jerked them up my back. He wedged his hip against mine so I couldn't move. "I warned you," he said. I nodded yes, and began to cry. I felt miserable. It was on the way! *THWICK!*

"*YAlllEEEOWWW!*" I screamed. I struggled, but there was nowhere to go. He was going to do it again. "No-o-o, please," I begged.

THWICK! "YlllEEE!" I shrieked. "Look at the welts—!" Nevil exclaimed.

"What won't you do with boys anymore?" Mom said.

She loved to make me spell it out. "I won't suck them," I sobbed. I felt Nevil's hard-on sticking into my side. Sucking it would be a relief. The awful part of all this was that after he whipped me, Nevil would leave me crying my eyes out while he and Mom fucked up a storm.

"What else?" Mom inquired.

I hurt too much back there to think. "Nothing," I moaned, "I won't do anything."

"Liar," Mom said. A little twist of Nevil's body, and then, *THWICK!*

"*WAHHHN-AHHHN!*" I bawled, wiggled my ass.

THWICK!

"*AWWWHN!*"

I didn't even think of promising not to screw, 'cause it wasn't in my repertoire. For a moment I thought of saying, "I won't take Nevil's prick up my ass,"—'cause Nevil was angling for that, but I decided to spare Mom the details.

THWICK!

"*WAHHHN-AWWW-AWWWN!*"

I cried hysterically trying to get free. I was so turned

on to Nevil I couldn't stand it. His prick was rubbing against me and heat from my rear cheeks radiated through my cunt. I was outrageously wet down there.

"That was seven," Mom said, grimly ignoring that I was flooding my vanilla pajamas, which were soggy gray below. "What else will you not do with boys?"

A wild hope—I say the right thing, the caning's over. "No hand-jobs?" I said.

"You know all the words," Mom said. To her, knowing what to call it was as bad as doing it. "What else?"

"I won't let boys finger me," I said dully.

"Or, play with your tits," Mom said. She was testing me and I fell for it. I wanted to say, "The other girls do stuff," but I couldn't take the chance. "No, no more playing with my tits," I repeated hopefully.

"You're such a slut," Mom said, giving up on me. The caning would go on. It wasn't my fault the crotch of my pajamas was wet. I bawled to Nevil that he better stop right now!

THWICK

"YAAOWWWW!" I struggled in Nevil's grip, but he was too strong, I wound up in the same place. All I could do was waggle my ass furiously, maybe getting me a few precious seconds before the next one. My pajama bottoms slipped, I couldn't feel how far down, 'cause my rear cheeks are all shredded with flaming red welts and puffy.

THWICK!

It hurts so much I can't describe it. I slip out of his grip and stagger up to my feet so I'm facing them. My pajama bottoms are down around my ankles, but maybe my bush is covered by the top. I don't care. I blab what Nevil's doing to me behind Mom's back—I don't see what I have to lose anymore—but Mom doesn't get it, 'cause I'm screeching and crying and hiccoughing, too.

Nevil knows what I'm saying. He takes me by my wrist, puts one foot up on my desk chair and jerks me up over his thigh. He hurts my wrist, twisting it way up my back. For a moment his mouth is near my ear. "Shut up," he suggests.

He's raising the cane! I pump my bare red-hot can and kick my heels up.

THWICK! Right on my raw flesh! I tried to scream, but nothing came out. I felt whipped all over, in my fingertips and toes and in my face. And, in my tits and my cunt.

THWICK! The pain's thrilling, like I know nothing can ever hurt more than this, it's the worst, if I can just live to the next second, it'll get better, but it gets worse and worse—and I'm out of my head crying and apologizing and begging.

There was a long pause while I recovered, and I figured I miscounted. I thought it was eleven, and I had one more coming, but it must've been twelve. But, if it was over, why was Nevil still holding me over his thigh? Then, I felt him lift the cane again.

"No-o-o, please," I cried.

THWICK!

"YAAAlllEEE! YAAAOWWWOWWW!" I screeched and groaned.

Mom told me to pull my bottoms up and stand in the corner and think about behaving myself like a high school girl instead of a whore. I jumped up and down holding my behind and bawling. It wasn't fair, 'cause a lot of what I did was to stay virgin for her.

I glared at Nevil through my tears and swore I'd never do anything for him again. He was putting the cane back in its case. At the same moment, I realized I was turned on to him worse than ever. I wished he'd fuck me one last time in the mouth, and once the regular way, to get me started. And maybe once in the behind like he wanted, and then I'd tell him good-bye, and he'd miss me forever. I was hopeless. At least, I knew it.

They headed for Mom's bed, as horny as grown-ups ever get. I was still sobbing. I played with myself, imagining Nevil doing it all to me, and then two guys from St. Deems, then Mark, then Cathy doing herself thinking of my ass getting caned, and then me and Nevil caning her while Mark watched. I wanted to walk away from Nevil wiggling my ass and make him regret what he was going to miss without me.

In the weeks after this, I went wild. Not just from the caning, but from knowing that it turned-on Nevil and Mom so much they were fucking up a storm. I couldn't help myself. You know how sex-crazy some boys are? That's how I got with boys. I wanted to get into their pants! You're supposed to look into a boy's eyes to tell what he's thinking. But, what if you already know what he's thinking? Look below, there's a snake in a bag trying to fight its way up. Help the snake straighten out. Nice snake. Unbuckle a belt, undo a button or two, unzip, pet the snake. I was sexy out of my gourd. Remember, people said I was a good girl and a virgin till Tom Thomas ruined me. It's true, I was a virgin, and very, very good at what I was good at.

Mom knew I sneaked out five or six nights a week. She kept threatening to get me locked up in a private mental clinic and make Dad pay for it. Every week or so, she'd catch me coming back in the wee hours, needing a bath more than another lecture on my low morals. The next day Nevil would come to my room with the cane case—always with Mom now—and say, "Your mother tells me you've been a slut and I'm here to discipline you. Bend over the desk and raise your skirt." "I'm studying!" I'd protest, when I had time to grab a book. Or, "Do you mind?—I'm on the phone!" They didn't care. Mom would yell, "Get off the phone!" But, I covered up the mouthpiece as soon as I heard them come down the hall toward my room. Once, I'd already made a date with a new guy, Dirk, but I wanted to get off the phone smoothly, so I kept listening and covering up the mouthpiece, and with my other hand, slowly, without paying any attention to it, raised my skirt in back and began rolling my panties down, like I was telling Nevil and Mom, *This bores me.* Nevil took the cane out. I said a sweet good-bye to Dirk and bent over to hang the phone up. I think they got the message, *I'm not bending over for you, I have to hang the phone up.* But, I stayed bending over till Nevil finished flaying my hiney. As usual, I wound up whimpering, "It's over, I'll never do anything for you, Nevil!" He knew what I was saying, but I was crying too hard for Mom to get it. She thought I was promising not to mess around with boys anymore.

Instead, I got worse. I needed more comforting from boys. Also, Nevil's caning hurt so bad, I figured I should get all the pleasure I could to make it worthwhile.

Mom couldn't stand Nevil seeing my cunt when I bent over. For a few canings, exactly two, I think, she made me wear panties, the most ordinary ones she could find. All at once, the scene didn't turn them on much. Mom was still outraged at my promiscuity, Nevil was still indignant about me putting out for anyone but him, and now he had more rivals than ever. But, erotically, caning me in panties was a step back. Nevil was bored. Mom wanted him steaming hot. Her compromise was to have me roll my panties down to just below my rear cheeks. That was supposed to keep my quim covered. Nevil told me privately it didn't work. When the cane made my rear cheeks dance, he could still see my quim lips writhe. Mom could have seen that too, if she'd wanted to. But, she was getting too much out of Nevil's turn-on.

One day I refused to submit to any more caning, I said I'd come and go as I pleased. They tied me over the desk. Nevil caned me extra on the back of my thighs for kicking him while he tied me. I'd have left home, even if I'd wound up a whore, but I stayed 'cause I was crazy about Nevil. Whether I was tied down or not, I shimmied right in his face. Mom yelled at me, "Stop that, you slut!" but, screw her, my hiney was stinging, it had a mind of its own. Nevil got more and more turned on to me. He'd rather have made love to me than Mom anytime. He just balled her so he could be with me. He never said that, though. How do I know? Easy, a Shame Artist just knows.

— 12 —

NEVIL'S OTHER WAY

Nevil liked living high off Mom and putting it to me under her nose. Then, he punished me for being sexy! Isn't that like the Devil, tempting people to sin and then roasting their asses in Hell? I mentioned to Nevil that his name sounds like "Devil," and both have "-evil" in them. Nevil claimed that adding up the letters, a = 1, b = 2, proved he wasn't the Devil. I said it didn't prove anything, since number games, flashy card tricks and pocket miracles are what you would expect from the Devil.

That startled him. I told him he was thinking, "What've we got here, a little bitch that thinks?" A few days later I overheard Mom asking him to punish me for my grades, which were about average. "She's as smart as the Devil!" said Nevil. "I wonder why she doesn't do better in school?" Somehow, Mom took credit for my brains, while blaming me for just getting by at St. Deems.

One day when I was sucking Nevil an hour before Mom was expected home from the beauty parlor, he told me that putting my ass up for a trick was another way to stay virgin. I didn't need another way. I pretended my mouth was enjoying itself too much to say yes or no.

Nevil didn't mention that his pet project would hurt. When he goosed me, it was sensual, but scary, 'cause I knew he was getting me ready for serious ass-fucking. I goosed myself and imagine him screwing me back there. I was curious how it would feel if we could. I asked him if he did Mom that way. He nodded yes, but I could tell he was lying. "Not much?" I said, giving him an out. "As a special treat," he said, "like spicy food you wouldn't eat every day." That settled it. I'd try it eventually, if he promised to stop right away when I said so.

Nevil said it was a way to show I loved him. What did he think I was doing when I sucked him off three times a week? I would've told him to go fuck himself in the ass, but he was close to coming. I was so mad, I sucked furiously, and a moment later I got my reward. Maybe he just turned himself on talking about doing me that way.

No, he meant it. Two days later he had a different, totally wacko slant. This time, he told me that he'd prove how much *he* loved *me* by screwing my behind. "What!" I gasped, so outraged I was breathless. "Sure," he said, "ask a hundred men, what part of their own body's their favorite, what are they going to say?" "Their cocks." "Good, now, you want to call anybody by a body part as an insult, what do you say?" "Asshole," I said, kind of getting it. "Well, if a man's willing to put his favorite part in your least esteemed part, doesn't that prove he loves you?"

Of course, we both knew guys would put it anywhere that felt good. I was stunned by the effort he put into conning me with this bullshit. How can you help loving a man who'd try to trick you with this one? If you're a Shame Artist, a really stupid bullshit story melts you inside.

A while after Mom set Nevil up to cane me for coming in late spangled with cum, we made up and I was blowing him every chance I got. One day he took his hot prick out of my mouth and set me greasing it with Vaseline. Then, he put my face down and my rear end up. I was still dressed. I sucked him with my clothes on when we didn't have a lot of time. We didn't have a lot of time today, but he wanted what he wanted. He flipped my skirt up in back. I ordered him not to get Vaseline on it. I sounded like my Mom, "Keep your feet off the sofa!" Nevil pulled my panties down below my knees.

He assured me I was such a slut I was going to love anal screwing, but I wasn't sure. When I sucked him, the head of his cock filled my mouth. How could he get that monster, no matter how greasy it was, into my delicate little asshole? Slowly and uncomfortably, hurting me all the way in, that's how. I squealed the whole time. It took forever to get the head in. I sobbed, "Maybe, this isn't such a good idea." If he'd only quit, I'd never, ever let anyone do this. Then, I'd never know what was good about this way, if there was anything, and I wouldn't even care. Nevil didn't quit. He had me by the hips and he was going to ram his prick in no matter what, the apartment house could burn down, we'd have to run out into the street hooked up this way.

Once the head was all the way in, it was almost bearable. I looked through my thighs at the shaft of his prick pushing in and his balls hanging down. Would it hurt as much coming out? What if he couldn't get it out? He swiveled in deeper, a half-inch at a time. I groaned till the shaft was all the way in me and his groin pressed against my behind. I liked that feeling.

I suspected there was more to it, and I was right. He said, "Now, move, little slut!" He'd already forgotten that this was a way to show how much he loved me. I ground around as well as I could with his prick skewering me. Holding me by the hips, he drew halfway out and pushed all the way up.

Exciting! Finally, fucking—even though in the wrong place! "Keep moving, bitch!" he cried. He gave me a lusty, all-out butt-screwing, in and out, on and on. I swiveled and squeezed, grunted, squealed, and moaned. I ploughed my clit, too. I bet Nevil thought my taking his prick up my rear end was just another way to accommodate him, till he felt me clinching and releasing, churning wildly and thrusting backward. He stopped humping and tried to hold back to make it last, but I milked him. Nevil told me later it wasn't only my terrific humping that got to him, it was the sight of my school-girl dirndl flipped up my back, my ass speared by his cock, and my gorgeous rear cheeks working. At last, he machine-gunned me, pumping his stuff high up into me. The instant I felt his hot spurt into my bowels, I came!

Afterward, I wanted Nevil to cuddle me, but he sent me to the bathroom to sit on the pot. He explained that it would trickle out of me, like a cum enema. I had to wee, anyway. He stood in the doorway watching me. That was so embarrassing it turned me on all over again. He could see that. "Play with yourself," he ordered me. I rolled my clit obediently until I came again, sitting on the pot, with him watching and getting hard again. He stood in front of me, his cock rising up to my mouth level.

"Nnn—" I started to say, but he took me firmly by my ears, reminded me what a slut I was, and said I better lick his cock clean so Mom wouldn't know. It took a lot of licking, considering where it'd been. The weird taste was my punishment for letting him screw my hiney and for liking it so much.

I got used to putting my hiney up for Nevil. I was still a virgin at an age when that seemed important. Now, it seems dumb. I was delighted to do something extra naughty and shameful and get back another way at Mom. I took a little hurt at my tender asshole as punishment "for being a naughty girl," but I was such a horny bitch, the pleasure went all through me. Also,

I was doing more for Nevil than if it didn't hurt, and now he'd really be hooked on me.

I looked at the tense little man who taught second period (9:45 A.M.) American History and I thought, *I lick my Mom's boyfriend's balls and then he screws me up my ass. What're you getting lately?* The teacher saw me smirk and looked away.

Nevil and his ways are background stuff you might want to know when you hear someone say Tom Thomas ruined my morals, like they charged in the campaign. Tom wanted to fuck me the regular way from our first date. I told him, "Slow down," but he wouldn't, so I had to go down on him. I sucked him off three times that night. Sometimes, you bend the rules. He was a high school football star, he had lots of girlfriends, and I didn't want to act too young for him.

He wanted to fuck me on our second date, big surprise, but I claimed there was a problem, without saying what, and blew him again. And again and again. I considered letting Tom take my cherry on our third date, but it was hard to weigh the pros and cons, 'cause I was sitting on his lap and we were kissing and he was strumming my bare tits. Then, his hand went under my dress in back and he felt my rear cheeks through my panties. His thumb slipped right over the damp lower strip and into my quim. He could tell how turned on I was. I thought this is it, I'm going to lose my cherry right now. Instead, he pulled down my panties in back and petted my hiney. When I realized how much he was into rolling and rubbing and pinching my rear cheeks, I stretched out so he could see what he was playing with. I was facedown across his knees like for a spanking, but this time for caressing. He played with my gorgeous hiney and my virgin quim and my eager clit till my head was spinning.

"You're naughty," he said, and lightly patted my rear end. "I ought to spank you." "Promise?" I murmured. Since we were in my love nest in front of our apartment, it wasn't going to happen right then. "Yes!" he said, and his cock rubbing against my side all at once got hard as a curtain rod. He gave me a pretend-spanking and I shimmied for him. Then, I slipped off his lap and sucked him out of his mind. He probably could have fucked me, but as he told me a long time later, he knew I didn't want that. He kept hearing my "no's" in his mind. He ate me out and we were carnally bonded to each other forever.

On our fourth date we were at his father's apartment. His father was in Geneva. Tom spanked me soundly with his hand. After a half dozen good smacks I began to bawl. Tom said he couldn't allow that, and if I didn't stop he's gag me. So, I bit my lip and suffered quietly. But his spanks made plenty of noise! Afterward, I was still lying across his knees, sobbing, waggling my red bottom, when he drew a finger up and down my crack and trolled 'round my asshole, which was a lot more experienced than he could have guessed. Tom thought I held back 'cause I was afraid of getting pregnant. I'd seen the round impression of a condom in his leather wallet when he paid for dinner, but he didn't say he had one, maybe to see what else he could do. You get the upper hand by not letting guys know you know.

Tom said, lightly goosing me, "We could do it here." And, we did. I let him think he was a pioneer, but I used all the great technique I developed with Nevil. I swiveled, I humped, I squeezed. Tom was amazed.

I liked to be fresh to Tom, see what I could get away with. I could call him "bonehead" or anything like that in front of our friends, and sometimes he'd spin me around so I was facing away from him and slap my butt. I loved that! But when I went too far, like calling him "asshole," he steamed up. If we were alone, he'd take me right across his knees and use his belt on my bare bottom. When we were out somewhere with people, he'd hiss, "I'll warm your behind later!" I'd be in disgrace till he punished me. "Warming" makes it sound cozier than it was. Five to ten minutes of agony and my butt wound up not just warm, but red hot. And it hurt so much biting my lip didn't help. So, he'd gag me with my panties. My crotch was always damp on a date, 'specially with Tom, 'specially when I knew I was going to get a whipping. I got pretty familiar with how I smelled and tasted. Never cared for it much, though lots of men told me my sex gravy was delicious.

My two gripes about Tom were, he wouldn't go steady with me and he bragged. It's mortifying to walk past high school boys who know you take it in your mouth and your hiney. The girls knew it, too. Someone taped a cartoon on my gym locker of a girl sitting on a long stout cock. She was pictured from the back and one side, hunching forward so you could see the prick was up her big ass—no, it was *my* ass, the girl was supposed to be me. She had a curvy voluptuous ass. There were wavy lines radiating from the asshole, my asshole, which might've meant it hurt, but who knows? She had hair like mine and big boobs. Her big mouth, grinning up to the ear you could see, proclaimed in capital letters "I LOVE ASS-FUCKING!" in case you couldn't tell from the picture. The sketch was so crude only a boy could have drawn it, but it had to be a girl who put it on my locker right before my gym class. What did they get out of doing that?

I couldn't pin Tom down. He even went after Cathy and my other friends. Cathy insisted she was blowing him two weeks before I did, but she didn't get around to telling me about it. We decided not to fight over Tom, since neither of us was going to get him, anyway. We'd share him and stay friends.

Before long, I was taking it my new shameful way from a clique of senior boys at St. Deems. They all knew Tom, they were all primed, there was no tension at the end of a date. After enough petting, I greased them up and tipped onto my face, showed them my gorgeous butt. They had no idea how I got off on them, taking their most valued part in my least esteemed part. I squealed when a lovely broad one poked in. I kept a little jar of Vaseline in my purse. I put the Vaseline on their cocks myself, 'cause they liked that, and they would've used too much if I'd let them do it.

Nevil was right, I loved it. I thought, Mom should

see me getting this! There weren't a lot of girls as raunchy as me, carrying their own jar of Vaseline. The first moment hurt less now and it was groovy all the way up. Squirming on it, and rolling my clit with my fingertip, I could almost always come. The only part of me I held back was my cunt. I wouldn't lay the regular way for anybody. By our junior year at St. Deems, all the "in" girls were sucking their boyfriends and most of them had found a way to lose their virginity, too, so one of the few tricks left to me if I didn't want to be like everybody else was taking it in my behind. I had my cherry until my freshman year in college, when Tom came back to pluck it.

13

INITIALS

Tom took me to hear jazz. I played his father's classical tapes for him on his father's stereo. He loved Boccherini and Schubert. You won't find that in the other books about us.

We did everything but screw the regular way. He was delighted to do kinky "Nevil" stuff with me, 'cause he had plenty of girls for ordinary screwing. While I was seeing him, Tom misplaced his little black book. Actually, it fell out of his pocket at his father's place when his pants were around his ankles and Cathy was kneeling between his legs. He alternated between us for this treat. She batted the book under a sofa and later slipped it into her handbag. Tom had fifty-eight girls' names and numbers in it. There were little code letters, circled, by almost every name. Sure enough, Cathy had a circled "bj" by her name. "You slut!" I yelled at Cathy. It was okay to tease her. She was slow getting started, but her blow jobs were already a legend. I wasn't sure I was the best mouth at St. Deems anymore, which is one reason I let guys do me "Nevil's other way." In these times you have to specialize.

Cathy looked blank when Tom asked her whether she'd seen the book. Cathy never loved Tom like I did. She knew she'd get revenge with the book someday. Eventually, she sold the book to gossip reporters, and what with the "MRG'd" videotape of Tom and me at the motel pool and Dr. Wurst's old affidavit that I was a virgin three hours before Tom date-raped me in the dorm (okay, we had a date for him to rape me), the Benedict-Thomas ticket got flushed.

Tom's black book went back to when he was a fresh-man at St. Deems. Most boys start a new book every year, but some of Tom's names and numbers were so old we couldn't read them. It was a diary in shorthand. The earlier the entries, the more innocent the action. Three girls had nothing but a faded "bt" by their names. It's okay if you don't get that. These three got into Tom's Honor Roll more than five years before me by letting him fondle their bare tits. It was funny to see as classmate's name with an "ff" circle: More than four years before Cathy hooked the book, Karen let Tom "f" her with his finger. "Shame on her!" we both cried. Cathy showed me Alice's name afloat in a bubble bath of circles. Me and Cathy couldn't even figure out some of Alice's tricks.

Five girls, two on one crowded page, had a circle without initials in it, but a little stem growing out of the top of the circle. "Looks like an apple," I said. "Close," Cathy said, "try again." "Cherry!" I exclaimed. We talked to three of them and they admitted giving Tom their cherries.

I was awarded a "bj" and the exotic "af." Tom wanted to "f" Cathy's "a," but she was afraid it would hurt too much. Me and Cathy and two other girls earned an "ak." Cathy blotted out her name and all her tricks before she sold the book. "I only 'k'd his 'a' once!" she blurted out, "he kept pushing me there and I wanted to see . . . how low I could get!" "Same for me!" I whooped.

I gave Tom that treat more than once, but he wasn't first. I met Buzz through my sexpot Aunt Deedee. He was in New York for spring break from Peddie. Cute, dark red hair that stood up like a brush, hard muscles. He was into pumping iron. He bragged about smoking dope, but only came up with one joint for both of us.

Buzz was more polite than the boys at St. Deems. I sucked him good-night on our second date, 'cause I didn't know whether I'd see him again before he went back to school. He was white-skinned, his body hairless except for tight curls of dark red, almost black pubic hair. His prick was sensitive. I couldn't believe how fast he came in my mouth. I bet he jerked off all the time. He said he was sorry and I was so good at blowing, he wished it lasted longer. I was flattered, I glommed on again. This time, it took only a little longer. I licked his balls real well. He said nobody ever did any of this for him. Maybe four minutes and he was coming again and screaming, even though we were in the love nest in front of my front door. He said he was sorry about screaming, and also, this time he came fast 'cause he didn't want to impose on me! I was so touched I bet I could get him to number three, if he promised not to scream. I pitched in. I was on my knees and he was sitting on the quilted bench. He was semi-hard. It was late, I regretted promising, but I didn't quit. I'm macho about blow jobs.

Then, we were both on the thick pile rug. I licked Buzz behind his balls, a dynamite spot, but tricky 'cause you're getting close to the asshole, and if the guy's a head-pusher you can wind up doing something you don't plan on. Buzz was a head-pusher, fake-polite, a phony when you come down to it, and I came down to it. I didn't have a choice, my face was so far under, it was behind him, in his crack, we were cheek-to-cheek, and my mouth was guess where. I kissed his cute white cheeks, all I could reach of them where they curved into his crack, a lick to the left of his brown crinkled hole, a lick to the right of it, but his legs were over my shoulders and he was pushing the back of my head. *"Yech!"* A slip of the tongue! Then, he responded so marvelously I thought I might as well do it and get it over with. I turned on from being completely humiliated. Anyway, he was going back to boarding school, he wasn't going to tell anyone I knew. Even my sexpot Aunt Deedee wouldn't approve of this kiss! He wasn't holding my head down anymore, I was into it like it was another mouth. I rolled over so I could my hands on his prick at the same time. His cock was hard as a rock. When I sensed number three was on the way, I rolled back over, licked quick up his balls and the shaft of his prick, racing his cum all the way, and we both got there the same instant and he spurted into my mouth. He gasped loudly, didn't scream. This time, he didn't apologize, either. He wanted to turn away when I kissed him on the mouth! I didn't let him! He clenched his teeth, but I parted his lips with my wicked tongue. Got the bastard!

I guess I would've kissed somebody's ass, someday, certainly I did Tom's 'cause I adored his backside, but there was no reason for me to start with Buzz. Once it was in my repertory, when I wanted to give Tom a special treat on his birthday, I told him to roll over and lie on his cock, I wanted to hunt for the end of his tailbone. I ran the tip of my nose sniffing like a beagle down his backbone and going, *"woof-woof,"* to where it curled between his rear cheeks. I didn't tell Cathy about licking Tom's behind, 'though we told each other everything else.

Cathy was still trying to explain away her "ak." "One day Tom turned over on his belly," she said, "and made me burrow in and hunt his tailbone with my nose, like a hound dog!" "Made you?" "Well, he didn't twist my arm, but it was such a charming way to get me to kiss ass, how could I say no?"

I wasn't sure I wanted to take credit for that charming idea. "Before," Cathy went on, "I said no to everything new, but wound up doing it anyway. Like, 'I'll never, ever suck a cock, I don't care how many Sarah does!"

"I remember that one," I said.

"But, I never resolved not to kiss ass, just 'cause I never pictured people really doing it. I thought it was just street talk for apple-polishing."

I also had a circled "sp," which mystified Cathy, 'til she remembered I told her about it ages ago, the first time Tom spanked me. Cathy was wild to hear all about it again. Tom tried to spank her once, but she told him, "No way," and he backed off.

A few guys spank you any chance they get. Tom was one. His parents were divorced and neither of them lived in New York. Tom had keys to both his parents' "pied-a-terre" apartments. Mostly, he took girls to his Dad's.

Kinky stuff got around. Tom liked to spank pretty asses so much he didn't care. Four girls besides me had "sp" circles over their names, which meant he had warmed their hinies at least once. We knew he went with Patti, who admitted to Cathy that she "needed discipline," but didn't go into details. Patti wore tight skirts and squirmed in her seat in class.

I loved Tom's fiendish glee when he ordered me across his knees. He relished raising my skirt in back and taking my panties down. He gloated as my rear cheeks swelled out. Mostly, he used his lean, bony hand, and it hurt plenty. I bit my lip so I wouldn't alarm his Dad's neighbors.

One wall of his father's bedroom was mirrored. Tom

knew I was watching him raise his hand high above my bare bottom. He feinted, making me tense my cheeks. He waited till I stopped flinching and smacked me good. Seeing him aim spanks and watching my white hiney turn blotchy red made it twice as exciting for me. I loved the sensual high when the heat from my flaming bottom spread to my cunt and all over me. I got wet below as though he was caressing me. Even my tits became more sensitive, they burned, they itched. He paused in the middle of warming my ass to tweak my tits, or made me stand in front of him afterward biting my lip, and pinched them hard. I groaned with pleasure. As soon as he reached between my thighs, I went berserk. "You're coming?" he said. He saw my cunt wet and writhing, but he liked me to say it.

The biggest turn-on was knowing ahead of time. When Tom called me "naughty," like the first time he hinted at it, I felt my ass tingle. "What are you going to do about it?" I teased. "Give you what you deserve." "Promise?" I always said in my bitchiest voice. I knew I'd soon be facedown across his knees or bending over with my big round ass up in the air. I felt damp seeping into the cunt strip of my panties.

Tom always had a script in his mind. He'd tell me, like, "You'll lift your skirt in back and kneel in the big leather chair and take your panties down." When I was fresh to him and hurt his feelings, he'd tap his belt and tell me I would be keeping my bare ass turned up for punishment all evening. He'd threaten to give me the reddest rear end in Manhattan, which I knew he probably would. If his plans for me sounded too brutal, I felt like bolting, but I never did. Since he was taking the chance of warning me early in the evening when I could've still gotten away, I felt I should "hold up my end."

What turned Tom on was me submitting reluctantly when he told me to drop my panties. I'd pout as I slowly raised my skirt, hooked my thumbs into the waistband of my panties and pushed them down a few inches, showing my curly blonde bush and a glimpse of quim. Sometimes, I'd change my mind and run away, still holding my skirt up behind me. There was only so far I could run in his Dad's apartment, so I'd hide.

One Saturday evening when Tom was super-steamed at me, we went shopping for a paddle. I told him it wasn't fair! What happened between me and his kid brother was his own fault for going out of town Friday, the day before, without calling me. When I arrived at his Dad's on Friday evening, his kid brother was there. Jimmy was only fifteen, gawky tall and handsome, with soulful brown eyes and long eyelashes. He tried to make me feel better about being stood up. He said he hoped he'd have a beautiful girlfriend like me someday. I kissed him for that and asked him what he would do with his beautiful girlfriend. All at once he couldn't say a word. I could tell he was holding back 'cause of Tom. I told him to close his big brown eyes. I walked around and around him stripping. He knew, 'cause he peeked! Huge boner in his pants! He wanted to grope my boobs, but I made him stand up with his arms by his sides as I took his clothes off. He never dreamed a beautiful girl like me would adore taking down his pants and his underpants, and squeezing his cute young butt with both hands! And, teach him how to please her! We pleased each other too much, 'cause when Tom let himself in the next morning he saw my clothes scattered around and me asleep with my cheek on Jimmy's underpants. I dressed and tried to scoot out while Tom ranted at Jimmy. But Tom pinned me to the door frame and hissed that I would pay later—with my ass. I was afraid Tom was getting bored with the routine of keeping me in line. So, I offered to buy a special paddle for the occasion.

That evening Tom and I went to a sex shop. I criticized every paddle, just to be bitchy. The manager kept telling us to take our time. He was practically drooling. I could tell the swine was picturing me naked, getting a red hiney. I posed bending 'way over, thrusting my backside out, to drive him crazy. It was a warm June evening and I was wearing silky harem pants that cleaved to each cheek right into my crack. Tom wanted to try out the paddles on me then and there. The manager said he couldn't allow that. I put my hands at my hips, showing I was ready to drop my pants, but the manager gasped that he absolutely couldn't allow that, though there was hardly anybody in the store and no one else in the discipline aisle. He sounded like somebody was strangling him. Maybe he thought we were cops trying to shake him down. Finally, he croaked that we should come back when he was closing, at eleven that evening, for a private party with him and his girl, whom he described as having an open mind. Tom said, "Sure," and I licked my lips slowly, but we didn't.

I recalled seeing the perfect paddle in a bath shop. Tom said right away, "She'll take it." It was a long-handled wooden hairbrush with a curved oval back, the right size, not too big like some sports paddles. It let Tom put a spank where he wanted it. It cost me less than any paddle in the sex shop, and I got a hairbrush out of it that I could use anytime at Tom's Dad's place. A few hours later I brushed my hair with it while my bottom was still tender from vigorous use of its other side.

When we got back to his Dad's apartment, Tom marched me right into the study, no kiss or anything. I unbuttoned my blouse, took off my harem pants, un-hooked my bra. I thought Tom might go easy on me 'cause of my pretty tits jiggling in his face, like they were begging for mercy, but maybe to him they looked like they were just trying to get attention for themselves. I was inching my panties down when Tom took the hair-brush out of its wrap. I panicked and ran out of the study, blouse fluttering behind me, panties bunched into a ribbon below my rear cheeks. I was down the hall before I heard him coming after me. I fled into the liv-ing room, flung myself head and boobs onto the big L-shaped sofa and burrowed facedown under the corner bolsters. I got almost all of me hidden under pillows. It was a brilliant plan. Only one foot stuck out and guess what else? I balanced a pillow behind me to cover the crack of my ass. The paddle came down SMACK on the pillow! That didn't hurt, but I could feel the terrific force right through it. Then, Tom lifted my pillow off. All at once I felt naked back there and very obedient! I pushed my panties down all the way and raised my trembling butt a few inches for the paddle. "Tom, I love you!" I pleaded from the depths of the sofa seat under the heap of pillows. "*Oh?* What's that supposed to mean?" he shot back.

"It means . . . please, don't hurt me too much," I cried. I knew by now I deserved a red hiney. Also, if I didn't take my punishment for blowing his kid brother, I wouldn't have a chance with Tom ever again. I decided to prove how much I loved him by keeping my backside turned up no matter how bad it hurt.

SMACK! The first spank caught me right across both cheeks. I could feel the hard curved wood cut into my tender flesh and bounce off. I couldn't help flutter-kicking my heels, knocking the pillows off my calves. SMACK! Another spank in the same place! SMACK! I knew red roses were blooming on either side of my crack. I sobbed, "I thought you wanted me to take care of Jimmy!" into the corner of the sofa seat. I don't know whether he understood what I said, or maybe he didn't like it, 'cause the next spank was low and wicked, right over my asshole. I howled. Tom put my panties to my lips. I opened wide and he stuffed them in. That was our deal, if I made too much noise, I got gagged. He spanked me again in the same tender place. I humped my rear end furiously. Without thinking, I guess what I was trying to do was waggle my butt so wildly that he couldn't aim his next smack. It worked for a minute, but I wore myself out, collapsed all at once, and tried to hide my backside among the pillows. Tom lifted my middle and put a bolster under me. In a way that was thoughtful, now I could just lie on the bolster, I didn't have to work at keeping my backside up. It was up. And the backs of my thighs were bare.

SMACK! SMACK! A spank to each cheek! Then, three to the right, three to the left! Each buttock burned with its own fire and wobbled on its own. Spanks to the tender under curves that caught the backs of my thighs! The wicked paddle fit right in there! The cruelest part was, Tom made me spread my legs all the way and he spanked my inner thighs, first with the hairbrush and then with his hand. Letting a guy chastise you on your inner thighs proves you really love him.

Every now and then Tom reached between my legs, cupped my quim and rolled my clit. The shame of it all excited me so, I came violently to his touch. Later, he told me he loved to give me a red ass and watch my bare legs kicking up and my naughty backside wiggling among the pillows, which I knew, 'cause his prick stayed hard for an hour, no matter how many times he kneeled behind me on the couch and pumped his stuff 'way up into my bowels, or pulled me out from under the pillows by my hair and came down my throat. I was so ashamed I couldn't look at him, and I felt relieved each time he put me back over the bolster and my face back down under the pillows, even though it meant my ass was in for more paddling and screwing.

When Tom spanked me, I couldn't think anything except, how many more? His idea of how much was enough was 'way past mine. Afterward, while I was sucking him, I'd sneak one of my hands behind me to rub my flaming rear end, and I'd think, *Other girls have boyfriends and never get spanked. Why do I wind up suffering back here so often?*

Part of the answer was, my sassy round ass, too lush if I gain weight, but just right if I starve a little, and creamy smooth. I'm sway-backed, not so much you'd see it as bad posture, but even when I stand up straight, it looks like I'm offering my hiney. If my rear end was shapeless, it's doubtful every other man would want to punish it. But, my perfect backside drives men crazy. It's like they have to get even with me for showing off such a terrific ass! Even when guys pinch and tweak and roll my rear cheeks, my ass frustrates them, like, there's something more they have to do. Sometimes, it's a sincere goose, or spanking me and then fucking me from the rear. The only thing that satisfies some guys is screwing my hiney.

Another reason I get my bottom warmed so often is that I'm a naughty bitch who has it coming. Now, if you're a nice guy reading this, you want to tell me I'm not so bad. You nice guys bore me. When I'm super horny, I feel my bitchiness roaming from my cunt to my tits and to my ass and back again. I know what I need. My tits pinched, a good hard fuck, yes, but it gets so bad I need a guy to dominate me completely. A sound spanking first loosens me up, makes me wild, puts me in the mood to fuck a guy any way, every way he wants.

I never brag about doing more guys than I do, or say I enjoy some exotic sex trick if I really don't. My naughty streak comes from being oversexed. A good fuck whets my appetite. Then, I have to have more. My puss is a tiger, you can't tame it with a hamburger. Men don't know women get as horny as the horniest boy. I know beautiful models who are dying for it, they whine they haven't been screwed for months. It's their own fault, they'd rather spread for their vibrators than come out and say, "Fuck me."

For me, sex is a hurricane that never ends, getting soaked and blown back and forth all over the street, forever. Partly, I blame it on my tits. They're a good size now, and the nipples are long, pink and pointy-up, like men love. But, years ago, I tweaked and rubbed my nipples every night before I fell asleep, imagining Artie was doing it, trying to get my boobs to grow. The drawback was, my tits became incredibly needy. Now, they zing all the time, begging for a touch. Even my bra touching my nipples turns me on. I want to ask men on the street, total strangers, "Would you mind—?"

I can't describe what goes on in my cunt without sounding like a nympho. I once asked a woman gynecologist whether I was a nympho, and she said it was better not to think in those terms. Later, I realized she hadn't said whether I was or not. Anyway, it churns. It drips, it gushes. When I see a hunk or sense what his cock looks like, my cunt jumps. A handsome mouth or long sensuous fingers drag me toward a guy like he's a vacuum cleaner and I'm lint.

Most guys are so busy undressing women mentally that they're not aware we do the same thing. We're sneakier about it and we have to be a hundred times as clever to know what we're looking at. If you can't tell a woman has beautiful boobs when she's dressed, believe me, she hasn't. But can you tell when you meet a guy in a suit how big his cock is or the shape of the head of it? Can you tell whether his balls are two wren eggs in a tight pink sack, or two purple eggplants in a grocery bag? How hairy his balls are, and how much hair grows up behind into his crack? Men's clothes hide all that. You can guess—and check it out later when he drops his pants. You can tell about his chest muscles and his tummy and his butt. When I'm with a new guy I imagine playing with his chest or pinching his butt. If I'm turned on, I imagine how heavy his balls would be to lift on the tip of my tongue or how far down my throat his cock could go. Surprised? Like, I don't know when a guy's looking at my lips as I speak and thinking about me sucking him?

Any touch, I'm gone. A man's chest against my nippies in slow dancing drives me wild. At school dances boys would lift their thigh between your legs. My quim would twitch and I'd get so hot, I'd make a boy take me to a deserted classroom for relief. We could be gone for forty-five minutes. Another boy would ask me to dance, and it would start all over again. Most dances, I'd get seduced by three or four boys. They absolutely had to play with my boobs first. High school boys can't skip that! So, I wore a nothing-bra to make it easy for them. When they'd push my sweater up, my bra'd go up with it and my boobs would be out. They'd tweak my nippies 'til I couldn't take any more, and then I'd unzip them and take care of them real well, and they'd finger me, and then I'd take care of them again. Sometimes, I'd make a boy lie on his back and kneel over him and suck him off twice without stopping while he played with me. You bet I carried mints! Once, I forgot them. I asked Cathy, but she had only one left, so I didn't take it. After I gulped cum four or five times, my breath smelled like the barrel behind the fish store.

My panties were so wet after the first boy, they were useless. They'd go into my handbag and I'd go bare. We're all naked under our clothes. Some girls just dance. They have no idea what it does for high school boys when you mouth their earlobe and whisper that you haven't got anything on under your skirt. Besides, when you're in heat—especially when you're not wearing panties!—boys can smell it. They all wanted to do their part. I liked to reach down for a moment when nobody could see and feel their hard hot cock throbbing in their pants, and then we were out of there.

When a guy tweaks my tits, my cunt surges right away, like you push the button outside the front door and you hear the bell ring inside. A touch on my inner thigh, and my legs spread. It's not just my titties, clit, quim, it's every inch of me. A tickly touch on my asshole makes me squirm and long for more. I can't stop after one touch anywhere, even if it means I wind up taking a cock this way or that way.

I love to fondle guys. They tell me I have terrific hands. Sometimes, I'm kneeling to give a blow-job, but after cradling the guy's balls and kneading up and down his shaft with my patented squeeze and jerk, I feel his spasms starting, there's not much left for my mouth to do but glom on and gulp.

I warned cute guys I would spank them if they misbehaved, but it didn't happen as much as I would have liked. I tried ordering Tom to drop his pants and go across my knees, but it was never worth it. He always got uptight. The words would scarcely be out of my mouth, when Tom would turn the tables—take me across his knees, bare my bottom, and make my rear cheeks bounce till I apologized.

It wasn't enough to sing out, "I apologize, I apologize!" after half a dozen spanks. He'd say I wasn't sincere and punish me more sternly. When I suffered enough hiney pain, I'd cry "I'm sorry" with feeling, and he'd let me up. Then, I'd begin to feel better; but, sometimes, I could see Tom's dignity was still wounded. There was one tried and true way to bring him around. I'd woof like a hound dog. He'd lie on his belly. I'd plant warm moist kisses all over his handsome buttocks and hunt with the tip of my nose for his tailbone. I loved to lick and draw back, making him wait, lick again, and draw back. Teasing with my tongue was okay, so long as I finished with the Ultimate Submissive Kiss.

I told Tom early on a date when I needed my hiney warmed. He'd get so hard he couldn't walk down the street. During the evening I'd remind him of what I "deserved" by backing into him or patting his behind, giving him a pretend-spanking. A long time ago, I hoped the next all-out spanking Tom gave me would cure my naughty cravings, but it just made them worse. Until Tom took my cherry in my freshman year of college, the naughtiest part of me was—no matter how juicy my cunt and how much a guy wanted a plain vanilla screwing—I gave him something else. Like, I went down on him so fast he was speechless. Or I greased his cock and funneled him into my ass. I loved being the naughtiest! The nuns were right, it's all about Pride.

— 14 —

SKIING NEW SLOPES

For all the TV stories about what happened on a certain Tuesday afternoon on an old sofa in our dorm, no one brought out that Tom Thomas and I went away together the whole weekend before. We were guests of Alice Krieger's parents at their weekend home 'way upstate in ski country. Alice was my friend from St. Deems. She had her own dorm room at Belmont down the hall from me.

The Kriegers invited Alice to bring home a man she was talking about. They worried that anyone Alice mentioned wanted to marry her and live off their money. Alice got permission to invite Tom and me. Alice didn't want to be alone with her eager suitor, which I understood completely the minute I saw him. Also, she thought getting Tom and me together might be the solution to my virginity problem. And, just maybe, she had feelings for me that could only come out under ideal circumstances—such as we had that weekend. I was amazed that Alice was always friendly to me. She never held it against me how I took care of Josh in the back seat of Mark's car.

Tom volunteered to drive. He had a big roomy car with snow tires and a ski rack. He picked up Alice's date for the weekend from his business school and they drove to our Belmont College dorm, where Alice and I waited with our valises and skis. I went into shock when Tom's companion got out of the car. It was Alan Darshow, whom I goofed up the day we graduated from St. Deems. I made a sound—*"Gaaa!"*—like when Cathy made lemonade with salt instead of sugar. "Good to see you again, too," said Alan.

Tom had never met Alan. On the drive over, Alan asked him personal questions about me, till Tom, who was not usually the most discreet guy in the world, became fed up with him.

I took Alice aside. "I did so tell you, 'Alan Darshow,' " she said. "He's been after me since high school. He calls it, 'staying in touch.' He says you went with him in high school. When was that?"

"I never went with him!" I wailed. Alice spoke softly and you had to listen when she trailed off. Maybe, she said "Darshow" under her breath 'cause she wasn't too happy about being with him.

"Well, he's my problem now, not yours," Alice said. Alice didn't give Alan a chance to say how he felt about me coming, but she picked up that he liked the plan. He knew Alice had less interest in laying him than working in a slaughterhouse; but he figured me and Tom would be kissing and fondling all over the place; so, we were supposed to light the fire, and then maybe everybody would go up in flames!

We set out for the Krieger chateau, Tom and I in front, Alice and Alan in the rear. Tom told us about a civil law suit and let us guess what the rival attorneys said and how the case came out. A coed was suing an acquaintance for raping her. Did she consent or was she raped? Get it?—Within a week, it looked as though Tom and I were going to be on opposite sides of a case like that.

What was Alice doing with Alan? Alice had perfect features and an elegant body. She never wore makeup. Alice was smart, and she'd been around, though you'd never know it from seeing her. Just the opposite of me. I blush, my nippies get hard and poke out at the wrong time, and I always look like I'm misbehaving, even when I'm not. I want to be Alice!

The road ran into dark shadows while there was still some light in the sky. Alice and Alan didn't talk at all. Tom held my hand loosely on his right thigh. The seat went straight across. I knew what Tom liked. Looking straight forward, I quietly unbuttoned the top buttons of his wool pants. One button faced out and one faced in. Slowly, slowly, I unzipped him and lifted his stiff cock out. No one in back could see anything.

I stroked Tom languidly so he wouldn't forget he was

driving. From time to time my left hand cramped. I was reaching at an awkward angle. "Are you tired?" he said. I admitted I was. "You can put your head on my lap, it won't disturb me," he said considerately. "Love to," I said sleepily.

Tom's sports coat loosely covered his mushroom waving an inch in front of my face. Lots of time to re-acquaint myself with every vein and wrinkle. Love the ridge where the shaft became the head. Could lick the head, too, so long as don't take it all in my mouth. That would give him the wrong message. Tom grinned. I wonder if Alan could see Tom's grin in the rearview mirror. I turned on thinking how this must be driving Alan crazy. Even if he leaned 'way forward and looked down into the front seat he'd see only the right side of Tom's long sport coat draped over my head and shoulders.

I licked Tom, never too much, gave him a rest. A rhythm he could enjoy without worrying it would overwhelm him. Once, the car swerved. I thought it was my fault, but from Alan's remarks I gathered that a car cut us off making a left turn. Still, if Tom had been too distracted to respond, we could've been totaled. I remember Alice snapping at Mark when he was driving, "Don't play in traffic." I tongued and smooched Tom for an hour. Ready to take my cherry! I wondered, would I wind up in a new black book (Cathy had the old one three years now) with a cherry over my name? I kissed his cock tenderly, thinking, This is the one that's going to do it, tonight. I was ready, too.

Enough is enough. I put his cock back in his pants, zipped him up, buttoned the outside button. He grimaced, meaning, he was going to get painful "blue balls" if he didn't come soon. I stretched one hand straight up above the front seat, yawned, "How long did I sleep?" and sat up.

We were told to drive straight to the Krieger chateau, where dinner would be served on our arrival. It was after nine when we turned into the long private driveway up to the estate. The security fences and gates with identification checks and call boxes were formidable. These people could buy Alice the Darshow sports car franchise for her birthday. And, it turned out at dinner, they were so right-wing that offhand remarks by Tom Thomas, future Republican candidate for vice president, made them uncomfortable. However, Alan did well at dinner. He had good table manners and his criticism of the unemployed gratified his hosts. *How nice for Alan, I thought, that he'll never have to look for a job.*

Alice's mother was a frail aristocrat with a bell-like voice who didn't say much. She, like, had to haul herself out of a cozy bed of contempt to be polite to us. She was afraid of our sexiness, Tom's and mine. All I had to do was make her feel we weren't sexy or she was.

Alice's father toasted us, "Our youth: the future of our country!" He had mean, hooded eyes. This man was a killer. He ruled here with an iron hand. I decided to stay out of his way.

The high-domed dining room had old paintings each with its own light every six feet along the walls. The

Virgin held her baby on her right arm, where in a painting just like it at the Met she holds the baby with both arms. An extra long, narrow Dutch dining table, which Alice said was sixteenth century, heavy white-brocaded tablecloth and tons of gleaming silver. Mom always had good silver, but the tableware here was two centuries older, heavier, richer in styling. I never saw anything like it before or since.

Four dobermans sat at the table with us. I'd never seen that, either. I asked Alice about it. She explained that the fifth house doberman was ill and was being restricted to water in the kitchen. The dobermans sat up in narrow chairs with napkins in their laps. Everybody was impressed that they had been trained in the American style, cutting meat with the knife in the right front paw, transferring the knife to the left paw, and then eating with the fork in the right paw. Mrs. Krieger pointed out that it would have been much easier to train them in the European custom of not switching cutlery between paws.

Mr. Krieger did not permit the dobermans to speak at dinner. Neither me nor Alice said anything, either. Dinner here was not a forum for dogs or co-eds. The portions were small. The white wine was super. I let my wine glass be refilled often. I was celebrating in advance, Tom knew, Alice knew. But, after dinner came a surprise.

Tom said he was tired from the drive and begged to retire. He winked at me as if to say, "It's cherry-pricking time!" I swore to myself, *On my back, legs spread wide, no excuses, no blowing, no funneling into my expert ass, but taking Tom's cock right where it belongs, and be glad it's over.* I said, I'm tired, too. Alan agreed, to be agreeable, but with less enthusiasm. He knew he wasn't getting anything tonight. Alice was ready for bed, too, to avoid her parents' questioning and to be up early tomorrow to ski.

Mr. Krieger told Alice and me that our valises were in our rooms and waved us off to the second floor, where her bedroom is. He directed a servant to show Tom and Alan their rooms in the opposite direction on the ground floor. Tom looked ill. Alice went up to her father and whispered something, but his eyes flashed and he rasped, "Absolutely not!" loud enough for everyone to hear. The dogs trembled. Mrs. Krieger soothed them. Two weeks before, Mr. Krieger promised Alice we'd each get one of the four bedrooms in her wing on the second floor. Sometime afterward, he changed his mind.

There was nothing to be done. None of us were happily tired anymore, except Alan, who looked smirky-glad that Tom and I would be separated. We all trooped off to our rooms. The common halls and rooms were crisscrossed by invisible light beams that set off alarms when anyone moved through them, once the master of the house decided everyone had retired to the bedroom wings for the night. That was the least of it. As we left the dining room, we saw the dobermans crossing the grand reception hall from different directions as they prowled their different routes. Alice had been raised with dobermans and they had never harmed her, but she had never gotten completely over her fear of them. They turned me stone cold. She said there were usually five dogs guarding the house and eight patrolling the grounds. The house dogs would not come into the bedroom wings, but it would be impossible for anyone except Alice's father to roam around the house at night. "What if you want a snack at three in the morning?" I asked. "Easy," Alice said, "there's a snack pantry and refrigerator in each bedroom wing."

The servant who showed Tom and Alan their rooms told them lurid details about the dobermans. If the boys wandered out of their wing, the dogs would pin them to the ground, fangs an inch from their throats, and keep them there until the master of the house called them off, even if he didn't come till noon the next day!

I gave up. I bet Tom gave up, too. I bet he jerked off. If he put himself in his famous black book, there'd be a circle with tiny letters "jo" by his name.

The evening was young for Alice and me. On the way up to our rooms, she apologized for her father. She described Tom and me to her parents as "practically engaged," but that didn't fly. In this house, you were married or you were not married. There was no sex outside of marriage and probably not a whole lot in marriage.

Alice drew a bath for me, saying, if we'd gotten in earlier the servants would've. She added, "I'll leave if you want to be alone. Or shall I stay and wash your back?"

"Stay," I said. At the same instant, I wished she'd go. I was terribly horny, and I could take care of myself in the tub. Now, I'd have to wait.

"I'm terribly horny," Alice said, as she washed my back.

"You're horny!" I exclaimed. "What do think I was doing in Tom's lap?"

"I knew you were," Alice said, "that's one reason I'm so horny. Tom's cute. I regret giving him a hard time years ago."

I recalled Alice's name with the bubble-bath of circled initials in Tom's book. "How were you hard on him?" I giggled.

"We only had one date. I could see he thought he was a stud, so I decided to screw him silly. I made him do me every which way, non-stop, plain wore him out. Then, I just looked at him, and said, "That's it? Fucked out?"

"I love it!" I turned and looked up to her so she could see I was beaming. A woman after my own heart! I was impressed she earned all those initials in one night! I wished I had the book so I could ask her what some of them stood for.

"He never called me again!" Alice chortled.

I dried myself in front of her, blushing as usual. No, not as usual, women didn't usually make me blush! I came to the Kriegers' expecting to try something new, but I was beginning to sense I might wind up trying something else new.

"Will you wash my back?" Alice asked softly. We went to her bathroom.

"You're beautiful!" I said as she stripped. She had pert breasts, a tiny waist, and a charming rear end. Her limbs, her neck were drawn out an extra inch beyond ordinary attractive lengths, giving her the elegance of a fantasy drawing. I saw that in high school, but it was a lot more seductive now than back then in the gym shower. Alice knew this was new to me.

"No, you're beautiful!" she laughed. "You have much more of what men like! If I were a man, I'd jump all over you!" She dried off.

Why drag men into it? We adored each other! I could have said that. I could have said anything to her! But there was one thing I was dying to ask her: "What the fuck are you doing with Darshow?"

"I haven't decided. Maybe shove him down the slope backwards? Or have the chef skin him? Don't you think he'd make a good sausage?" I giggled, but her jokes scared me. *Something of her father in her?*

Alice admitted Alan was a screen. This semester she was screwing two men, her economics professor, who was married, and a Jew lawyer who wanted to save rain forests. She never wanted her parents to know anything about her love life, so from thirteen on she chattered to them about boys she despised. Which was just as well, 'cause her heavy romances were with black poets and social activists. The Kriegers would not have been thrilled with these beaux.

"I still don't see why Alan Darshow?" I shrugged,

meaning, *You don't have to stoop that low to mislead the old folks*.

"I'll tell you," she said, "give me your hand." By now, we were back in my room, on my bed, both in nightgowns. From the moment she took my hand, I knew the answer.

"I have doubts whom to go to bed with," Alice said. "Sometimes, it's not enough to say you're not hungry. You carry a rotten fish around to remind you not to eat."

"Alan is the rotten fish? You don't like sex with men at all?" I said, but her grin said she did. I didn't count Mark's stories about Alice riding him ragged, or the initials stacked above her name and cascading down the page in Tom's book, 'cause all that could be for show. I changed my question, "What do you like better, men or women?"

"Can't say, love men, everything we do, and women, everything with women, too. Feel safer with men, but closer to women." All this time she held my hand in her delicate warm hand. I swear, our hearts beat in sync, thump-thump, thump-thump. She brought her face to mine—kissing range—and said, "I feel safe with you." I closed my eyes and parted my lips. We kissed. I thought I was going to faint, I was going to die—no! I was going to be just fine.

But after a minute I joked, "Was that from Tom?" God, how stupid! I was just afraid. "No, that's from me," she said. "Here's one from Tom." She cradled my head in her arm. I'll be damned, she got it exactly right!

She went out with him once, years ago, and she can kiss like him! "Here's one from Mark!" she declared, and she kissed me like Mark! "Now, how about one from Alan?" she laughed, sticking her tongue three miles out and grabbing at my boobs.

"Spare me," I begged. "Give me another from Alice."

She smiled and pulled her nightgown over her head. I understood I was to do the same. Then, she guided me onto my back. My thighs were open—just as I thought they'd be about now! She rested one hand on each thigh. "Here's one from Alice," she said. It was marvelous. If you want your cunt done right, sometimes it helps to go to someone who owns one. Not that Alice did anything men haven't done, but her mouth was more subtle. It was crepes suzettes at Pavilion compared to the Pancake House Cinnamon Special.

And, then, I did her. Just coming off great tutoring, I was inspired. I knew what I liked and I fine-tuned it to what Alice liked! I loved her delicate, wispy bush, her sensitive quim. Most of all, I loved her taste. I had tried tasting my sex gravy to see what men enjoyed so much, but I never cared for it. But, Alice's! Imagine a sauce created for the emperor of China!

We both went crazy and did everything! We didn't know when dawn came, 'cause our faces were so deep in each other. But, once the sun was up, we fell asleep cuddling like spoons. Someone woke us up knocking on the locked door to our wing, then went away. Mr. Krieger rang up at eight-thirty. Alice got in and out of her bed so it looked slept in. We sponged off, dressed in our ski togs, and went down for breakfast.

Alan was rested and ready to ski. Tom had switched gears. He was eager to ski, too. Alice looked full of energy. I was frazzled and wrung out in a good way. Yesterday, licking Tom in the car, I pretended to nap. Now, I was pretending to be awake. I thought nobody could tell, but Alan teased me, "What's the matter, didn't get your beauty rest?" He thought being horny for Tom kept me up all night.

Mr. Krieger was an avid skier. Mrs. Krieger volunteered that when he courted her he went down an advanced slope on one ski. That was as chatty as she got. Mr. Krieger took us to his ski club, Three Mountains. He pointed out the cluster of three mountains the club owned, one for skiing, the other two to keep the wrong kind of people away.

The skiing was great, and I forgot I was tired. Tom wanted to tell me his plan. "This evening—"

"We'll have to wait and see," I said.

Alice and I had a moment alone behind a snowy mound. We hugged.

We got back to the chateau late in the afternoon and I fell sound asleep at once. Tom had hoped to be alone with me before dinner, and he was annoyed.

The Kriegers invited two couples from the ski club to dinner. Tom and I were seated at the "kids' end" of the table, the Kriegers and guests at the "grown-ups' end." The table was so long, it was like being at separate tables. The fifth doberman had recovered, and all five dogs sat between us and them. Alice sat next to Tom, and Alan next to me. I couldn't help beaming at her. She smiled pleasantly like nothing was going on. Alan, across from Alice, kept saying things to get her to notice him. Tom tried to curry favor with the doberman next to him by offering it half of his tiny portion of veal, but the dogs were incorruptible. He might as well have offered them his salad.

As I finished my soup, I felt it. Someone's bare foot was lifting my dress, grazing my thigh, inching toward my cunt. At first, I thought it was Alice. Her expression didn't give anything away, but it never does. Then, I thought it was Tom's foot. I saw his face strain as he deployed his leg. I could have checked, but that would have been cheating, and I didn't want Alan to notice! The big toe landed, a little high but prodding lower. It was right on! Then, it was off to one side, trying to find a way inside my panties. Tom was talking business law to Alan, it couldn't be him! But I knew it was! The strain was going to make Tom lurch and yank the tablecloth! I sat on the edge of my chair and eased my panties down two inches and tried to feel the size of the toe, but it withdrew a moment, till I took my hand away. Alan was busy trying to impress Alice, so he didn't pick up this maneuver.

The toe came back, landed right on my clit. I went nuts. It dipped into me and back to my clit, into me, back to my clit. Too agile to be Tom! It was Alice! "Are you okay?" Alice said. It was Tom, alright. The first time we connected, he toe'd my tit when I was sitting on a rug at a party.

I wanted to save myself for Alice, but I always loved sex under people's noses. I was hot and damp down there, craving more. This was bizarre, being served seconds in veal and veggies, having my wine glass filled, composing my face while getting thoroughly toe'd by a lover. If Tom had a new black book, I might or might not achieve a cherry over my name, but I was earning a "tf."

The dobermans sniffed the air and stirred uneasily. I've heard dogs can smell when a woman's aroused. I was close to coming, but my lover (whoever) pulled away. Then, the toe was back, and I came at once, hard, 'cause I was trying not to. Everyone thought I was choking. Alan dragged me out of my chair from behind and performed the Heimlich maneuver on me. I defy anyone to enjoy an orgasm while a fist rams you in the belly. I signalled wildly and muttered between clenched teeth, "I'm going to barf!"

"You may be barfing up the wrong tree," Alice said. She could have been more concerned. I spotted Tom putting his sock back on in the confusion.

After dinner, we lost Alan for a few minutes. Tom told Alice and me his schemes. First, I was to pretend I was too ill to be alone, but not so ill the Kriegers would feel compelled to call a doctor. I would ask Tom to stay with me while I rested. That might've worked, but Tom missed that one of the guests tonight was a big-shot internist. To get invited here, it helped to be a billionaire, a senator, or a celebrity doctor. The physician had watched in awe as Alan bounced me around like a rag doll, every few seconds squeezing the daylights out of me. Alice scooted over to the doctor and pleaded with him to intercede, but he deferred to the first aid in progress. However, if I hadn't recovered fairly soon, or if Alan had broken a couple of my ribs, our hosts would have asked him to take over the case.

Tom's second plan: He thought he could creep under the invisible beams and not trip the alarm. And, having eaten dinner cheek by jowl with a doberman, he was less afraid of the dogs. "What are you going to do when you're on your back and a doberman's fangs are an inch from your throat?" I asked. Tom explained that the doberman's quarry had to start his escape or counter-attack "from nothing," while the dog was trained to respond to his movement. Tom's theory was, that gave the dog an advantage, because responding to a stimulus is faster.

"So?" I said. It's easy to please men in bed, but impossible to understand how they think.

"Simple," Tom said. "I count to three and respond to my own count instead of starting from nothing. That way's faster. On 'three,' I kick the dog off me."

"But the doberman counts by three's," Alice said.

At last, it was Alice and me again, her bed this time.

"Sarah," she said, "we can do it all again like last night. But there's another way to be with each other, a way you never get with a man."

"What—?"

"It's fantasy, a memory, or anything you've heard of. Any time or place, you can be a man or an animal, give me any role you want me to play, man, woman, animal, a god or a movie star. We talk through the scene 'til we come together in our minds."

I was afraid I wouldn't be as imaginative as her. "Don't you want to touch?" I said.

"Sure, we make love, too. But when one of us sets a scene, we go with it. Let's say—have you ever wanted to be a handsome man walking around with a stiff cock"—Alice bounds off the bed and struts around stroking an enormous imaginary cock growing out of her bush—"and women are crazy for it, they're all falling at your feet and licking it?"

"Not exactly—"

"Well, that's my fantasy, then! But, you must have your own!"

Alice wasn't altogether wrong. Now, I remembered day-dreaming once that it'd be great to be a stud where there's no other men and fuck five pretty women a day. It was on a desert island! Or did I see a cartoon like that in one of Tom's girlie magazines? I told Alice about seeing myself walking up and down a beach full of women waving my cock around.

"Great!" Alice cries. She takes my hand, draws me off the bed. "Here's the beach, there's the blue ocean with gentle waves rolling in. I'm one of the luscious women—how many?—fifty?—waiting for you to saunter by. What're we wearing?" She lies down on the beach. "Thong bikinis, Okay? Topless? Okay. Lots of shade trees on the beach. Good, you strut by. Wave it at us! Feel your big balls swing! We adore it!" She walked over to me on her knees, started to lick the air—my pretend-cock!—and told me how she loved it. She was generous, shared me with other beauties who wanted a piece.

"I'll fuck the juiciest one!" I announced, pointing to Alice, "You!" I was about to throw her on her back, but she said softly, "Terrific, Sarah, now, just talk through it, how you'll fuck me."

So, I imagined how I'd mount her and thrust my huge cock in her and she'd wrap her legs around me and I'd fuck her with long, hard, swively strokes. She told me how every bit of her responds and how her womb goes *Whomp!* At times, she got carried away and cried aloud. She mimed—what? Scratching my back! I could feel her nails! She was also the other women licking me while waiting their turns. "May we kiss your handsome backside while you're fucking Alice?" they begged. They complained about my muscular male butt moving too fast. One got a good grip and locked on to lick my crack. She told me I tasted salty. Could have been the ocean. I felt something shift in my balls! I was going to come—as a man!

I came like a male ape, making sounds I'd never made before, *"Rrrraaah—"* We rolled around on the rug, laughing. Then, we cuddled up and caressed each other.

"I've got a sci-fi one!" Alice said. She discovered she acquired mental qualities she lacked by blowing men who had them. Not just their talents, their enthusiasm for their work. Alice was talented in a dozen ways, but she didn't have a passion for anything. This evening her idea was, she wanted to write music, not just any old music, but jazz Schubert would improvise if he were a student at Belmont.

Okay. I did classical music and jazz greats for her and she sucked her heart out. Bach was stern, didn't approve of her project, wound up holding her by the ears. She swilled down Bach's genius. Mozart was tender, playful, and oddly sad. Beethoven was demanding and distrustful, wound up ecstatic. Schubert was grateful, but kept trying to get away to finish a symphony he was working on. Alice suspected I'd known a few jazz musicians myself, the way I guided her face to my big black cock and cried, *"Wooo-wooo-wooo-eee!"*

We made love the old-fashioned way. I doubted I could think of anything else. Then, I did. "I'm a nun, a teacher, you're a naughty schoolgirl, say, eleven years old. You steal your mother's lipstick and show boys your hiney. I take you into the washroom and warm your ass." Alice came to St. Deems in high school, years after the reign of Sister Martin.

"And, then—?"

"We'll see."

"How do you look?—like yourself?"

"Not really, no. I'm about thirty-two, lean, athletic body and a pretty Irish face, with freckles. Red hair, green eyes. I look strict."

Alice smirked like an eleven-year-old brat. She bent

over, flipped her pretend-skirt up, showed her hiney to a boy. I compressed my lips in rage. I mimed dragging her by her ear to the washroom. She stumbled a few steps sideways, ear-first. She begged me not to spank her, but she oozed sex like a little tart, so there was no chance I'd relent. I ordered her to take her panties down, lie across my knees. She obeyed. When I lifted her dress in back, her hiney trembled.

I thought I'd have a ruler, but I found myself holding a riding whip. Alice promised to be good. I was merciless. "When I'm done with you, you'll behave!" I hissed. She tensed her delicious hiney. I went, *"Hwisss-plik!"* and touched her bare buttocks smartly with the edge of my index finger.

"Ylll!" she screamed, sticking her behind up a bit, touched the whipped flesh gingerly. I pinned her hand behind her, *"hwisss!"* and tapped her behind again. *"Ylll! Ylll!"* Alice shimmied prettily and sobbed. I put more wrist into the whipping. She tried to cover her raw bottom with her free hand, but I trapped both hands at the small of her back. I informed her in my severest voice that now she would get more for trying to shield herself. *"Hwisss!"* and tap! She flutter-kicked her heels and howled, *"YAAAlll! YAAAlll!"* Squinting, I saw her backside thatched with purplish red welts.

When I gave her a chance, she confessed she was naughty and deserved whipping. I asked whether she felt satisfactorily punished. She said she did, added that she loved me for disciplining her. I refused to let her off that easily. I went, *"Hwisss!"* and tapped her rear cheeks six times, rapidly. She pumped her rear end madly at each tap, blurted out that she'd never steal lipstick or let boys see her private parts. Her legs were splayed, she was turned on. I doubt she knew how raunchy she looked.

Whimpering, Alice asked me how it felt to give her red stripes and watch her squirm. I admitted it was exciting, yet a struggle to stay strict and not let myself be seduced or take pity. She murmured, "You can do anything you want to me." I let her up. She jumped up and down in front of me, rubbing her painful butt. Her eyelashes were wet.

"Real tears," I observed. She went down on her knees, kissed her way up my thighs. Later, when we were resting cuddled up, she said, "You can punish me sometime. Use a real whip if you want to."

"I thought you said it was better in the mind," I said.

"Still, you might want to."

However, I felt only loving to her. What intrigued me was that she assumed we'd have other times, even when we weren't locked up together. "I have another one!" I said. "Can I have two in a row? You get to be a man in this one."

I was Captain Sarah Moons of a magical pirate ship. It disappeared when I snapped my fingers and said, "Night!" and it reappeared when I snapped my fingers and said, "Day!"

I wasn't making this up on the spot. A long time ago I lived on a magical pirate ship when I couldn't stand Mom lecturing me. I added stuff to impress Alice.

All the pirates loved me. There were a dozen men in the crew for every woman, so I was in demand. The few women on board were scared of me, but I treated them well so long as they remembered who was captain. From time to time, when we needed a new crew member, we raided another ship or a port. Everyone wanted to join the crew of the magical pirate ship. I tested the handsomest, most virile men myself.

Alice played a handsome would-be pirate eager to please Captain Sarah Moons in her broad love hammock on deck. Her description of what she was doing to me knocked me out. "God, Alice, you can fuck! I'm still coming!"

"So, I'm signed on?" Alice cried. She was thrilled to be aboard. We drifted to sleep in each other's arms, feeling the waves rock us in the love hammock. We must have slept for at least two hours. Then, we woke and raided the refrigerator. There were fresh raspberries and blackberries.

"I have one!" Alice cried. "Or would you rather sleep?" I was ready to play. "Okay," Alice said, "but it's tricky. I'm dressed as a man. You're a beautiful girl who comes on to me. We kiss, but no fondling. Then, I suspect you're a man with beautiful features, in drag. I try to decide, Are you a man or a woman, and do you think I'm a woman dressed as a man or a man playing a woman dressed as a man? Your responses are completely ambiguous. Then, I doubt myself. Maybe, I really am a man playing a woman?"

"I don't get it," I said. "Why don't you know what

you are? What do you want me to think?"

"We respond to each other. You think what you think, depending on what you're getting from me, and I think what I think, depending on what I'm getting from you."

I confessed this one was over my head, but she struck her pose as a woman in drag, and I wanted to come on to her! It was that simple, not a great stretch, as we actors say. We kissed, and I found the right way, playing it moment by moment, responding to what she was giving me. Now, I felt she was a woman, now, a man. Now, I was a woman, now, a man. All our selves and roles paired off in a Virginia reel.

It took concentration, because we were both naked the whole time, although we were supposed to be dressed, cross-dressed, or cross-cross-dressed! At last, I clasped Alice's hand to my breasts and cried, "I want you whoever you are!" She shouted, "And I want you whoever I am!" and pressed one of my hands to her quim. We made love again and fell asleep again. When we woke, sunshine streamed through the window.

"I have one more!" I said. "I know what it is!" Alice laughed, but she was wrong, it wasn't about Tom, at least not at first. I told her my fantasy was—to be Alice!

"Be me? What would that mean?" she wondered.

I was sorry I said it, 'cause all I was thinking of was that Alice could have all the sex she wanted under people's noses and not give it away. Alice asked me what I'd do if I could get away with it. I told her one of my favorite day-dreams: I'm a TV anchor woman. I keep a man under my desk, and no one knows but a few insiders on the program. I blow him during commercials, and he plays with me when I'm on camera. He's always trying to get me to give myself away, so he fingers me, eats me, uses a vibrator on me—drives the sound people crazy trying to find the source of the buzz. Imagine reporting the news while you're being eaten! I have to keep cool, reading my lines from the teleprompter as though nothing's going on.

"Who's the man?" Alice asked. "Tom!" I said. He just popped into my mind.

There was a desk in Alice's room, but we didn't use it. Instead, I sat on the edge of the bed to play a TV anchor woman. Alice, as Tom, sat between my legs on the floor. I announced a longevity tax bill being debated in Congress, and Tom gave me the works. My only relief was to call for a commercial, when I got to suck him. Then, it was back to work and he was at me. He wanted to fuck me, but with me in the chair and him crouching under the desk, there was no way Sir Cock can reach Mistress Quim. I was cool as Alice would have been, never letting the cameras catch me laughing at him as he tried one contortion after another.

We showered together. Alice said she waited all night for me to ask her to play Tom deflowering me. But it never occurred to me! I only thought of it when the "Tom" under my anchor desk tried to reach me with his cock.

Mr. Krieger called us to breakfast. I was stiff from yesterday's skiing, but feeling content. I skied better than ever. Shifts in balance I'd been told about came to me naturally.

We left late in the afternoon. The Kriegers warned Alice that Alan wasn't good enough for her, but they were hard people to please. And, Mr. Krieger was satisfied that separating Alice and me from the men prevented any hanky-panky.

— 15 —

FORBIDDEN PLEASURES

I've filled five tape cassettes talking about my life with Sofi and Francis the August before my first TV commercial. We practically invented each other. Without the video of me, not many people would've heard of them. And you'd really be reading this without Sofi's agency and Francis's video of me and Tom Thomas!

Sofi thought I could run GAM for her someday and she'd sleep till noon. In the meantime, I dropped like a roller coaster from Fifth Avenue brat to low-rent sex toy. When Mom cut me off, I ran through my savings in no time. I needed money from somewhere. Francis wouldn't just give me an allowance. He'd give me a twenty when I did something exotic for him. "Hey," I said one time, "that was worth three hundred!" "You have a big ego," he snorted. "You're lucky I don't have any smaller bills on me." A few days later he made me do the same trick for the change in his bathrobe, a quarter, a dime, six pennies. I said, "Thank you, sir."

I told myself I wasn't exactly a hooker, 'cause a hooker who looked like me could make a thousand a night just for the basics. But I loved whoring for Francis, and he loved making me jump through hoops for small bills. "What?" he would say, "you need *how much*? What're you going to do for me for that?"

I'd recite my repertory, which was growing lately. It was simpler to say, "Whatever you want, sir." And do whatever it was—all the way. If I held back, he'd refuse to pay me until I did it right.

Francis and Sofi were both into domestic discipline. When Francis was edgy, he would tell Sofi she was "this close" to a spanking. She would get quiet and submissive. She didn't beg or try to slip away. At a word from Francis, she presented her backside for the strap with dignity. But she hardly ever had to do that, at least not when Francis had me to whip instead. I was the opposite of Sofi: I blushed, I wiggled, I tried to tease my way out of it.

Francis would coo, "Come here, Sarah, darling," in a voice that still calls to me in my mind and makes me horny. I kept falling for that trick, even when he sat straight up with his belt doubled in his hand. I'd go to him blushing furiously. He made me stand right in front of him and drop my panties. I'd reach up under my skirt and tug them a little down my hips, all the while searching his face for a sign he loved me. He took me

[219]

by a wrist, a tit, an ear, or my hair and put me over his left knee. One time Francis did seem to relent, laid the belt aside and sat me on his lap. We kissed. My senses reeling, I forgot the danger. All at once he flipped again and put me in my place—head down, ass up!

When Mr. Hardon was around, Sofi brought him to watch. I hated that wimp seeing me bawl and kick my heels up, my gorgeous bare cheeks bouncing, showing my crack, my cunt, everything. And, afterward, Mr. Hardon watching me, still whimpering and waggling my red rear end, on my knees in front of Francis. To my surprise, none of this lowered me in Mr. Hardon's eyes. When we were alone, he still sucked up to me.

I went around the house with a rosy bottom and glowing with shame. In that state, I was super-excitable. Sofi called me, "Ms. Anytime," 'cause whenever Francis and I crossed paths, I was ready the moment he pulled the string on my bikini. He screwed me rolling on the wet sand at the shoreline, on a lifeguard stand, on a wooden bench beside a "nature trail," in a rowboat on a pond. One of his favorite ways was at a window, making me bend over the sill, bare boobs swaying in the breeze. Sofi called it, "broadcasting." Anybody in the neighborhood could see Francis close behind me and guess what was happening to my bottom half when I hollered and my upper half lurched forward again and again and flopped around outside the window.

When we visited people out here, Francis slipped his huge adorable cock into me on their lawns and sun-decks, in their bedrooms, bathrooms, and basement playrooms. I bit my arm so I wouldn't squeal, but our hosts knew Francis liked to do me "under their noses." I'd wear just a short summer dress, no underwear, on these trips, like, telling Francis, "Ready when you are." One time on someone's sundeck, not knowing how long we had to be alone, I unbuttoned him, unzipped him, dragged his warm lovely monster out and squirmed down on it. I spread my dress around us, so you might think I was just sitting on his lap. Our hosts came out and talked to us. I posted and swirled on Francis, squeezed him inside me. Marvelous!

This trick depended on staying cool—one thing I can't do. I blushed deep red. I moaned, tried to disguise it by clearing my throat. Our hosts looked at each other. They knew. The lady of the house said, "Do you like modeling, dear?" It was a bad moment to answer. I was afraid if I opened my mouth, I'd scream. "Love it," I gasped, begging Sofi with my eyes to back me up, 'cause I wasn't starting till the fall.

At a neighbor's I heard Sofi say, "Francis and Ms. Anytime'll be down in a few minutes. He's nailing her in your bedroom." Actually, he was nailing me in a hallway a few feet away, up against the wall. My skirt was up, my legs around him, his hands under my butt, and when I came, everybody knew where we were.

Francis was into bondage. Sofi was, too, 'cause he was. We tied Francis up and made him crazy. Like, one day, we kissed him up and down, front and back, and walked out. We went into another room and fooled with each other till he began to think we weren't coming back.

He was beyond mad. We came back and teased him silly all over again. I mouthed his big, sweet, kissable cock while Sofi smooched his ass. She asked in her tourist voice, "Are you having fun yet, dear?" which guaranteed I'd have to gulp enough cum to whitewash the Vatican. You stayed on Francis till he was done. You didn't get excused 'cause your jaw ached from being wide open and your tummy was full of hot salty cream.

I saw where they were coming from. Sofi was head of an agency, but Francis was only a white-collar working stiff. At home it was reversed. When Francis fucked her, she was overwhelmed. She could float for a week on one fuck. But Francis would want five different sex trips in the next two days.

Maybe, Sofi got huge to keep Francis off her. I wanted to ask her how she blew up to four times her size and then came down again in six seconds. When I was alone, I practiced asking her casually, like, *By the way, how d'you do that*? But I was supposed to act like it was no big deal. Except, if Sofi ever decided to blow up when she was sitting on my face, I'd be a goner.

Sofi likes a beautiful young woman taking care of her. Lounging in a deck chair, looking at me over her magazine. "Come here, Sarah!" Doesn't exert herself beyond loosening her bikini, flipping it down so her auburn bush shows. Doesn't pretend to read while I lick her, but keeps her place in the magazine with one finger. My way is to eat her out earnestly so she doesn't know how mad that makes me.

Being a pinball bouncing between them was good

raunchy fun. I was too busy trying to please them to think, I just went with it. Francis made me write down the ten most humiliating sex tricks I could imagine doing for the two of them. Of course, they were already making me do eight of them, and by the end of the week they hit all ten.

I was supposed to clean the kitchen and bathrooms and make the beds, but Sofi complained I lived in their house "like an American teenager" and didn't even clean up after myself. For punishment I got tied up, naked, in ridiculous positions. I was like a goose-neck lamp you bend any way you want. I would've stayed without being tied down, but it was considerate of them to tie me, 'cause it made submitting easier. I couldn't even think about running away when I was lying on my back, legs spread wide and ankles tied way up in the air over my head. Or, when I was tied bending over, ass up for whipping and whatever, elbows tied together behind my back pushing out my boobs, I didn't have to worry about shielding my titties or my ass.

Sofi had a hood she dropped over my face. She called it the "bonnet" 'cause it tied under my chin. The bonnet had a hole as big as my mouth wide open. The idea was, I licked whatever anybody put to my lips. Sofi made me wear the bonnet to entertain people who dropped by. Some were her advertising clients. Visitors tweaked my tits and gave me different body parts to kiss. A few tweaks were familiar, partly 'cause of the sex club Francis and Sofi belonged to. I thought I recognized one woman's nipples, a few cocks, balls, butts, clits, quims, and big toes. It was like *Guess*, this time with lousy odds.

One afternoon, Sofi gave a plasterer permission to maul my tits. He said his hands were clean, but they were coated with plaster flakes. I was tied down in the seat of a chair, kneeling backside up, head and boobs over the back of the chair. He kissed my neck, and called me, "honey." "I'm not your honey," I said. He stopped playing with my nipples, thought that over, then went back to it. Sofi blindfolded me with my bikini bottom. The fragrant crotch was right over my nose! The workman touched my hiney low and goosey, and said to Sofi, "You're sure?" and Sofi said, "It's all right, she's being punished." I strained against my bonds, 'cause I was sensitive back there! A moment later he grabbed me below, the bowling-ball grip, middle finger in my cunt and thumb up my ass. I clenched to keep his thumb out, but it won, 'cause I was also thinking, why not play along and see if I could like it? Thick stubby fingers with plaster, in and out, 'round and 'round. I decided not to come, but I did. He took his fingers out of me. I listened for the sound of him taking his pants off. I was sure he was going fuck me, maybe in both places. I cursed him and Sofi.

Cursing was forbidden, I just forgot. Sofi declared she was going to whip me. She'd never done that herself. She strode out of the room, saying, "Don't go away," her idea of a joke, 'cause I was tied ass-up kneeling in a chair. It wasn't just cursing, it was daring to go against her. She'd decided to use the plasterer to fuck me, and I was supposed to go along. The plasterer didn't say a word, didn't touch me. I guessed he was content to watch me get a whipping and then fuck me.

Sofi came back with a leather strap cut into three strips at one end. It had a little knot tied at each of the three ends. She described it to me, dangled the three strands against my backside. She hurt my bottom as much as any man ever did. Only one other guy, Walter the thug, was in her league for cruel. Sofi said she was going to make my ass dance. I didn't like the sound of that. I begged her not to, but she flogged me. I screamed "*YAAAIIIEEEOWWW*!" It hurt so much she gave me a whole minute to writhe and scream. I completely broke down after the second lash, offered to screw the plasterer any way he wanted. Sofi said, "That's the right attitude, but he left when you started cursing." That didn't make sense. Would a little cursing drive a workman out of a room where I was tied up naked and blindfolded and the lady of the house was egging him on? A few moments later I realized what was going on. Sofi must have swelled up. That's what made the plasterer flee, when he saw her going gigantic.

Sofi gave me an order I couldn't grasp 'cause I was bawling. Then, I got it. I was collapsed across the back of the chair, but she wanted me to put my backside up for her as cute as I did for Francis! I didn't want to do that for her. It's something I do for men. But I had to obey. Even with men, I'm faking when I make it look like my butt's begging for it. After each lash, my ass danced for Sofi at least a minute, and then I forced myself to turn it up like I was seducing her to flog me again. She'd say, "Good, Sarah," and flay my rear end.

I hate being punished by a woman. At least with a man, you get a frisky cock afterward. You say, "I'm sorry" and swear "I won't do it again," and he takes your word even if it's something you couldn't possibly not do again, 'cause all he cares about is getting in, one way or another. Then, it's a comfort to feel his hot hard cock enjoying itself in you and spurting every glop he can make, and he's so pleased, usually you can cuddle up and everything's okay.

But what did I get from Sofi? I sensed her arranging a chair so that she could sit in front of me, her quim in my face. Her odor overwhelmed the one from the crotch of my bikini blindfold. It was a familiar subtle raunchy scent, elegant and commanding like Sofi herself. That scent said, *"Lick me!"* I thought of lion tamers who put their heads in the lion's mouth. No! I refused to die that way!

Relieved Sofi had stopped flogging my behind, I gave tongue with gusto. In the midst of her giant, quaking, moaning climax my blindfold fell off. At that exact instant she was rapidly shrinking to normal size. Afterward, *she* was all smiles, but I didn't get anything out of it. My ass was tender for days, and there was some plaster flakes up in me that took a while to come out. Francis examined the welts on my bottom when he got home and said they would *probably* heal, and in the meantime I should be extra submissive and stay out of trouble. I cleaned the house and kissed ass, and the welts healed by the end of the week. It seemed to me Francis treated Sofi with more respect for a few days.

Francis hated Sofi and me fooling around without him. Once, when he caught us on my bed, he whipped both of us. Too bad he interrupted us, 'cause Sofi was giving me more than she usually did. Anyway, we both had to kneel face down on the bed with our behinds up in the air. Francis strolled back and forth brandishing his belt. I teased him, "Feel like a big shot whipping two asses?" My reward was, he smacked my bottom three times as much as hers. I sobbed, "That's not fair!" He gave Sofi quite a few red stripes, but she kept her tail turned up and never howled, not once, from the hurt. She bit her lip when the strap landed, and once she sighed like she was offended. It was all foreplay for them. They got into a great endless fuck. I was left rubbing my hiney and watching them. I tried distracting Francis with kisses here and there, but he mostly ignored me.

Sofi and Francis belonged to Forbidden Pleasures, an S-M club that met once a week at different members' houses. It was for couples and it was exclusive. The women had to be beautiful and the men handsome or rugged, in good shape, not pigs or dorks. You had to own or rent a house in the Hamptons with a room where about thirty-five people could party. Going as Francis and Sofi's guest to my first meeting, I worried that my summer party dress showed too much cleavage and was too short. It hung off my hips like I was going out in my panties and the dress was a frilly afterthought. Francis said skimpy clothing was forbidden. Sofi smirked. We were already in his car down the driveway.

My dress was too tempting and I would get fucked silly. But if everything was forbidden, fucking had to be, too. On the way all I could think about was, Who was I going to do what with? Francis and Sofi? Our neighbors? Strange men? Women? One after another or all in a heap? Would they get into me every which way? Would I be punished, would I get to punish anyone, or just watch? Sofi said many came to watch and stayed to play. The car ride was like a sex dream. I got so horny I could smell odor of bitch wafting up from my own cunt. I clamped my dress tight to my thighs to keep the scent in. Sofi would have teased me.

The first thing I saw as we entered was a girl on her back on a couch with a guy kneeling, head between her legs, eating her out. Tongue all the way up, nosing her clit. I thought, I want that now! She was a sexy kid, younger than me. Oscar, an almost bald, wiry ex-boxer who always acted like some kind of official, ticked off the rules these two were breaking.

The girl's skirt was up, her great legs over the guy's back, toes curled tight. She yelped in short bursts of joy as she neared coming, clutched her panties in one hand and flipped the other hand in the air, like she was sprinkling pleasure through her fingers into the room. The guy was wearing denim shorts and polo shirt. She was his wife's sister! Sofi pointed out his wife, who looked like the girl on the couch, but five years older.

The story was, the week before the guy had walked in on his kid sister-in-law when she was blowing her date. It spooked the boy, who ran off still buttoning up.

All week the girl carried on about how she couldn't face anybody, till her older sister came up with the idea hubby could square matters by eating her at the Club.

Sofi said the main idea of the Club was a place where you were forbidden to do whatever you felt like doing. If you got an urge to feel a man's butt, you weren't supposed to. If he wanted to kiss you or take your boobs out and pet them, you weren't supposed to let him. My boobs got played with more than any time since high school. One sweet guy said they were the hit of the evening. Also, I was not supposed to let a man introduce himself by putting a hand under my frilly micro dress and fondling me underneath. He might just feel the storm brewing there, and that could cut through a lot of bullshit conversation. However, this was a standard greeting at the Club, like a handshake anywhere else.

There was plenty of forbidden woman-on-woman sex, but in the five weeks I went as Francis and Sofi's guest I didn't see any man-on-man sex at all. I don't think there was a rule against it, just the men in this crowd were uptight about that. The only rule that wasn't broken was, you did whatever in front of everybody. No sneaking off into other rooms, 'cause that would've made it like other Hamptons parties. A few women, once they got their clothes off, walked around nude, which was strictly forbidden. Also, men who were extra well hung strutted around. None of them could compare to our Francis, the horse, who was in and out of his pants all night.

There was a nice rhythm to the evening. Lots of

forbidden fondling and sucking all the time. Men would say, "Would you blow me?" And you could say, "No," or "Not right now," and a minute later you'd both be talking to different people. I generally said "OK" if a guy said, "I want *you* to blow me," like it was personal and urgent. I did a couple of blow-jobs soon after I arrived at these meetings when I was a bit jittery. Sucking a guy off relaxes me and makes me comfortable with him. When I want to feel I belong at an orgy, my trick is to blow three guys right away. Then, I'd have three friends there. Here, it was risky.

The S-M stuff tended to be routine girlfriend-or wife-spanking. A jealous guy, or a man taking his "disobedient" wife across his knees and baring her bottom—that sort of thing. You heard phrases like "old-fashioned spanking." Hubby raising his hand 'way up each time and pausing dramatically over bare cheeks.

I remember what happened to me better than stuff I just watched, but somehow one flagrant bit of misbehavior, and 'specially how a certain slut was punished for it, pop into my mind when I think about the Club. Ellen was a newcomer in the middle of August, a tall, slightly horsey brunette with large boobs. She took over an alcove and arranged herself naked on some throw pillows. There were usually more studs than ladies at the Club, and some of the women were into each other, so Ellen was a big relief to the extra guys—helped them get a leg up on what they came for. Anyway, four guys laid Ellen one after another, and everyone saw she didn't close her thighs between screws. She just stretched, which isn't the same. Talk about forbidden! There might have been a fifth if the boyfriend had not pulled her out of her nest. She was leaking cum and sex gravy. He called her slut and blotted her underneath with a towel (there were stacks of towels everywhere), which she said was sweet, and leaned her big boobs into him. She was tipsy and chagrined. Screwing all comers wasn't her thing, she was just taking advantage of the Club to feel what it would be like to be totally screwed out. She didn't quite get there. The boyfriend took off his belt, doubled it, and put her across his knees. Her boobs wobbled when he strapped her. She had broad hips and voluptuous rear cheeks rather like mine, so it was fascinating to watch her get it. I could almost feel the searing pain in my hiney! And, since it was hers, not mine, I could enjoy it! She bawled, "I thought we were supposed to—!" She was slow catching on.

My first evening at the Club, Mitch and his wife Rona were the stars. He said she was "withholding," meaning she wasn't sucking him off with the same enthusiasm as before they were married. Now, there's an original complaint! I think Rona had come with Mitch to a few meetings to gawk at the rest of us, and suddenly she was the center of attention, facedown and skirt up, hands scrabbling behind her to keep her panties up. It wasn't as brutal as it sounds, 'cause she was embarrassed but laughing, too. My guess was Rona had been spanked at home, but never in public before. She craned her head around trying to see if anyone was watching her lose the battle of the panties. Hubby got them down below the high curve of her butt for an instant before she yanked them up. "I don't want—all these [men] seeing—the crack of my ass!" she hissed.

Oh? Fine for the rest of us, but not for her? Too bad, a dozen guys were locked into watching Mitch bare her firm round backside. He was cute in his sleeveless T-shirt, athletic like her, with wavy hair and gleaming white teeth. He was determined, trapped both her wrists with one hand behind her back. She cried in frustration. Mitch plucked at her panties with his free hand, worked them down on one side, then the other, till they were clear of her backside and dropped between her thighs. Rona knew she was all exposed, more than just her crack, but I think she was too horrified to object. She kept her thighs pressed together, but from where I was standing I could see curls of her luxuriant black bush and a little of her cunt. Her quim was delicate and rather pretty, I thought.

Mitch gave Rona a sincere handspanking in loud clapping salvos. His pattern was five or six on one cheek, five or six on the other, ten or so right across her crack, and then again . . . and again. Rona's firm, rubbery cheeks bounced like two basketballs as fast as he spanked them—but they weren't basketballs. Her bottom suffered plenty. Mitch had broad, muscular shoulders and a good arm. His hand left brief white imprints in her pink, blotchy-red butt. The triple-time spanking raced ahead of the hiney pain, so Rona knew that her ass would hurt more and more. She got angry, didn't care who saw what, bucked her head up and down and kicked wildly. Her reward was several spanks on the back of each thigh, which persuaded her to stop kicking that way. She tried to heave herself off his lap, but she couldn't. The spanking went right on. Rona broke down and sobbed. All she could do was kick up her heels a few inches, a rapid flutter-kick in time with the spanks. She moaned something I didn't get through her blubbering, but you can guess. Hubby's let her slip to her knees right in front of him. She unbuckled, unbuttoned, unzipped him, and began a long passionate smooch up and down his cock. And casually tried to pull her panties up. Mitch ordered her to leave 'em down till she was done. Her skirt covered her rosy backside, but having to perform with her panties still down was a reminder she better not slack off. She took his cock all the way down her throat, her forehead touched his groin. Some guy applauded, and me and some others joined in. Mitch came and roared like an ape. He couldn't complain this time!

No one announced a spanking. Even before the first smack there was a hush and people gathered around. Some women came expecting to get their bottoms warmed, they had been "promised" a spanking for days. A few were rosy-bottom regulars who got punished at every meeting I went to. One was Milly, a Shame Artist even though she might not have thought of herself in those terms.

Milly's vice was that she talked and talked. You might think she was insecure, but she had no reason to be. She had doe eyes and up-turned nose, light red hair and curly bush to match, tiny waist, perfect boobs, long legs and a high, tight, round ass. But, Milly never shut up unless her pretty mouth was filled. One week when her boyfriend couldn't come, she showed up alone and said her boyfriend sent her and said we'd know what to do with her! Our host that week stripped her naked, took her across his knees and spanked her soundly. Milly had a long curl of red hair that kept falling across her face each time the host's hand smacked her butt. She kept pushing the curl back and chatting away. Meanwhile, the hostess hid Milly's clothes and armed herself with a paddle. She took Milly from her husband's lap right over her own lap and gave her pink butt a half dozen meaty smacks. This surprised Milly and delighted the rest of us. Men love watching one woman spank another. I love watching that, too. Our host announced that Milly would be coming around to each of us carrying the paddle. She was not to eat or drink or use the ladies' without permission till she was done.

Milly put men and women in a good humor and we weren't too strict with her. Men tweaked her nippies affectionately before they punished her. No one had it in for her, except her devil who wasn't there. For the rest of the evening she wandered around nude, handing over the paddle and presenting her rosy rear end. She did as she was told, kneeling, bending over, kissing here, licking there, but she wouldn't completely cease her running commentary until a prick or quim required her mouth's full attention. I didn't want to miss my turn. I timed it perfectly so I was able to take Milly across my knees. All right, I was sterner and I paddled her well-punished bottom more than the others. I just felt like it. I made her count the spanks aloud. I can still hear her counting tearfully, "fourteen, fifteen . . ." She squirmed and mewed like a pussycat, which made it more enjoyable for me. I also liked holding her hot cheeks. She sighed. I rolled them gently. She told me she loved that. I set her down to kiss my cunt. She was splendid. Her cute nose played hockey with my clit. I came quick with shallow tremors and mashed her face lightly into me. When I let her come up for air, her face was completely coated with my sex goo. She knew I'd creamed her with love, and I could tell she was turned on to me, but afraid of me.

"Oh, no, no more!" Milly pouted when the next guy beckoned her for punishment. Her face was still a mess after taking care of me. He wouldn't give her permission to clean it off! "I'm too tender back there!" she protested, "see how red I am!" She actually showed him— can you imagine! He took her paddle and pulled her by one nippy—"Okay, okay," she cried, "I'll go across your knees! OW! OW! OW! You're strong! What's your name? OWWW! That hurts!"—squirming—"Would you rub it?—OWWW! Please, I'll be good! OWWW! I'll do anything you want! OWWW! I'm Milly, what's— WAHHN! WAHHN! WAHHN! Okay, I'll go down, let me ahhhwggg—"

After this evening there was a twist: Milly's boyfriend denied he'd sent her, or even known she was going on her own! But I'd met him. He ogled me the week before. He was the sort who would get a thrill from sending his girl to put out at an orgy. Milly told me she was so attracted to him she agreed to be his sex slave. She said she even signed a paper like a marriage contract, but it was one-sided, it just said she had to do his bidding. I asked her how she met him. He was a salesman of novelty items who happened to have the seat next to hers on a plane. He did magic tricks and told her corny jokes. "With rhymes!" I exclaimed, and she vaguely recalled "something like that." He didn't look much like my magician-joker, not that he'd have to. I hadn't noticed whether her boyfriend wore a special ring, but later I was certain he did, and that I had seen it on his finger without realizing what it was. Milly thought he wore a high school graduation ring. I had nightmares for weeks mixing up my devil and hers. Sofi said, even if Milly's lover did send her, she came, so it was all the same.

Oscar, who liked to remind people that he was a founder of the Club, insisted he had to have a hairbrush to punish his wife, 'cause that's what they were accustomed to at home, so the host went off to get one. It was a long five minutes for Patti to lie across his lap with her face down on the sofa seat and her bare bottom up. A few women came by, whispered in Oscar's ear, and left lipstick "kisses" on his bald pate. Whatever they were into, Oscar wasn't going to give it to them until he got the hairbrush and took care of Patti. Oscar was a super lay. I told him he should use one of the paddles lying around. People came by and asked, "What are you waiting for?"

Patti was slender, with delicate shoulders and waist, small pert breasts, and little round ass cheeks. I knew girls like her in high school who made up for their slightness by their readiness to please. Patti's charming backside was especially sensitive: It seemed to hurt more than better-padded bottoms like mine. At the first smacks of the hairbrush Patti's little cheeks turned red. She waggled, cried, kicked up her heels, and showed every sign of exquisite suffering. Taking his time, Oscar spanked her with the hairbrush on and off for more than ten minutes, with time between smacks for her to hump his knee, cry, and recover.

It was fun to flirt or mess around with a guy while some slut or "disobedient wife" was being chastised nearby. It was like background music. You both refrained from looking most of the time, even when you were distracted by a SMACK! and a cry. Then, when you couldn't stand it anymore and looked, it was twice as exciting. After being punished and giving the spanker a blow-job or whatever he wanted, some women got real quiet and stood around discreetly rubbing their bottoms. Other women acted sluttier than before, which made sense to me. You need consolation then more than ever, and the fire in your tail makes you raunchier than the guy who punished you can satisfy, or even imagine, especially if all he gives you is a mouthful. Also, you tend to think, "I've already paid with my ass, so why not have as much fun as I can?"

I asked everybody, "What's the Club mean to you?" and got a lot of different answers: "liberating," "sharing what we do with like-minded maniacs," "communal blah blah." I liked what Pam and her boyfriend T J said. For them S and M went better with an audience. So much was theatrical, anyway. When T J ordered Pam to drop her panties or assume a pose for punishment at home, he didn't know how dominating to sound! If he wasn't strict enough, the act lost its excitement. If he was too loud and authoritarian, his voice sounded hollow. As for her, she could submit at home, but it wasn't humiliating anymore, and the spark was going out. With us looking on, T J knew the bossier and stricter he was, the more entertaining it was, the better it felt, and Pam could be totally humiliated and turned-on.

Pam was tall and slender, with olive skin and black straight shoulder-length hair. She wandered around at Club meetings in silky lingerie, a scooped-out bra showing her stand-up nippies, bikini panties, a garter belt and stockings. Her round suntanned ass was bare. So much for my worries about my dress! Pam was hot like me. Once she got started, she took guys on greedily, like how many could she do before she had to face the music. Her panties were sopping wet below. She had to wear them till T J punished her. When T J decided she was ripe, he made her drop the disgraceful panties, took her giggling across his knees and doubled his belt. At each spank Pam's head shot up, her perky tits quivered, and she complained, like, reproaching him, "*WAHHN!*

That hurts!" "Good!" he would shoot back. Soon she was crimson back there and bawling.

T J liked being the center of attention as much as Pam did. He joked with his audience between spanks. He put down his belt, swilled sangria, dripped the iced sangria into her crack, rubbed ice on her cute rosy cheeks. He spread her cheeks a little and tried to insert an irregular ice cube in her asshole. The ice melted while he was working at it, but he got some of it in. That set Pam into a frenzy of lust. T J picked up the strap again. For all her whining, you could tell she loved it. Her quim twitched. She was a swamp underneath of sex juice and sangria and melted ice. T J shoved his thumb into her. She squealed and squeezed. He pretended he couldn't get his thumb free, but of course he could—finally, he "wrenched" his gloppy thumb out of her. And, raised the belt again. I was utterly turned on watching her pump her flaming behind in the air every time T J strapped her, 'cause I knew how it felt, all the shame and hiney pain and the horniness. I'd have thought there was nothing more exciting than getting a good spanking when you know you're a total slut and deserve it. Well, watching Pam get hers was as much of a turn-on for me without the stinging butt.

It made me so hot I raped George, the guy I happened to be talking to. Blond, curly-haired George was a hunk. I could feel my titties stiffen and stand out, always a sign for me. I was wearing a sheer bra that didn't hide my response at all. He didn't seem to notice! I put his hands down the front of my dress on my boobs.

George was new to this scene—hard as a lead pipe, but he offered to take me out on a date! I wanted him now, not sometime next week after three hours with him, when I might not want him! I unbuttoned the top buttons of his slacks (forbidden! I thought) and pulled on his cock. I love pulling on a beautiful cock like his, 'specially the first time. At the same time I knew I was 'way over the line into forbidden stuff, and I could feel my backside quiver. *Going to pay with my ass, anyway,* I figured, *might as well make it worthwhile.* I told George he wasn't going anywhere till I had him where I wanted him. There weren't any free sofas or chairs, so he leaned back against the bar, half sitting on it. I dropped my panties on the carpet and climbed on him still wearing my dress, and he held me by my butt and went right into me. I humped him like crazy and I came twice, and then he came and that set me off and I came again. George was still hard. From the beginning of this fuck I had my eye on an abandoned glass with ice cubes. It was so close I thought he was going to knock it off the bar with his elbow. I could reach it. I gave it to George and told him exactly what to do with the ice. He'd seen Pam and her friend, and he said, "Copycat," but I slowed down in mid-fuck and he did what I wanted, and I came again with a big whoop. I was totally satisfied and collapsed on his chest.

I thought I was in luck, 'cause Francis was at the other end of the room and didn't notice us. But when I came over to him and the group around him to make sure I was in the clear, he cooed, "Come here, Sarah, darling," in that voice he used to pull me in for a thrashing. This time, I wasn't fooled. I was sexy as I ever get, but I didn't need Francis. I felt grand, warm all over except for a pleasant chilly tingle around my asshole and a little ways inside. He insisted. I saw he had a paddle on his lap. It was a wooden spatula, with a strong narrow shaft and a small fan-shaped flat end. I still don't know what it was designed for—working with pie crust?—but I knew what it was going to do to my bottom. I could have laughed at him and walked away, the first time I ever felt that way toward Francis. But I didn't dare. If I disobeyed him here, I would get it three times as bad at home. Besides, I didn't completely hate the prospect of Francis warming my ass here. It could be deliciously shameful and enjoyable, 'specially if it led to some sensual treat. I'd doubted he'd want to screw me at the Club, with all those women hanging all over him. But he'd probably had all of them at one time or another. I felt possessive. So, I went up to him. "Strip!" he barked. "Everything?" I whispered. "What's the matter, ass too cold?" he said. Apparently, everybody saw my ice trick. I took my party dress over my head, and got a nice *"Wow!"* from one guy. I wasn't wearing my panties at the moment. There I stood, blushing red down to my sheer bra, which was all I had on. The first instant was a rush, all eyes going right to Ms. Quimmy, who twitched with delight. I unhooked my bra, shrugged it off. My nippies perked up. "Look at those breasts!" a woman said, which was nice in a room with lots of pretty pairs on display at any moment. Francis told me to turn around, hold my knees, and stick my butt out. He made me stand right in front of his chair so he could smack me with the paddle without exerting himself. 'Course, he was just displaying his power over me to his fans. I showed off my gorgeous ass to his group. I was so close they could see the blonde curls of my bush and the pink wrinkles of my quim. Francis felt me underneath, goosing me, probably checking whether there was any chill left there.

Francis's touch turned me on, as always. I was sick with lust all over again. He sensed that, 'cause he stopped playing with me and boasted he was going to teach me a lesson. What did I do that was so bad? Screw someone younger than Francis? Screw a younger guy in public? Get him to insert a wedge of ice in my asshole? Men like Francis make up the rules as they go along. You can go along, too, if you want. But it's not always fun.

I braced myself, dug my nails into my knees. *SMACK!* The wicked fan of the paddle sank in, I could feel it! It brought tears to my eyes. I shimmied, more or less holding my knees, and then Francis told me to stop wiggling and put my ass up. "It is up!" I cried. I couldn't stop every wiggle. *SMACK!* I bawled. The fan was like a small strict hand. It caught me on the big rearmost curve of my left cheek, then on the right, then 'cross my crack. Francis didn't just spank you, he aimed every smack so you knew you would not be spared anything. Your hiney would suffer! The mean fan sank into the lowest, tenderest curve of each cheek. As near to my asshole as any paddle could get! I howled. After six smacks my backside hurt so much it wasn't part of me anymore, it had a life of its own. He let me pump and waggle my ass in the air until . . . I was even more worried about the next smack than I was hurting from the past one. He knew when the pain fades from the last one, before I get too scared of the next one, I turn on. He let me have the moment and then—again!— *SMACK!*

After ten I begged for mercy. Some man said, "That's enough!" but a woman snickered, "No! At least twenty! Better, forty!" It was Sofi's voice. Where was she? I was delirious from rump pain, I thought she had swelled up so big she was everywhere, as big as the room, she was the room itself, we were inside her. *SMACK! SMACK!*

That was it, although nobody told me. Francis just let me struggle to keep my legs straight and my hot red rear end pointing out and up. I never let go of my knees the whole time. Nobody had to hold me in place or tie my wrists and ankles like they did at home. I think Francis and everybody appreciated how hard it is to work the pain off after each spank and keep putting your ass up for the next one. My backside hurt so much, I couldn't be sure I was putting it up prettily anymore. Francis got out of his easy chair and splayed me over its low padded back, spreading my legs. I was still standing, but my face was down in the seat of the chair. He dropped his pants and undershorts and grabbed me by my hipbones and had me extra roughly.

Two women helped me into the ladies' to clean

myself up. One wanted to quiz me about Francis, like, how close we were (apparently, she didn't know about Sofi and I didn't tell her) and was he always that brutal? My backside was blotchy red and I was leaking tears. The other woman blew cool air on my raw bottom that magically made it feel better. She complimented me on my breasts and kissed away my tears. She was beautiful herself. I let her kiss my boobs 'cause she was expert and sensitive while I chatted with my latest "rival" about Francis. "We should take this out there," I murmured to my new admirer. I thought I would put my clothes on, but she led me out into the living room still naked and laid me out on a couch and kissed me all over. "Who are you?" I sighed. "You don't recognize me?" she laughed. It was Ethyl. She could come in any form. I blinked in wonder and she slipped away. Gone!

Now, I've been carrying on about the spicy S and M stuff, but there was also lots of eating and drinking and pot-smoking and coke-snorting and plain sex going on. S and M is more fun to write and read about. The pleasure of sex is harder to describe than the shame of S and M, at least for me. On the other hand, the skit the hosts of the week put on always had a Forbidden Pleasures theme. Not everybody was up to planning and rehearsing, so some hosts just winged it. When the Club met at our house, me and Francis and Sofi cooked for more than thirty people, and we had our skit ready. I was a naughty schoolgirl with pigtails. I wore a mini and carried three books tied with a strap. I pretended to study in the school library, but I was more interested in playing with myself. I had fun with that, swinging my knees in and out, doing myself like it was a new discovery, one hand, then both hands, I was one horny little bitch. Sofi was the librarian who caught me moaning. She pulled me once around the stage by my ear to the principal, who was Francis. He said he would have to "chastise" me, and I looked at him like I had no idea what that meant. A few people laughed. He told me to drop my panties and show him my "buttocks." The principal was the kind of older gent who would use words like that.

I was also showing my rear end to the audience— once again! The principal chastised me on my buttocks with the book strap. I shimmied after each smack. I didn't have to pretend to cry, I really did, 'cause it hurt more than in our rehearsals, and 'cause I really got into being a schoolgirl caught with her hands in her panties. The skit ended with me kicked out of the principal's office. Sobbing and rubbing my rosy buttocks, I try to peek back in through the keyhole in the pretend-door. The librarian and the principal look each other over and begin to strip. Everybody loved us.

— 16 —

MRG: How We Know What's Going On

Silas Hardon was at Sofi and Francis's house often. He preferred watching to mixing it up with us. One liberty Mr. Hardon took, when I was blindfolded and tied over a hassock with my hiney in the air, was playing with my tits. He twiddled them and sucked them till I went out of my mind. He grooved on that, playing with himself, I think. Then, he sneaked around behind me and pinched my rear cheeks. He thought I didn't know who he was! I cursed him and growled, "Fuck me right now, asshole, or, when I get out of this, you're going to be sorry!" I could sense he was getting his courage up. He was more afraid to back off than just do it. A moment later he was screwing me from the rear. He did a good job of it, made me pant like a bitch till I came, but right after he pumped his load into me, he wanted to apologize—for screwing me?—for screwing me when I was tied up? Silas, you always drive me crazy! What a super lover you would make if you weren't such a wimp!

I still got to humiliate Mr. Hardon, but I didn't have as free a hand with him as I did at the artists'. That's 'cause he was Sofi's major client, and also Francis's boss. Mr. Hardon was merely the founder and CEO of MRG! I never heard this from Mr. Hardon and Sofi didn't tell me till the day after he screwed me. I was amazed. In the meanwhile, he told her what he wanted and she passed it on to me as though it was her idea. Like, "Sarah, Mr. Hardon has been a naughty boy," meaning, he showed a flicker of interest in me or her— "you'd best make him drop his pants and put him across your knees."

Mr. Hardon was a Shame Artist, too. Francis and Sofi were triple cautious not to do or say anything to embarrass him, even though he'd have loved it. I bet if Sofi had slapped his face, he would've died of happiness. They couldn't touch him, 'cause they were too dependent on him. Through me, they already had Mr. Hardon where they wanted him. Why risk changing anything? Such is the power of the buck.

Silas Hardon didn't look like he had the right stuff to build a big media company. But he acted totally different in business. Like me: I was two different people with him and with Francis.

Sofi told me Mr. Hardon made his mark by observing that TV news directors ran whatever footage they had, even when it didn't match a breaking story. They had to get shots fast, even if they had to stage them. Mr. Hardon said that the famous photo of raising the American flag at Iwo Jima told the story 'cause it was posed, but in the photos of the scene as the photographer came on it, you can't tell what the men are doing. It was smart to stage an event any way it might go. Once in a blue moon, Mr. Hardon said, you might shoot something useful as it actually happened, and then the video editor could combine it with what you set up before. None of this escaped journalists with half a brain. What set Mr Hardon apart was, he realized it was a waste of money to stage phony shoots for each news event. He pointed out that when low-budget movie directors want to show action is happening in San Francisco, they don't hire a helicopter to shoot new footage of the Golden Gate Bridge. Stock footage works just as well. If you're selling over-the-counter grease for hemorrhoids, you can hire an actor to play a doctor saying he recommends your grease for his wife's problem. Or you can use stock footage of a man in a white coat and stethoscope plus a voice-over on your grease.

Mr. Hardon told Francis and the other MRG execs, "Give me every scene that comes up in the news. We'll adapt stock scenes to fit stories as they break and sell the networks all they want cheaper than they can set up a live news shoot."

Take riots. Mr. Hardon made a riot street in a studio that went from paving to tar to packed dirt in ten minutes. You could light it for any time of day or night.

You could have mongrels, pigs, or chickens wandering across the street. There was a grocery store and a hardware store in a sad, wooden one-story shack. Mr. Hardon shot twenty variations a day for three days. One scene showed a dark-skinned proprietor boarding up the window of his grocery store. Another showed a man heaving a garbage can through a storefront window. Looters entered through the broken window and hurried away with TV's, a carpet sweeper, chrome kitchen cabinet knobs and drawer pulls.

We see MRG's of these standard sixty scenes anytime there's a riot, whether in Asia, Latin America, Africa, or a barrio here. The language of the shop signs change. The skins are black, white, brown, bronze, or yellow. A bash! Free things!

Sometimes, a riot's shown as a night scene to black out details that don't work. All this is a lot easier to do in the lab than to fly a crew to a slum where beer bottles come crashing down from roof tops. And then, six weeks later, to send the crew half way round the world to shoot practically the same scene, if they can even get there before the riots are over.

In the bad old days before Mr. Hardon took charge, reporters paid a bunch of locals to play rioters. A citizen got twenty bucks to go home, pick up the TV he looted the day before, bring it back through the shop window, and let himself be videotaped looting it all over again. That's why, in old pre-Hardon riots, looters were always grinning into the camera, then stopping and looking confused. You didn't hear the director's translator yell at the looters not to look at the camera, that was edited out. Francis figured that the stock footage of third world riots he directed for Mr. Hardon saved the networks one point two million dollars just in the first year.

Or take when a Wall Street manipulator is indicted. The first news always shows his lawyer at the top of the Court steps, saying, "My client has no comment at this time. This indictment is hogwash. My client has done nothing wrong and he will be vindicated." You also get a shot of the back of the money-man's head as he's hustled into a limo after posting bail. Simon Hardon asked, "Is it a good use of network resources to send out a crew every two or three weeks to shoot a different lawyer saying, "My client has no comment. . . ."

Mr. Hardon shot the classic scene using actors, and that's what you see nowadays whenever anybody with clout is indicted. If the lawyer is one of the three lawyers recognizable to anyone besides his family and cronies, his face is MRG'd onto the standard footage. Also, the networks can buy a composite video clip from the MRG lab wizards that shows any celebrity brought into the halls of justice in handcuffs. Since a Democratic candidate for national office is accused of high jinks with a floozy every four years, it made sense to have a cassette ready and stick the lucky candidate's image in as the story broke. That's how I got to play the "show girl." But, this time, the scandal concerned staunch Republican Tom Thomas. MRG never intended to sell any "MRG'd" tape of a politician to the opposing party. MRG's market was news directors, period.

The Republicans found out about the tape and paid Mr. Hardon big bucks not to sell it to the news. Enter Sofi, who always thought she was going broke, pushing Francis to make his "Show Girl Minus Candidate" tape pay off. He sold the final job to the Democrats, double-crossing his boss, Mr. Hardon, and then he double-double-crossed the Democrats by selling the solo tape of me to the Republicans. He got paid up front and under the table by both parties! That's why he didn't go to jail. There's an unwritten law, if you catch both parties with their snouts in the trough, it isn't crooked.

The summer I met Sofi and Francis was the first year of President Chase's first term. In the fall I got a studio apartment in Manhattan with Julie, a new girl from a cow town in Minnesota. I also made my first TV commercial. The personal stuff was over between me and Sofi and Francis. I was one of the girls, now, they expected me to pull away. A week after I got my first check for the commercial, I gave Julie a month's rent and moved into my own place. On a roll, I made a play for Francis. A disaster! It earned me ten minutes in Hell.

The following year, I nestled up to an empty poolside chair in a studio for the video, "Show Girl Minus Candidate." Sofi sent me over to MRG for this gig and Francis was the director. The Tom Thomas scandal broke nearly two years later.

—— 17 ——

GAM AS IT WAS

Fat Sofi! That's what everybody at Gorjus Actors and
Models called the boss behind her back. At first, I
couldn't believe my ears. True, Sofi swelled up at work,
but discreetly, so no one saw her do it, and once she
was enormous, she could scarcely be recognized as Sofi.
When she was thin, she lived on grapefruit, bran flakes,
and steamed veggies, jogged and exercised at a club
every day. We all did.

Fat Sofi! Nobody I talked to at GAM would say why
they called her that. They just did. They thought I asked
'cause I was new. I got the message, if I wanted to be
one of them and not stand out, I'd better call her that
behind her back, too.

The Tom Thomas scandal drew a lot of attention to
GAM, what we girls did for our clients, and what we

did for fun after hours. When I joined the agency, it was seedy, 'cause there was a standoff with Ron, the landlord and super. GAM occupied the whole top floor, the sixth, of Ron's building. We were the last tenants, and we were moving the last week of January. Ron said he was doing the building over. There would be two condo apartments per floor. Meantime, Ron wouldn't fix anything, 'cause Sofi was behind in the rent. She refused to pay a cent or send a girl down to him until he fixed the plumbing and caulked a drafty window.

To Sofi, the best things in life were free. No matter how well we did, Sofi thought everything would crumble if she spent a buck. Remember, how the furniture at her beach house kept flashing in and out? It was rented, Sofi had the money, but waited too long to pay the bill.

When Sofi was a week late with GAM's rent, Ron started dropping eviction warnings. Sofi sent girls who weren't getting work down to the basement, where he lived. Ron's basement was Hell. His walls were covered with girlie shots, the crudest, not even from the better mags. Hell was muggy all summer and overheated all winter. It was right up against the building's boiler. The two windows were a room away. One window was closed, the other was boarded up. To get to them you had to cross an obstacle course of pipes and old sinks, toilets, and burned-out electric motors.

Rent payment went this: *"Hi!"* the girl would say, "I'm here to take care of the rent!" *"Uhhh,"* Ron would say, "You owe month. One week, this, understand?"

Ron wanted it the same way every time, nothing

fancy. He took off his shoes, pants, jockey shorts, and sat on his bed. He was thin and wiry, with a long thin prick to match. Not circumcised. The girl stripped everything off, kneeled, licked him for one minute. Then, she lay on her back on his grungy bed, spread. He never took more than two minutes. A girl could be back in seven minutes when the elevator was with her.

Once, Denise was on the rag and that put Ron off. Imagine, a pig like him turned off by a little blood. So, he agreed to let her blow him. But he couldn't come in her mouth! His religious training, something I know about. It never inhibited me, 'cause I saw the nuns go crazy from not getting laid. Anyway, Denise was a pro. One time she sucked off twenty-eight guys at a convention and made $1,400 in three hours. But she couldn't get Ron to come. Finally, she goosed him, he howled and gave her a mouthful against his will! He wasn't grateful. That was too far-out for him. He threw her a black look. She thought he was going to hit her. She grabbed her clothes and scooted out of there, dressed waiting for the elevator.

I paid a week's rent in October. I made the mistake of trying to hook Francis away from Sofi. I wanted to prove I could do it. Sofi never mentioned it, just called me a cunt and sent me down to Ron to pay the rent. As she threw me out of her office, I sensed her beginning to blow up huge. Her monstrous arm dripping fat flattened against the other side of an opaque glass panel in her door. I fled down the stairs, I didn't even wait for the elevator.

Ron sat on his bed, ready to be served. I stripped naked. He pointed to the spot on his fake oriental rug where I should kneel between his legs. I licked his prick counting in my head to sixty. He put me on my back on his bed and lay on me. I held my breath. He never took his plaid shirt or socks off, even though his bedroom was roasting. He swiveled around in me. His whole idea of how to do it was based on the word "screw." Afterward, I showered, gargled, douched, gargled, douched and showered.

January, our last month in his building, Ron turned the heat off altogether. The agency was drafty and cold as the streets. Droplets of water from leaky overhead pipes froze into icicles. There was a mush of ice water around the toilet. Half of us had the flu. I planned to stay home unless I was called for a job, which I didn't expect this time of year. Also, I was lying low after the Solstice Orgy, where me and Julie were disciplined and decorated.

Santa gave out filigree gold bracelets to most of the girls, although nobody would've said they were well-behaved. Nobody got cash bonuses, 'cause the star actors and models earned a fortune, while beginners and losers were a drain on Sofi.

GAM was the only agency I ever heard of where Santa brought switches and used them. Maybe, something like that goes on in out-and-out whorehouses.

My former roommate Julie was a new print model from Minnesota. She was twenty-one, an ash blonde with lanky legs. Her face was blah-pretty. Who knows what men read into her face? She had creamy boobs with a freckle on her left boob. Men asked for "the one with the freckle." She got kicked out of her home for screwing all the local boys, and after her first day here, which she spent in her hotel room, afraid to go out because of all she'd heard about the big city, she carried right on.

A week after Julie showed up at GAM we heard a racket from the can, the loose toilet seat rocking, the toilet tank lid scraping the tank, Julie's squeals of pleasure, "Oooo-eeee," and male grunts. A while later Julie came out, shivering, and then the salesman who was trying to sell us a huge paper copier. He looked like he'd done something wonderful—become the first man in history to soak his shoes in icy water fucking a beautiful model who straddled him where he sat on the pink shaggy-rug covered lid of a toilet in a freezing agency can with leaky plumbing.

The clients loved Julie, the art directors loved Julie, the photographers and their assistants loved her, passing salesman loved her. What was wrong with that? Just that she lost it in front of the camera. She was not getting enough sleep. It all wound up on Sofi's desk—stacks of spoiled shots from photographers, Julie's eyelids drooping closed. Drugs? Sofi didn't give her a chance to deny it. She chewed her out so Julie thought she was fired. Julie was too green to know that when you're really fired, the boss starts by saying what a wonderful girl you are. Instead, Sofi offered her a starring role, bare-ass, bending over, at the Winter Solstice Orgy. And more pricks than even Julie would normally get in a month. That was the stick. The carrot was, Julie would get one more chance as a Gorjus model if she gave up drugs altogether and sex binges the night before a shoot. Women who were punished at the Winter Solstice Orgy and had to take all that cock at once tended to be chaste for weeks afterward. It was like making a child smoke a whole pack of cigarettes, so he gets sick and doesn't want to smoke anymore.

Sofi pointed out that business fell dead for the holidays. If Julie's ass was going to show purple welts for a week, this was a good time.

Julie scuffed around bitching "Fat Sofi!" for the ten days till the orgy. You'd think, since we were going to suffer together, we'd have gotten closer. Instead, Julie acted like she couldn't stand me. I tried to warn her it could be incredibly painful, if the whipper tries to fulfill everyone's fantasy of a public whipping, but, it could also be a terrific turn-on. She bit my head off.

I starred at the Solstice Orgy for offending a client. Mr. Soap turned up at a video shoot, although normally he was too big to be concerned with details. Sofi got a call from an art director that brought her quick. Mr. Soap was trying to pitch me between takes, him in his fine tailored threads and me in a bath towel.

In the first scene of the commercial, which we shot a few days later, I was dressed in a business suit. I turn off a handsome executive with my body odor. Then, I realize it, look mortified. Another woman tells me about the sponsor's product. In the third scene, which we shot the same morning, I'm dressed in a different business suit, the handsome executive approaches me cautiously at first and finally breaks out in a happy smile.

It was the shower scene where I got into trouble. I showered using the client's soap. I was nude or in a towel the whole session. You might guess I was wearing pasties or a tiny bra and bikini panties that they artfully framed out of the videotape. I could have, but I didn't.

Going for it nude is professional. Everybody said I was at ease with my body. I teased the camera with the bath towel. That wasn't professional, come to think of it, but a perk for the guys. I love to tease. Me nude, back to the camera, bending forward a bit, backside sticking out covered by the towel, a wiggle, like I have an itch and I'm trying to rub it with the towel. Lowering the towel inch by inch, dimples showing, a little of my crack showing, raunchy ass grinding, the towel dipping more, my terrific rear cheeks swelling over the towel, a humpy bump! backward, and the towel's all the way down beneath my butt and you can see my quim, twitchy and wet and crying out to be screwed I can't help it, that's where my itch is, and if you're a man you're dying to ram your cock in there. I look back at you, like, pleading, *Please, kind sir, give it to me! Help me out of my misery!* It was my trademark shot, like MGM's roaring lion.

I turned-on all the men at the shoot. Why the art director called Sofi was, I turned-on to a lighting technician. It just happened. One of the strongest instant turn-ons I've ever felt. I saw a long bulge in his pants and I wanted to blow him on the spot, but all I could do was lick my lips and throw him a humpy wiggle. When he came near to adjust a scrim, I touched him. Only a light caress on his ribs, but I was nude. Nude actresses aren't supposed to touch techies! Especially, not with a big client stewing in his own juices ten feet away!

The orgy was in GAM's playroom, which took up the whole rear of the office. The space doubled as a photo set, but all the photographers had better studios of their own, so mostly it was a place to flop or play ping-pong. Sofi refused to admit the air-conditioner didn't work. It was just a big clunky fan that collected dirt and dead flies in the vents. In the summer we had a shelf for street clothes, and models (male models, too) stripped to their underpants. Bikini panties were standard for the girls.

It was fun to watch the girls play ping-pong, boobs swinging side to side. The men who turned up to watch the prettiest bare tits, the sexiest bottoms and longest legs in town were art directors or businessmen who used us in their ads. GAM's playroom was a sales come-on. Clients popped in for a few minutes after lunch. Most advertising people were too busy to hang out in our playroom, or had to look like they were.

No invitations were sent out for the Winter Solstice Orgy, no one was phoned and reminded to come. Somehow, the food and booze, body paints and sponges, dildoes, clip-on baubles, and tinsel arrived on time, all us actors and models were there by 10 P.M., the horniest big shots in our industry always turned up by 10:30, and Santa always came before 11 with gifts and switches. So, someone must have planned it all.

Before Santa came, the playroom was jumping with loud rock that made it impossible to talk. Everyone milled about, looking for someone or avoiding someone. More hugs, kisses, fondling, more unbuttoning and un-hooking, more hands under skirts than at the sex club last summer, maybe more than anything since the St. Deems parties. A bra was tossed in the air, and then there were bare boobs everywhere.

Men hung around me and Julie, but they didn't talk to us or grope us. Some were awed and speechless. Some were beaming, probably tickled they'd soon be watching our asses squirm, but still keeping their dis-tance, like we might be contagious. Maybe they thought they'd catch what we had and get whipped too!

Santa came into the playroom wearing a mask with a woolly white mustache and beard, but *(Ho-ho-ho!)* I knew he was Mr. Soap, the client I burned at the shoot when I turned on to the techie. Fat Sofi turned the rock tape off. Santa gave out gold filigree bracelets to all the girls but me and Julie. Then, he took four light, flexible switches bound at one end to form a handle out of his red sack and swished them in the air. I gagged, 'cause I knew how much they could hurt, even if Santa didn't exert himself. I whispered to him to take it easy on me and I'd take care of him. I wasn't wearing anything underneath my white leotard and my longish nippies stuck out. He nodded okay.

A mob of regular agency clients, male actors, and

god-knows-who rushed at me and stripped off my leotard, spread me over the arm of a couch. Two guys held
me down, one on each of my wrists. I couldn't move an
inch. My boobs hung down almost to the seat of the
couch. My ass was up, my knees straight, 'cause I was
right against the arm rest. I spread my legs to keep my
balance. Santa and anybody else behind me got a good
show.

Julie dressed for the orgy in a low cut sweater, a push-
up bra showing the famous freckle on one boob, and a
micro skirt. When your skirt barely covers your ash
blonde bush, your panties are your most important ac-
cessory. Julie's panties were filmy black with a hot pink
quim panel. Sounds provocative if you don't know Julie.
She dressed like that all the time.

They mobbed Julie and stripped her. Three guys
pulled Julie's sweater over her head so fast her creamy
boobs jounced around, like her nippies didn't know
where to point. Someone balled her sweater up and
threw it against a wall. A moment later her tiny black
and pink panties fluttered a few feet in the same direction.

They bent Julie over an armchair to my right. There
was a commotion at her chair. The guys were too eager
and they jammed the zipper of her micro skirt. They
couldn't get it off. All she was wearing was her skirt and
a pout. They flipped the skirt up in back. She was bare
ass up, head down. There were two guys in the way, I
couldn't see much of Julie, but I saw Santa swishing his
switches, practically drooling. "Bastard!" I wanted to

yell, but I didn't. Actually, I envied him. There were times I would've loved to whip that slut's rear end.

Julie yowled like she didn't believe how much switches hurt. What'd she expect? She said later Santa's thrashing was meaner than the ones her father gave her when he heard what she was doing for the local farm boys. It was my turn! The first one made me scream and wiggle. He wasn't going easy on me! Later, he told me he couldn't fake it with everybody watching him! What an idiot! My boobs swung up to my chin and plopped back against the arm rest. I drowned out Julie's yowls!

Fat Sofi! I knew that gloating laugh! Nobody wanted her blocking the view, so they elbowed and shoved her blubber back into a corner of the playroom. They didn't know who she was!

When they finally let me and Julie go, we jumped up and down holding our bottoms and bawled. We were raw back there, but not bleeding. We got passed around and mauled. Everyone was high on something, booze, cocaine, hash. Men were taking their pants down all around us. We were in the middle of a mushroom patch. We mouthed one mushroom after another. I drew the next mushroom to me while I finished one off. It's easy to be wild when your hiney's on fire.

Fat Sofi! She was back leading the celebration. It was time for everyone to decorate us stars. That meant Sofi had to pry me and Julie from the men, which would not have been easy for anyone without her obese authority. Somehow, she got Julie and me standing up naked in the center, and they finally got Julie's skirt off over her head. At Sofi's order, everybody picked up sponges and dipped into the body paints and filed by me and Julie and daubed us. I got blue paint in my hair and purple on my face, red and yellow on my boobs, black on my belly, orange and more red on my thighs, and forest green on my back. Julie got the same colors in different places. Our butts were already purplish pink and too raw to paint.

This year the dildoes were soap bars shaped like phalluses. Each one was a monster of a different color. I got a big peppermint prick inserted into my cunt—about ten times!—by a kneeling gentleman sporting a toupee; a red-brown prick in my mouth, offered with sly humor by a woman casting agent; and at the same time, a creamy white one screwed up my ass and twirled by two young men I didn't get a good look at. I think Sofi sent them to do that, at least, I saw her dipping the white soap phallus in a bowl of water to make it slippery half a minute before. Julie got two sky blue pricks in her mouth and up her ass, and a canary yellow one in her cunt.

Sofi shoveled her huge hands into boxes and held up bells and baubles, and then everybody took them and clipped them on us wherever they could go, on our nippies of course, but also, on our hair, head and bush. Finally, the tinsel: They finished by wrapping us in yards of glittery tinsel.

There were other women at the orgy, not all models or actresses, who stripped off and joined in. Everyone in the room was fondling, kissing, or fucking somebody.

Me and Julie were supposed to just stand there clench-ing our dildoes and watch all this until midnight, which was a long twelve minutes away. No use objecting you didn't care for the taste of soap in your mouth. When the dildo in my cunt slipped a few inches, someone was right there to screw it back in. The soap prick in my rear didn't need any attention. At midnight Sofi laughed, and popped the cork on her cheap champagne. We got plenty of help removing our dildoes, and a mo-ment later I got pushed over the love seat again and fucked I don't know how many times. My tinsel broke away, though some stuck in my body paint. Most of the clip-on baubles fell off, but the bells stayed in my hair and I sounded like an ice-cream truck when I came. My body paint smeared all over me and onto guys who screwed me.

Some gentlemen didn't say a word when they did me, which would ordinarily be rude, but at the Solstice Orgy it was what went down. Santa fucked me extra hard. Maybe, that was all he wanted. I didn't have the strength to hate him. I was already coming, I kept com-ing with him. Couldn't stop, anyway, even though I knew he would brag about it.

This always happens at an orgy: A stranger's behind you, screwing the daylights out of you, and here comes a cock right at your mouth. So, you open wide. I think I saw this guy once before, clothes on, in an art direc-tor's office.

I got so busy finding the rhythm to please two guys at once, I forgot Julie. When I looked over, there she was, painted and tinseled, with one line of guys at her head and another at her tail, and she was totally into it, with a head-bob-bob, hump, squeeze and swivel, bump! head-bob-bob, shimmy and bump! Her pretty red hiney was working as hard as mine, and maybe even faster, 'cause there was less of it.

I heard Julie bleat, "I don't do anal!" so loud the whole room could hear. As her ex-roommate I knew that was a whopper. Some of Sofi's clients knew it, too. Julie made it worse for herself with her attitude. A moment later she squawked, and I caught a glimpse of her hindquarters. The guy behind her was in there! She was grinding and thrusting her ass back, sticking her tongue all the way out and squealing, 'Ooo-eee! Eee-ooo-eee!' If you want to get every man at an orgy lining up to screw you in the ass, all you have to do is squeal like a pig. Gentlemen love making you squeal even more than shooting their wad 'way up into your bowels. Already, there were two art directors behind Julie waiting their turn. The slut! I wasn't going to compete with her, if that's what she wanted, she could have it. Only one guy seemed to want to put his prick into me "Nevil's other way." I let him. I'm not sure anyone noticed. He was so drunk, maybe he didn't, either.

If you don't know GAM from being in the ad business, you may be thinking the agency was just a specialty whorehouse. It wasn't. Sofi ran a few hookers on the side, but Gorjus itself was a real agency for runway and photo models and video actors. A few girls gave clients something extra.

Most of us didn't screw clients as a rule, but we knew a male client was more likely to ask for us next time if we changed in front of him. We scorned dressing rooms and screens and we all wore sheer underwear. Some girls didn't need bras and never wore them. Nobody objected when a model whipped off a dress and was just in her panties for a moment until she got into the next one. Of course, when we modeled lingerie or swimsuits, changing in front of the client meant baring it all over and over every few minutes.

Married actresses and models said, "Look, don't touch." A girl can build a career on that, if she is good other ways. Some girls said things like, "I have to make a down payment on a car. I need eight hundred." The client could come up with it or ignore it. If he came up with it, he got a great time.

A few girls were hookers, not part of GAM. They needed to write home that they were models. Sofi made them pay eighty bucks for one modeling lesson, three hundred to have her photographer shoot a portfolio. The photographer got one hundred, plus fifty for expenses. Sofi took most of a hooker's earnings until she paid for the portfolio and the modeling lesson. Then, Sofi got one third, the hooker two-thirds. Hookers understood that if they cheated, they got tossed out. No goons beat them up, nobody threatened them. Just, out. Some who got tossed out begged to come back after two weeks on their own. Then, they paid back whatever Sofi thought they stole, they got punished, and all was forgiven.

Our reputation was tainted by the hookers more than the hookers were helped by going out as models. It was a lousy way to do business. But the Thomas scandal broke on the ninth year for Gorjus Actors and Models, which would be a hundred years for a shoe store.

Fat Sofi! If you think she was a madam with a soft heart, forget it. She was a monster. All her enormous cunt lacked was shark teeth. She didn't pamper the girls, took what they owed her, ripped them when she suspected they were cheating her. Every month or so, one or another of the under-employed models got paddled or whipped until her bottom was beyond red. Models got their hinies warmed more than the hookers, 'cause they were more likely to get out of line. The hookers caved in and cried when Sofi told them off. Models and actresses yessed her, but turned around and did as they liked.

Sofi was the fat woman at the artists' beach house. It was her disguise. She knew I wouldn't look her in the face when she weighed four hundred pounds. She was the one who laughed when Larry paddled me after I misbehaved with Carl. She laughed the same way when Francis spanked me and made me do tricks.

New girls always watched a paddling. An art director said it was an erotic ritual. Actually, it was Sofi's next-to-last resort for maintaining professional standards. Last was dropping you. She doubted a man could get away with managing an agency that way! After you saw three or four girls paddled, it was no big deal. You heard about any you missed. Everybody shaped up for days afterward.

Fat Sofi! The fact is, the girls adored her 'cause she was hard on them. The ping-pong paddles were always ready for use in our rear lounge, the notorious play-room. Also, and hardly anybody got to see this, Sofi had 8 × 10 color prints of girls bending over for punishment. In some shots, you could see the darlings were crying. There were slides across from the 8 × 10's, where a paddle blurs, swinging, about to smack a bare female butt, or bounces off. In one sequence, a man's fist clutches a belt landing on a voluptuous backside that has more crimson stripes in each shot. "Know whose red ass that is?" Sofi asked me. "No, should I?" I said, and then I recognized the ass! There was also a front shot of the girl holding her ankles and looking into the camera. My face! Scrunched up and bawling, I didn't recognize it! I felt the ghost of a sting in my bottom. The belt and knuckles were Louis's, an actor who went to Hollywood.

It was the September I started at GAM, before I got work as a model or a TV commercial actress. I deserved it for doing a photo shoot off the books. A guy at a bus stop offered me seventy-five an hour posing in the buff. The agency nude rate for me, back then, would've been three hundred an hour. I was supposed to say no or take the gig and give Sofi a third. I worked three hours and kept all the money. The guy tried to call me at GAM and said too much. Sofi marched me back to the playroom, picking up Louis and Greg the photographer along the way. I remember stepping out of my skirt at the same time Louis took off his belt. There were a couple of big umbrella flashes in the playroom. Greg checked his camera settings. Back then, I was still impressed when a guy didn't even glance my way while I dropped my panties. Sofi said to hold my ankles.

Everybody came into the playroom and joked about my gorgeous bare hiney while Louis spanked me soundly with his belt. He was quick and professional. Greg said he'd show me the shots, but he never got around to it, even though I took care of him real well one rainy afternoon in his pad near GAM. That happened all the time with shots you actually needed for your portfolio, photographers promised you slides, you put out for them, and then they never came up with the pictures.

Fat Sofi! Along with some of the red behinds in her portfolio, there was a note from the girl saying she deserved it and how good it was for her, how it changed her life, blah, blah, and signed, "Love." Before you think these weepy, grateful girls were all just dumb asses, you should know that three of us, two besides me, went on and made a half million dollars before we were twenty-three. Some of us said we were older when we were very young, and then we skipped so many birthdays between nineteen and twenty-two, we didn't know how old we were anymore.

─ 18 ─

TRIUMPH OF THE QUEEN OF THE NIGHT

As a Shame Artist, my friend Gina put me to shame. She always looked perky and sure of herself. Adorable button nose, glowing cheeks, a cheerleader smile, a helmet of thick black hair. An elegant runway model body, long legs, tiny waist, surprisingly voluptuous boobs and rear end for such a slender bird, but never too much in front or behind for any outfit.

Gina worked out of a rival agency. You know her TV commercials, where she goofs on men playing pool or one-on-one basketball. She flashes her terrific grin and her tits point up as she beats a guy. Off-camera, she does whatever guys want wearing her famous smile. All her men are hoods like Walt.

I knew right away Walt was more than a hood. First, his eyes were fascinating. They drew you in like whirlpools. Did you ever see a movie about evil demons, the dead come back, whatever, where they don't have weird eyes?

Second, the way I turned on to him. *Wham!* So fast and crazy, I had to run to catch up with my own cunt. I looked for a pinkie ring. "Whadt do you look—?" he said. "No ringk. Free man."

Third, Walt talked like a foreigner. You expect the Devil to come from somewhere else. Ask yourself, would the Devil come from Ohio? See what I mean? The Evil One comes down on ordinary folks from a castle with a green acid moat. He holds a cape up to his eyes as he rides his fiery horse across a cobblestone courtyard and a drawbridge that he commands with a flick of his whip. In his castle there are bedrooms with huge fireplaces, wood-paneled walls, and beds hung 'round with heavy curtains. Underground, wine cellars and torture chambers. Walt's disguise was that he didn't look one bit like a depraved aristocrat. More like an ordinary immigrant thug.

You could hear that Walt still talked sometimes like the Gestapo in a World War II movie—pretending to be a Nazi after it's been out of fashion all these years! He bragged that during the Cold War, he hid that he grew up in Russia, but I didn't see how, his KGB accent comes out whenever he gets worked up. And when the Arabian sheiks were the troublemakers, Walt denied he was spying for them and his mother was a Libyan, but, sometimes, he sounds exactly like those Arab weasels on TV. Now, with Eastern Europe fading and the Russian mafia coming on strong, Walt lets on his father was Bulgarian and, get this, he claims his parents settled in Albania to raise pigs. Albania is one of those places bad guys naturally come from. But who moves to Albania? It's like North Dakota, you don't move there, you move away from there.

Walt is not the Evil One. At most he is a humble servant. The Queen of the Night saw through his disguise and sent him where he belonged—to the slammer.

A women's-lib conference invited Gina to make the keynote speech. All they cared about was the role she played in the TV commercials. Her private stuff never came out. For a while, whenever they threw a conference where women told each other to demand their rights, they had to have Gina. She updated her famous speech to today's headlines.

Gina admitted to me that her stirring speech was a sham. After it, she kissed up to her lowlife lover Walt, who slapped her face, called her names. . . . Her eyes drifted low, she squirmed. "What else?" I wanted to hear her say it.

"Sometimes, he tests me," she said.

"Tests you?" I was expecting something else.

"For 'vetness,' " she said gaily. He says I'm, 'in luf too mach mit mein own vetness.' He makes me, 'Holdt dress hup!' He puts his big paw between my legs. I'm always wet. Even if I wasn't, making me lift my dress would do it."

"It would for me," I murmured, "and then what does he do?"

"He whips me," she chirped, patting her behind with one hand and covering her mouth with the other, like, she was saying too much. "What's he use?" She looked at me. I looked right back at her, keeping the question open. "A bullwhip," she said after a moment. I thought, that's definitely not normal.

Gina went back to her room first, so they weren't seen together. The swine liked her waiting for him bare-ass, kneeling on the bed, face down, ass up. Once Gina started confessing, she couldn't stop. I said, "How awful!" but she knew I was turning on. She wanted me to know Walt was cruder than any thug I'd ever met. She had to make me see it: "He says, 'poindt ahsz-hole at zeilingk!' " She giggled. I couldn't help it, I broke out into a big grin.

Gina felt so bad about fooling all those women that she went along with it. Or maybe she just pretended to feel bad. I never knew a single other bitch who loved pain like Gina. You know I don't. Gina swore that the more Walt whipped her, the more turned on she got. "I'd like to see that," I said.

One day Gina called me sounding weepy and snuffling. She said Walt just put down the long whip and walked out of the room. It was hard to understand her through all her whimpering, but she let on that she was crouching on the bed over the phone. Her behind was lined with mean red welts and she was waving it in the air to cool it. She had to wait like that anyway for Walt to come back and fuck her. I couldn't help thinking, *You deserve it, slut!* I felt my big bottom in sympathy and imagined her cute round cheeks dancing as the leather cut into them.

She kept blubbering about how much her hiney hurt. I reminded her she claimed she loved it. All at once she began to giggle and pant. "Maybe this is a bad time?" I said, like, I was supposed to forget she called me.

I heard Walt rumbling, "Tell her . . ." but, in his accent it came out, "Dhell hher I fock you lak beetch."

"He's doing me doggy-style," Gina translated, panting hard. I heard Walt behind her, "fockink" up a storm. The phone could have been right under her, 'cause of the rocking bed and slamming squishy sounds, on and on, the kind of long hard fucking I like myself and, it happens, could've used at the moment. I grabbed a turkish towel off the floor to sit on, hiked my dress up and pulled my panties down quick, not to miss a moment of this. I did myself with one hand and held the phone with the other. Gina groaned in pleasure and agony, 'cause her rump was on fire.

Then, I came! I actually came first! I dropped the phone for a moment, helpless. When I picked the phone up, a lot relieved, Gina was still panting, Walt was grunting, and the bed rocking and the sock-it-in squishy sounds were faster. *Enough, bitch, come already!* Would it be rude to hang up? Then, a sharp cry and a few long delicate Gina mews told me she was coming. I could see her quivering all over. Damn! Walt let go, roared. I could almost feel his hot jets creaming the north end of her cunt.

Calling me could've been Walt's idea, to impress me.

Well, he did. For days I kept thinking of that long hard fuck and getting all hot and bothered. I didn't want the whipping first, I just didn't think about it.

Walt has a baby face. When I met him, he didn't say a word, just pinched my titties, right in front of Gina. The amazing thing was that at that moment I knew my nippies were poking through my blouse and I expected they would impress Walt. It was almost as though my nippies and Walt conspired to get together quicker than I would've thought proper. Gina said, "Don't mind him, he does that to all my friends." "A simple 'Pleased to meet you' would do," I informed him, but he got to me. Gina told me, "Keep your panties on." I could keep them on, I just couldn't keep them dry around Walt. Later, I began to pick up the opposite message from Gina, that she wanted Walt to screw me and get it over with. One day we were at his place, Gina was out of the room, Walt stared at me. I turned on and blushed. I looked out a window so he wouldn't see he was wrecking me. He came up behind me. This was it, you can tell. He went under my short skirt, brushed my panties toward my crack and felt my hiney with both hands.

Hey, lover boy, is it round and creamy enough for you? Not too big, I hope? I kept looking away, but I was breathing hard, my quim was twitching and my knees turning to jelly. I couldn't help bending forward a little, thrusting back to him. He went down on one knee behind me. What was he doing? Gina was going to come back in on us! All at once, *YAAAlll!*

I screamed before I knew what was happening! Walt

had sunk his teeth into one ass cheek! I couldn't move, 'cause he held me firmly as he chomped down. "What are you, crazy?" I cried. He let go of the bite. As I got over the first rush of pain, I felt his tongue and lips soothing where he bit me.

We heard Gina on the way back calling, "What happened?" I straightened up, drew my panties out of my crack and covered my butt. I said, "Thanks," meaning, *That's enough!* He stood up, said, "Dhon'dt mendtion hit." I knew he wasn't a vampire, 'cause they bite you on the neck. Also, after this, I didn't have any more desire than I usually do to bite guys on the backside.

Come to think of it, I always want to bite men's asses, but almost never do. The crazy part is, I imagined Walt doing it to me while I looked out of the window, an instant before he took a step toward me. That told me something about Walt: He was just as bad as people needed him to be. He was everybody's favorite sadist thug, but it didn't stop there. It didn't stop anywhere, 'cause what Gina wanted was a guy brutal enough to make her do whatever he wanted. I wound up doing what he wanted, too. Guess I wanted it that way.

I still had teeth marks on my right buttock when Walt put Gina in the hospital for a month and I filled in for her. You'd think the terrible injury he gave her—which wasn't fun and games like spanking or ass-biting—would've tamed him, but it didn't. He was lucky Gina covered up for him and he wasn't charged.

I called him "bastard" on account of what he did to Gina. Walt warned me he would "varm" my butt for that. This was before I laid him, so he was upfront about it. I was on my way out to a shoot. I turned my back on him and gave him a wiggle. "Wish you would," I called over my shoulder. The next evening he took me out for dinner. I was almost sick with lust. We both knew my ass was dessert. We were sitting at the bar waiting for a table. I stroked his cock, nobody was looking. It was hard. I wanted to feel if it was as big as Gina said. I was more into his cock than anything he had to say. He said I made him hard. I murmured he made me warm and wet. I'd been at a shoot and hadn't eaten all day. The liquor loosened me up. I slid forward on the barstool and put his hand between my thighs. He went all the way up under my skirt and felt my quim through my damp panties.

He was amazed how sloppy I was. A storm wave flooding the dock. I told Walt I had to change my panties three times today, just thinking about our date. I was ready to fuck him right in the bar. His jacket more or less covered his hard-on as he followed me to our table. I'd rather have laid down on the table than sat down. It would've given everybody in the restaurant something to talk about the next day. *The one in the pantyhose commercial with the gorgeous ass! I saw it! She dropped her panties, lay down on the table, and spread! Her date, a thug type, unzipped and fucked her! They were like animals, they couldn't control themselves!*

We were sitting side by side on a banquette along the wall. I kept playing with his cock under his napkin. He told me people were staring, like, they'd never seen a woman do that in a restaurant. Give me a break, I see it all the time. I bet they also never saw a guy reach under his date's dress like Walt did when I slid by him to go the ladies'. He grabbed my sopping panties and squeezed my quim lips together. I couldn't get around the corner of the table. Also, I couldn't enjoy the grope, 'cause I'd waited too long and I really had to wee. Does that prove it was his idea, not mine? But I knew he would do that before I stood up. I gave him a look, and he took his hand away.

All I remember from dinner is Walt bragging about what a big shot he was and telling me what a slut I was. I wanted him to promise not to bite me, not to use a belt or a bullwhip, not to hit me with a closed fist or kick me in the cunt, which is how he broke Gina's pelvis, but just smack me with his hand where I was nice and round for smacking. With a guy who could do so much worse, keeping him down to a good hand spanking would help me feel safe. Walt wouldn't promise anything. "You vandt a guudt shpankink," he purred. I decided to be honest with him. I told him what I really wanted was a guudt fockink, but I'd go along with a guudt shpankink, too, if that's what he wanted. He didn't pick up that I was goofing on his accent. But I told him what he wanted to hear, how I'd love him to make me suffer back there.

When we got to his place, he made me apologize for calling him "bastard" while he wanked my tits 'til I was out of my mind. My panties were drenched, I couldn't wait to take them down and step out of them. I turned around and showed him my hiney. He was rougher putting me across his knees than he needed to be, that's where I was going. It's scary being yanked off your feet. I'd rather take my time lying across a man's knees and putting my behind up a few inches, like, offering him a gift. Also, Walt didn't have to clamp me in place, my ass would stay where he wanted it, and he didn't have to force my thighs apart, I spread them myself at the right moment, when I feel dominated and turned-on. For a moment I lost the delicious shame feeling and I was just scared. Is that what I wanted? I expected Walt to humiliate me and hurt me worse than anybody, and he obliged.

He started slow. He grooved on rolling and pinching my bare cheeks and patting them up. For him this was the evening's entertainment, or a good part of it. His belt lay across the hollow of my knees the whole time he played with my rear end. I felt his big cock pressing against my left thigh. He was a sauce freak. He dipped into my hot wet stew and smeared my gravy on my behind and thighs. I felt shame creeping back. He reached down and tweaked my left tit with his slippery fingers. Then, he picked up the strap. My butt flinched.

"Zhree more for zat," he said, poking my tight ass, "loozen!" I'd have played dumb, like I didn't know what he was talking about, but I was afraid that would get me more smacks. Walt ordered me to count the spanks. He wanted me to take it all and stay completely open. That wasn't easy, but a real Shame Artist could do it. I loosened up.

The first spank hurt like crazy. I yowled. It was amazing how much it stung. Most people work up to it. I counted, "One!" He told me it was for calling him "bastard." The second smack was worse. I cried "Two!" He didn't say anything, just watched me hump the air. I decided to take number two for moving in on Gina's boyfriend—him. The third smack was more than enough punishment for every slutty thing I'd done all year. I screamed and kicked my heels up. I broke off screaming just long enough to gasp, "Three!" After four spanks, I couldn't help trying to cover my butt. He pinned my wrist and told me, "Dventy-eight." That was three more for covering my butt! It wasn't fair! I cursed him and he said, "zhirty-zhree." All I could do was cry.

My rear was burning. Walt had strong wrists, and the way he swung the strap, all the force landed at once, WAP! I felt my cheeks bounce and I heard myself howl. There's no way I could take thirty-three! But he liked watching me wiggle my ass for half a minute after each spank, so I was able to recover a bit between spanks. I wasn't shimmying for him, I couldn't help myself. His leisurely pace meant I was going to be across his knees a long while. After nine spanks I offered, basically, stop now and I'll be your sex slave, anything you want. What I got was number ten. After that, I begged, I shrieked, I gave up and sobbed. I forgot to count fourteen, but he reminded me. At twenty, he began dipping into my cunt again after each spank and rubbing my gravy on my raw crimson cheeks. He rubbed viciously, it hurt, but felt good, too. By the time I bawled, "thirty-three,"

I was out of my mind, but I remembered to kneel and thank him and suck like this was the last cock I'd ever get. He came down my throat, on and on, a tummyful, but he was so turned on, he kept sticking it to me every which way. When I put my tender behind up for screwing, he slapped it a few times with his hand to keep it red. We had a hot time.

Gina said it was okay, she didn't expect Walt to jerk off for months just because her pelvis was in a cast. When she got out of the hospital, all she could do was lie on her back while Walt kneeled on the bed in front of her face. Even though she couldn't perform all that well, Walt was loyal and visited her every day for fifteen minutes. "He unzips coming through the door," Gina said. For a hood, Walt was a gentleman, meaning he brought her flowers and magazines, and started off leaning over to kiss her. Gina said he always asked her how she was doing while he took his pants off, and she got to tell him everything was fine before he straddled her boobs and gave her his thick cock to suck. "I can't move around enough to give a good blow job," Gina explained, "I just lie there and he fucks my face. He stays hard, I suck him five minutes more, he comes again. He dresses and splits while my tongue's still licking 'round my mouth, chasing down the last little gobs of his second dose."

Gina couldn't screw for months. I moved into her place to take care of her, and I subbed for her when Walt wanted anything besides her mouth. We did it on her bed. She watched from her wheelchair, one wheel touching the bed so she could feel our rhythm. I liked her watching me put out like a raunchy slut, which is the only way to act with Walt. She played with herself and moaned in her low-key way and got sloppy down there. The doctor warned her not to come or she would shake her mending bones loose, but she wouldn't stop ploughing herself, so Walt had to tie her wrists to the arms of the wheelchair. Gina begged Wait to touch her. Walt would take a moment while he was fucking me or when we were changing positions, to reach over and hold her underneath, but not too long, so she couldn't get off. All the time we were messing around, Gina begged for just one more touch, and then another one, she was desperate, she moaned and panted every time Walt touched her, which turned me on and Walt, too. I had to tie her wrists to her bed at night so she wouldn't do herself the moment I fell asleep. When Gina's pelvis healed, she wanted him to herself for a week to celebrate and I said okay.

Then, Gina asked me to come to a conference with them, and we all got down together. After her speech, we dined at the hotel with a dozen other people from the conference. Walt was respectful, didn't even sit next to her. It wouldn't do for her to be photographed with a hood. Even with his baby face, anybody could see he was a hood. Gina was smiling as always, but tense. I asked her what was bugging her.

She whispered that she wanted to stay awhile in the hotel restaurant, but Walt wanted her to go back to their suite. Her routine "Stand up for Ourselves!" speech drove him nuts, he had to whip her right away. We went back to their suite ahead of him. She stripped her dress off. She wasn't wearing a bra. Lovely boobs. She turned on the TV. "You're going to watch TV now?" I wondered aloud.

"No, silly," Gina said. "That's so people think it's just TV, when we make noise." She was taking too long fluttering around the room in her panties. I got nervous.

"Walt wants you bare-ass," I reminded her. She pointed out there wasn't much to her panties, especially in back. Each cute cheek swelled out mostly bare. I'd noticed that. "You better drop them, anyway," I said.

"Well, what if he said, 'Jump out of the window,' Would you think I should?"

That was just talk, no way would she stand up to him. I suspected she was disobeying Walt to annoy him, and I wanted to see how it played out. "It doesn't matter what I think," I said. "What would you do if I weren't here?"

"Drop 'em. Wait for Walt facedown on the bed, bare ass in the breeze. He likes me to leave the whip out, too."

"The bull whip! Show me!"

She took it out of its hidden sleeve in Walt's valise. He carried the terrifying bull whip the way billiards players travel with their own sticks. It was so scary, all I remember is a foot-long handle bound in plaited leather that extended three more feet and ended in a wicked spray of points.

"But I don't feel like dropping my panties now,"

Gina said, "or being whipped," and attempted to hide the whip under the bedspread.

"Because of me? I'll go."

She begged me to stay. Walt was at the door.

Gina raced into a closet. The sliding door was half open, but Walt didn't see her. He checked the bathroom, demanded, "Vhere she is?" I was too scared of him to speak. Gina was crazy. Behind the closet door, she put a finger to her lips, getting off on being naughty, frustrating Walt. Meanwhile, the TV was on, a lot of noise, a movie with sirens and car crashes.

Walt saw me glancing toward her hiding place. I was doing Gina a favor, giving her away before Walt got too mad. Besides, I was dying to see if whipping turned her on like she said. Walt dragged her out of the closet by her perky tits.

"What are you going to do to her?" I said. He practically ignored me. "You shtay, you shtreep," he said over his shoulder. "You heard him, strip!" Gina said, grinning. "Shudt hup!" Walt yelled at her. I stripped naked. Now, Walt was steamed that I was naked but Gina still had her panties on! He slapped her face, she winced, but got her smile half-way back as she wiggled out of her panties. He tugged her by her nippies across the room. I was sitting naked on the bed when the choo-choo passed. She was stumbling forward clutching his forearms, her face scared but smiley, her bare body bending forward, thin waist, flaring bony hips, elegant thighs and cute round white ass.

What a brute! He swung her around to the back of

a low easy chair and threw her across it. That put her pretty ass up over the back of the chair. He had already spotted the whip under the bedspread. He took it out and cracked it in the air. "I vant you zee how vet," he said, poking me off the bed with the whip to stand behind Gina. Her legs were spread. He ran two fingers inside her cunt lips, skimming off a good dollop of sauce.

"She's wet, so what?" I said. "You put your fingers in her cunt and she's used to you screwing her after you whip her."

"Dhon'dt be frosh!" Walt yelled, spinning me around. The next instant before I could think, *KEEE-SRICK!* The whip slashed across my rear end! I screamed, *"Ylll! Ylll! Ylll-EEE!"*

"Zhere!" Walt ordered me around in front of Gina's chair. "Grab hher teets, sqveeze zhem!"

My butt stung like crazy. That one vicious lick took away any desire I had to argue with Walt. I kneeled on the seat of Gina's easy chair, where she was hanging upside-down. My rear cheeks hurt so much from the one stripe I couldn't sit. Gina's head was almost down to my lap. I reached under her and gently tweaked her nippies, trying to give her what I liked. She didn't object. She looked up at me, kissy-face, and licked me wherever she could reach, my belly, the tops of my thighs. Her nippies were longish, swollen, warm and hard.

"Holdt hher down, yes?" Walt said.

"Yes, sir," I said. Gina was scared out of her mind but smiled her bitchy smile.

He raised the whip! *KEEE-SRICK!* I put a hand across her mouth to help muffle her yowl, which nobody would've mistaken for TV. Walt stood a yard to the side of her and laid on another one. *KEEE-SRICK!* She screeched and waggled her ass. I was so close I worried about the whip blinding me, but he was on target. Gina tried to escape by crawling toward me over the back of the chair. I was horrified by the welts on her rear cheeks. Walt dragged her ass back in place and ordered me to clamp her down. Gina kicked her heels up desperately. At one point she looked to me like I was supposed to stop him, but what could I do? Anyway, she had suffered like this before and always came back for more.

Walt gave her another one! *KEEE-SRICK!* "*AAAIIIEEE*" Gina screamed. Walt made me come around behind Gina and see her twat was a swamp, hot juice flowing down her legs and onto the hotel chair. "Fantastasch!" I said, one of his favorite words. I wondered whether the hotel would ever get her gunk out of the chair.

Gina cried, "Whip Sarah!" I didn't blame her. Walt glanced at me. I was turned on enough from watching, but afraid. I suppose I'd have put my ass up if he said to, but he didn't like her telling him what to do. He raised the whip! She knew it. I bet she was sorry she said that.

I stood back, trying to stay out of range of the whip. Normally, I don't like a man ignoring me when I'm naked, but this time it was fine. Gina pumped her striped hiney in the air as though she was being fucked. *KEEE-SRICK!* *"YAAAIIIEEE!"*

Walt took his pants off, threw them down, sat on a desk chair in front of Gina so she could suck him. His cock glided all the way in and up—she was still hanging down the front of the chair seat. I saw her swallow it and I watched it go all the way up her throat. Her face was down to his groin, she was blubbering, but the corners of her wide mouth kept turning up. It must be hard to smile when your ass is on fire and you're upside down, crying, and there's a long thick cock all the way up your throat, but Gina managed it. You had to admire her spirit.

I wanted to watch Walt shoot his wad. He did! Gina went cross-eyed, but took it like a trouper. When he was done, he was still hard and horny. Gina struggled trying to gulp cum up again as it trickled down. The worst feeling is glops trickling back down into your nose the back way.

Gina didn't actually say, "Whip Sarah!" She admitted later that's what she was thinking, though. I was thinking more along the lines of, *"Don't* whip Sarah!" when Walt took me by the neck and threw me over the back of the chair alongside Gina. So, he went along with what Gina wanted. There was barely room for both of us over the chair back. We linked arms to keep from falling off the sides. That was comforting, but tense, too. We were holding each other down for him, so both our asses got it.

KEEE-SRICK! One lash right across four cheeks! We screamed our heads off. Walt took a pillow from the bed and made us gag ourselves it. Since he was closer to me, and my hiney is bigger, I got it worse. Later, Gina said it was worse for her, 'cause the spray of points at the end of the whip hurt the most. All I know is, it was the cruelest whipping I ever got. Walt made sure the wicked points tickled my crack and the tender place underneath, I mean, the cheek 'way under curving right into my asshole. I guess Gina thought she was the only one getting that! We were so close hip-to-hip on the back of the chair, wiggling and humping the air like crazy, that the sides of our raw rear cheeks stuck together when they touched. That hurt, too, and we pulled apart a few inches.

A long while after Walt put the whip down, we lay bawling over the back of the chair. He strutted in front of us showing us his super pumped-up cock and put it between our faces, and we both got to lick it at the same time, one from each side. We touched tongues, too. We were both sobbing too hard to get into it.

Walt went back around behind us, fucked me about ten long strokes, all the way in, almost all the way out, then, he pulled out, fucked Gina a little, fucked me again. He fucked me more than her, not that it was some kind of contest, like, whose cunt he liked more.

One time after he pulled out of me, he scooped more gravy from my cunt and greased his cock with it. I knew what he was doing and I wanted it. Even more, I wanted to watch him to do it to Gina. Ever since she complained he fit too tight back there, I couldn't get the picture out of my mind of her taking it in her ass. I wasn't surprised when Gina groaned and stuck her tongue out. I felt her body stiffen. "Anal!" she grunted. "I know," I whispered. He rammed into her and swiveled. Me, next.

Walt stepped back around behind Gina and fucked her quivering juicy cunt. After a moment he remembered me and ordered me to lick his balls and behind his balls, while he was in Gina. Whatever I did for Walt made him screw Gina crazy and she came again and again.

Walt's big sack of balls swung up and back slapping at my eyes, and his hard butt kept butting me in the forehead, while I dabbed with my tongue at this or that. My nose was in and out of his hairy crack. He reached with one hand around the back of my neck and pushed. I kissed close to his asshole, a little to one side, a little to the other. He wasn't even my boyfriend! I was certainly not going to—! But it felt like he could snap my neck with a twist of his wrist. I licked in a circle, trying to stay a good inch clear of his brown crinkly hole. His butt buffeted my face and it wasn't up to me where my tongue wound up. Walt said later I wanted him to force me to kiss his ass! What a treat for me! Like, nothing as degrading as tasting Walt's wrong end might ever come along again. He slowed down balling Gina so I could plant my lips dead center and fuck him with my tongue. Take *that*! You bastard! A big swirl to set him up, and, that! God, I was mad! I wished I had a red-hot poker!

A red-hot poker seared a hole in the air alongside me and dropped through it onto the rug! It's like I said, whatever you wanted with Walt came true! But I was terrified Walt would get his hands on the hot poker. Maybe, this was how Gina got hurt so bad. She might've wanted to kick him down there! I wished the poker away. It burned another hole in the air and dived out through it, leaving a little charred spot on the rug. Better to work with what I had.

Walt kept me licking his ass like that was all I was good for till he exploded in Gina. She didn't even know how much I helped Walt give it to her, 'cause she was facing the other way and her ass was on fire.

Then, Walt had to have a break. He told me lie on my back on the bed and spread, and he ordered Gina to eat me out. Gina and I might never've gotten to that by ourselves. I made a mental note to return the favor to her sometime. Once Gina had me coming, Walt pushed her aside and fucked me. We were face-to-face, he was over me, but we didn't kiss. I still had a gamy taste in my mouth. Walt slapped my face while he was balling me and called me an "ass-kissink hooer," even though he made me do it! Guys don't count that they get us to do tricks in the first place. I'd have slapped him back, but I was too scared, so I took a shot at him another way. I told him I adored licking his ass and I'd do it anytime. You have to be a Shame Artist to catch on to how I goofed on him. I was in my glory, flooded with shame, coming again and again while he was straining his balls going for number three. But, when I told him I loved kissing his behind, it pushed him over the top, again, just as if I was doing it.

The next morning at the Conference Wrap-up and Farewell Brunch, Walt was relaxed and charming. He looked twenty-four, though he must have been—who knows? Gina was all smiles. I felt close to her. We ate brunch standing up together, giggling 'cause we knew neither of us could sit down. We both had swollen, extremely tender bottoms. With help from the same hard prick, me and Gina had shared all the ways into our bodies.

Maryanne Hawkes, the women's libber who caused so much trouble in college, interviewed Gina for the role of keynote speaker at another women's conference. A half hour later Maryanne met Walt. Then she cornered Gina and me and quizzed us about Walt's bed manners, like it was her business, and whether I was still seeing Tom Thomas. We didn't tell her anything, but she found out about the original videotape of me from a Republican mole at her conference.

Maryanne got Walt hired to break into the MRG video stacks for the Democrats. It was ironic that Walt was the only one who actually did time. Not for kicking Gina's pussy so hard he shattered her pelvis, but for getting caught in the MRG warehouse trying to steal a video that wasn't even there. Of course, the Democrats sent him to steal the tape that would've demolished their frame-up of Candidate Thomas. Then, the Republicans, who'd already bought a copy of "Show Girl Minus Candidate X" from Francis, set Walt up to be caught. You can't put the Devil in the slammer. Walt wasn't the Devil, but the Devil used him a while and dropped him like a stone into a swamp.

I drove Walt to the MRG stacks and went in with him. On the way there, flying creatures kept brushing against the car. I thought at first that they were bats. Walt snarled, "Dhon't sink aboudt zhem—ignore zhem!" He knew what they were. At one moment they were so thick, I couldn't see to make a left turn. I slowed down to a few miles an hour. Everybody honked at me. They couldn't see the creatures covering our car.

Walt flourished a lock pick, pulled up on the oversized brass door knob, and the outer doors opened. It couldn't be that easy to get into the MRG storage building! Walt waved an electronic decoding gadget and the main vault opened for us like a garage door. I showed Walt the bin where my video was supposed to be, but it wasn't there. A voice from outside a high window of the vault advised me to split. It was the voice of Ethyl, the Queen of the Night. Walt wanted to keep searching. "Waidt for me in car," he said. The vault was open. The outer door was closed on a latch. I heard rustling, but still didn't know what was out there.

I cracked the door. They darted by me, three, three more, five more as I opened the door wide, six more, a flock of winged quims, each with its own luxurious bush! Azure wings complemented a blonde bush, mint green wings a maroon. Spotlights shone through their iridescent feathers, spraying the entry hall with delicate hues.

The winged avengers spiraled up over my head and took off toward the vault. "Go get him!" I chuckled. I turned and sauntered out swinging my hips. I threw a kiss to the Queen of the Night shimmering in the evening air, close as a smile, as far as a star.

By the time I reached Walt's car, TV news trucks from the major stations were all over the street, and the crews were pouring into the MRG building. I got in and drove. Walt's number was up, and I wasn't sorry the least bit. The cops arrived thirty seconds later, lights flashing. They found Walt lying on the floor of the vault, dazed.

Gina visited Walt in the fed pokey exactly once, just to see what it was like. He told her the winged quims got down his shirt, up his pants legs, they nibbled him and fucked him silly, made him give tongue all-out till he crashed into the storage bins on one side of an aisle, crashed into the bins on the other side, and fell. Walt was still slapping at his chest and thighs when the cops cuffed him.

Our cops don't like foreigners and they don't like law-breakers who pretend to be crazy. When they arrested a foreign burglar who talked about flying cunts down his shirt and up the legs of his pants, they roughed him up, naturally, and told him to save his insanity act for the judge. One of the cops wiped a rich coat of cunt gravy off Walt's face and threw the rag away.

As for Francis, he was grilled silly by federal, state, and local law enforcement, but never indicted, 'though everybody agreed he was guilty as sin. Some execs quit MRG so fast there was no one left to fire Francis except Mr. Hardon, who was saddened the way it turned out, but he reorganized MRG and a year later it was just as powerful as it was before the scandal.

As of now, I'm in exile in Mexico. I have a pretty villa in an artist colony near the Pacific. Pedro does the heavy work in the house and garden and drives me anywhere it's not safe. Rosario cooks. She's teaching me Spanish.

Nevil ditched Mom. She got a man closer to her own age. Now that I have more money than she does, we get along better.

The villa has two guest rooms. When Walt was in jail, the surgeon who rebuilt Gina's pelvis asked her out. "Your pelvis probably wasn't bad before," he said, "but now it's perfect." Six weeks later, they married. Gina and him stayed with me a week in June.

Babs visited me. Wild as ever. Pedro dropped her off at local bars, who knew how she got home?

Also, Alice came with her daughter. She's happily married. Her husband knows she needs freedom and doesn't try to restrict her. It turned out Alice and I could make love just as well without guard dogs patrolling the halls.

For six years, right through my year in college, acting in TV commercials, and the whole political mess, I corresponded with Billy and talked to him long distance. He's coming to see me in a few weeks. He says, if I'm as pretty as I look in the political killer video with the blinking rectangles, we might pick up where we left off in high school. I tell him I'm even better without the rectangles.

I would never goof on Billy. He knows all about me and Shame Art, 'cause he was there at the beginning. He gave me my first mouthful in Cathy's closet at her birthday party and rubbed cookie crumbs on my nippies in the science room at St. Deems before I had boobs.

Billy said he never in his life put a girlfriend across his knees or set her smooching his behind, but he's sure he could enjoy all that with me, 'specially if it turned me on.

Billy's got a steady job mixing music for network TV, and he plays piano and composes. I think Billy might be too young to settle down, but in the meantime there's nobody I'd rather jog along with.

Available now

The Captive
by Anonymous

When a wealthy Enlish man-about-town attempts to make advances to the beautiful twenty-year-old debutante Caroline Martin, she haughtily repels him. As revenge, he pays a white-slavery ring £30,000 to have Caroline abducted and spirited away to the remote Atlas Mountains of Morocco. There the mistress of the ring and her sinister assistant Jason begin Caroline's education—an abduction designed to break her will and prepare her for her mentor.

Available now

Captive II
by Richard Manton

Following the best-selling novel, *The Captive*, this sequel is set among the subtropical provinces of Cheluna, where white slavery remains an institution to this day. Brigid, with her dancing girl figure and sweeping tresses of red hair, has caused the prosecution of a rich admirer. As retribution, he employs the underground organization Rio 9 to abduct and transport her to Cambina Alta Plantation. Naked and bound before the Sadism of Col. Manrique and the perversities of the Comte de Zantra, Brigid endures an education in submission. Her training continues until she is ready to be the slave of the man who has chosen her.

Available now

Captive III: The Perfumed Trap
by Anonymous

The story of slavery and passionate training described first-hand in the spirited correspondence of two wealthy cousins, Alec and Miriam. The power wielded by them over the girls who cross their paths leads them beyond Cheluna to the remote settlement of Cambina Alta and a life of plantation discipline. On the way, Alec's passion for Julie, a golden-haired nymph, is rivaled by Miriam's disciplinary zeal for Jenny, a rebellious young woman under correction at a police barracks.

Forthcoming

Captive IV: The Eyes Behind the Mask
by Anonymous

The Captives of Cheluna feel a dread fascination for the boy whose duty it is to chastise. This narrative follows a masked apprentice who obeys his master's orders without pity or restraint. Emma Smith's birching would cause a reform school scandal. Secret additions to the frenzy of nineteen-year-old Karen and Noreen mingle the boy's fierce passion with lascivious punishment. Mature young women like Jenny Woodward pay dearly for defying their master, whose masked servant also prints the marks of slavery on Lesley Hollingsworth, following *Captive II*. The untrained and the self-assured alike learn to shiver, as they lie waiting, under the caress of the eyes behind the mask.

Available now

Captive V: The Soundproof Dream
by Richard Manton

Beauty lies in bondage everywhere in the tropical island of Cheluna. Joanne, a 19-year old rebel, is sent to detention on Krater Island where obedience and discipline occupy the secret hours of night. Like the dark beauty Shirley Wood and blond shopgirl Maggie Turnbull, Jo is subjected to unending punishment. When her Krater Island training is complete, Jo's fate is Metron, the palace home of the strange Colonel Mantrique.

Available now

Images of Ironwood
by Don Winslow

Ironwood. The very name of that unique institution remains strongly evocative, even to this day. In this, the third volume of the famous Ironwood trilogy, the reader is once again invited to share in the Ironwood experience. *Images of Ironwood* presents selected scenes of unrelenting sensuality, of erotic longing, and occasionally, of those bizarre proclivities which touch the outer fringe of human sexuality.

In these pages we renew our acquaintance with James, the lusty entrepreneur who now directs the Ironwood enterprise; with his bevy of young female students being trained in the many ways of love; and with Cora Blasingdale, the cold remote mistress of discipline. The images presented here capture the essence of the Ironwood experience.

Available Now

Ironwood
by Don Winslow

The harsh reality of disinheritance and poverty vanish from the world of our young narrator, James, when he discovers he's in line for a choice position at an exclusive and very strict school for girls. Ironwood becomes for him a fantastic dream world where discipline knows few boundaries, and where his role as master affords him free reign with the willing, well-trained and submissive young beauties in his charge. As overseer of Ironwood, Cora Blasingdale is well-equipped to keep her charges in line. Under her guidance the saucy girls are put through their paces and tamed. And for James, it seems, life has just begun.

Order These Selected Blue Moon Titles

Souvenirs From a Boarding School $7.95	Shades of Singapore $7.95
The Captive $7.95	Images of Ironwood $7.95
Ironwood Revisited $7.95	What Love $7.95
Sundancer $7.95	Sabine $7.95
Julia $7.95	An English Education $7.95
The Captive II $7.95	The Encounter $7.95
Shadow Lane $7.95	Tutor's Bride $7.95
Belle Sauvage $7.95	A Brief Education $7.95
Shadow Lane III $7.95	Love Lessons $7.95
My Secret Life $9.95	Shogun's Agent $7.95
Our Scene $7.95	The Sign of the Scorpion $7.95
Chrysanthemum, Rose & the Samurai $7.95	Women of Gion $7.95
Captive V $7.95	Mariska I $7.95
Bombay Bound $7.95	Secret Talents $7.95
Sadopaideia $7.95	Beatrice $7.95
The New Story of O $7.95	S&M: The Last Taboo $8.95
Shadow Lane IV $7.95	"Frank" & I $7.95
Beauty in the Birch $7.95	Lament $7.95
Laura $7.95	The Boudoir $7.95
The Reckoning $7.95	The Bitch Witch $7.95
Ironwood Continued $7.95	Story of O $5.95
In a Mist $7.95	Romance of Lust $9.95
The Prussian Girls $7.95	Ironwood $7.95
Blue Velvet $7.95	Virtue's Rewards $5.95
Shadow Lane V $7.95	The Correct Sadist $7.95
Deep South $7.95	The New Olympia Reader $15.95

Visit our website at www.bluemoonbooks.com

ORDER FORM
Attach a separate sheet for additional titles.

Title   Quantity   Price

_____   ____   _____

_____   ____   _____

_____   ____   _____

_____   ____   _____

Shipping and Handling (see charges below)   _____

Sales tax (in CA and NY)   _____

Total   _____

Name _____
Address _____
City _____ State _____ Zip _____
Daytime telephone number _____

❏ Check   ❏ Money Order   (US dollars only. No COD orders accepted.)

Credit Card # _____ Exp. Date _____

❏ MC   ❏ VISA   ❏ AMEX

Signature _____
(if paying with a credit card you must sign this form.)

Shipping and Handling charges:*

Domestic: $4 for 1st book, $.75 each additional book. International: $5 for 1st book, $1 each additional book
*rates in effect at time of publication. Subject to Change.

Mail order to Publishers Group West, Attention: Order Dept., 1700 Fourth St., Berkeley, CA 94710,
or fax to (510) 528-3444.

PLEASE ALLOW 4-6 WEEKS FOR DELIVERY. ALL ORDERS SHIP VIA 4TH CLASS MAIL.

**Look for Blue Moon Books at your favorite local bookseller
or from your favorite online bookseller.**